Daughter of the Gorge

By

Barbara Twibell

This book is a work of fiction. Places, events, and situations in this story are purely fictional. Any resemblance to actual persons, living or dead, is coincidental.

© 2003 by Barbara Twibell. All rights reserved.

No part of this book may be reproduced, stored in a retrieval system, or transmitted by any means, electronic, mechanical, photocopying, recording, or otherwise, without written permission from the author.

ISBN: 1-4107-1498-5 (e-book)
ISBN: 1-4107-1499-3 (Paperback)

Library of Congress Control Number: 2003091272

This book is printed on acid free paper.

Printed in the United States of America
Bloomington, IN

1stBooks - rev. 02/27/03

Dedication

I wish to dedicate this work to my husband Douglas. The love of my life.

I want to thank Betsy Seidel and Gloria Brown whose generosity and motivation helped keep me on track, and my whole family who can try to pick out the true spots!

1

"Mom, how can you do this to me?" Throwing my purse against the just slammed door, I turn and propel my body onto the bed. My heart bursts; the tears cascade down my cheeks. My mother has betrayed me.

"Jamie, you open this door right now!" My mother's voice sounds shaky and a little desperate.

"If I have to bust down this door to have you listen to me, I very darn well will, Young Lady." My Mother knocks again harder this time.

"Oh, all right. The door is not locked." I speedily brush away the tears and sit up in bed. I wish not to have her get the satisfaction of seeing how hurt I am.

"Jamie Dear, I need to let go of the house. There are too many memories here of your father. Please try to understand." Mom sits down on the bed and reaches for my hand.

"But Mom, you told me things would not change for us. You said that I could pay you some rent and stay on with you, and we could keep each other company. If you sell out and you want me to go, what are you up to?" I withdraw my hand from hers, slowly placing my hands in my lap, and adding a little sniff to keep from crying.

"Others have told me I can't just sit alone in this house. You have your work and your youth. I'm doing you no favors by monopolizing your life, too. I've made up my mind, Dear; I want to try a life... I want to live again. Your father's death was hard for both of us. I really did not know what to do or where to turn. I now have a better grasp of where I stand finance wise than a few weeks ago. Though I'm not left wealthy or wise, if I sell the house and move where it's not so expensive to survive and use your fathers retirement to supplement, maybe I can find something to fill my time." Mom looked up at me with such sad eyes and with such a heavy expression, I could not yell at her anymore.

I was beat. I could not argue anymore. She had to look out for herself. I know my mother well enough to know this was settled.

What about my plans? There really weren't any. Did I think I would live the rest of my life with Mom? I don't think I ever thought that. To be honest, I was just accessible each day. Go to work, and then go home. Repeat each day.

I think now that I have been pretty self-consumed, not giving any thought to my newly widowed mother.

"Jamie, what's going on in that head of yours?" Mom pulls back to look me square in the eyes.

"Guess I'm moving on, Mom. Got any ideas?"

2

It's party time! The signal for a party is when someone leaves work. It was hard to tell my co-workers I was going to leave, and very likely not return. I'm leaving the area, not to just change jobs, but to put my life together.

I attended a beauty college with a couple of my co-workers, and we were hired together by this large chain store company. We were thrilled to be hired right out of beauty school; it is unusual so close after graduation. Anyone with any knowledge in this profession knows graduation from beauty school is only a license to learn. With our new state licenses we were ready to go out and whip the world! This at least is what we were told in school.

Reality was near starvation. The only clients you get your hands on when you first start out are the ones no one else wants. You have to win them over, or take all the drop-ins you can get. So, we stuck together, and helped each other with our bookings. In about six months you might start to see over your bills! Without tips, especially when starting out, you just might fade into unemployment.

I did really well compared to some new girls, but I hustled. I shampooed other girls clients when they were overbooked (without them having to beg me,) folded towels, filled shampoo bottles, swept the floors after haircuts, and answered the telephone when the hairdressers were busy.

We became a family of sorts. Sometimes we saw more of each other than our real families. It is not surprising then, that we know when one another hurts, or how deep the hurt is. We are all young women, and this is usually the dating stages or the wedding times or the pregnancy stage of life. Some of the girls have husbands in the service; some have husbands leaving them. Others are just trying to get that M.R.S. degree.

I made up my mind early to be successful! I had planned to work my way through college. My mother did not have the means to pay my way, so it was up to me.

On the side, in another city, once a week I went to a beauty salon in Tacoma Washington, where I began advanced hairstyling lessons. The gentleman who taught me was a member of the National Hair Fashion Committee. Yes, this cost me. Nearly all my extra money, but I knew I had to become better than I was. The lessons were hard, but I learned shortcuts, and theory of movement, design, and confidence. My boss had been watching me more lately, but I was told not to work too much yet with what I learned. I feel better about what I do, and have fun with the flare of using my comb in a more showmanship way. That gives a customer that feeling "you know what you are doing."

My teacher told me that my improvement would become apparent to others little by little, until they became aware I was able to keep my ladies from week to week, and they were very happy with my work!

With everything going for me, it had to have been a shocker when I announced I was leaving.

They will miss me, but they will already be dividing up my customers. I will of course recommend to each of my customers which hairdresser would probably do her hair in the fashion she prefers. Each hairdresser has her own specialties, and cannot please everyone.

BACK to the party! It was great!! We had Mexican food, laughter, cards, and gifts. Plus some tears from my real friends. Sally couldn't wait to remind the others about the time in school, when the teacher yelled at me that my next customer was in! That was right except this was during my second shampoo. When I turned to acknowledge her, I also turned the hose with me. Four other ladies down the line of shampoo bowls shrieked with shock, as the water was now drenching them!!

Another true tale told was about the superior court judge's wife who sent me a live crated turkey. It was the day before Thanksgiving, and the salon was crowded. In walks this delivery service guy who asks for Jamie. He then goes back outside only to return with this huge crate, all wrapped in gift wrap, with a great deal of noise coming from inside. Imagine my surprise when I opened it!! GOBBLE, GOBBLE!!

I left the turkey in the middle of the salon the rest of the day, and named it Henrietta for my customer. I loved this lady a lot. She died of cancer a few months later.

I will miss my friends. Of course, my job is there anytime I need it! It's now time for me to drive home and leave the past and pick up the future.

Barbara Twibell

Mom and I agreed she would not be home this afternoon; so it might be easier to leave. Neither of us is great at saying goodbyes.

I've packed what I think I'll need to spend the summer with Gram. Other belongings I've packed into boxes and labeled. They can be sent another time.

I was hoping the weather would be nicer, but, this is Washington State. The Evergreen State (moss, mold, money, and migration.)

The rain today varies from a mist to a hard knock-down, try-to-find-your-lane, and please-don't-pass-me-truck, rain. My radio is tuned to KIRO from Seattle and some pretty grooving music surrounds me. I feel cozy in the auto cocoon.

I've driven, or, been driven over this same highway for years, and it does not get exciting to me until I pass the Camas pulp and paper mill and head on through Washougal, two very nice smaller towns that have a bundle of civic pride. These two towns are the kinds that make me want to remove my shoes and walk barefoot in their parks. Leaving Washougal one will notice the elevation start to rise. This will go on until the area called "Cape Horn." There is a dramatic viewing area set aside where one can see the whole panorama of the "Gorge" open up. The mountains rise to about four-thousand feet here, with densely timbered hills and spewing waterfalls down the Oregon side. The view is inconceivable and awesome.

Daughter of the Gorge

The beginning of the trip to Gram's seems almost boring as I pass through places like Tacoma and South Tacoma. Ft. Lewis, a famous and large military base, snuggles each side of the freeway. McChord Air Base and the turn off to Madigan Hospital are well known to military veterans sent home to be made better. Olympia, the state Capitol is absolutely gorgeous. A most beautiful city, lying at the base of Budd Inlet. Bustling urban area, the neatest thing about this city to me is the capitol building. It is modeled after the Washington D. C. Capitol. Other places that I pass through are Yelm, Tenino, Centralia, Toledo, and points south. Highway 99 just snakes around the prairies, farms, and fords various rivers, and criss-crosses the railroad tracks.

On a messy day such as today, I will fight staying awake, listening to the windshield wipers. That is why I enjoy breezing along listening to the radio playing a little too loudly. One of the great scenic views one misses while traveling in the rain are the majesties snow covered peaks of Mt. Raineer and St. Helens and Mt. Adams. On a sunny day these mountains seem to travel along with you as you go down the road toward Vancouver, Washington.

At Vancouver, Washington I make a left and go up the river, traveling east towards the "Gorge." At this turn, I will pass through old Fort Vancouver and will be able to see the Interstate Bridge that separates Washington and Oregon. The highway east will travel within view of the mighty Columbia River.

Barbara Twibell

The feeling inside of me is one of awe. I love this place with the deepest and most dedicated emotion I know. This has been home to me more than anywhere else.

In a lifetime of uprooting and moving, I was always brought here, back to "Gram's" to settle down, or visit for awhile.

Winding its way out of the distance, in a soft blue fog, the mighty Columbia River takes shape, getting sharper to the eye as it gets closer to the Cape, and bends its path around and to the side of me to go out of sight to Washougal, Camas, and finally Vancouver, Washington, and past the area mostly known as the greater Portland basin on the Oregon side. The Columbia feeds logging mills, paper mills, orchards, cattle ranches, dairies, wood pulp forests, fish hatcheries, and many cities.

The river naturally goes on to the ocean, but the part that I love, and is my life, is from this point east, past Beacon Rock, Bonneville, Stevenson, and so on to points east.

Sitting in my car at the Cape Horn overlook, the incredible view that forever haunts my memory floods my eyes. Looking over to the left at Gram's farm, it's setting in the saddle of the hillside. The forest looks as if hugging the pastures in the safe wrap of its arms. A rock fall, below the car spreads hundreds of feet down a steep cliff blending onto various beautiful fields, and ranches.

Jamie felt her heart flutter at the sight of the glorious four thousand foot bluffs and waterfalls of the Oregon State side. To my left, a saddle swale large enough for several other farms. The most prevalent and noticeable to me is my grandmother's home! I can see the barn and the house! Even though they look small to the naked eye, most persons would not notice them, tucked in and about tall stately evergreen trees. This is where I will spend another summer, or whatever time, to get my footing.

The time it takes to get to Gram's house is not fast enough. I know the joy we both feel when we are re-united.

The road has turned to gravel now, and I can smell that clean fresh woodsy smell that comes after a rain! The rain fog is just touching the tops of the evergreens.

I drive down to the house on the one lane dirt driveway that's broken down on each side of the center. The middle is filled with grass and dandelions and leads right to the side of the house. All the trees have been bathed by the rain and are vivid dark greens.

I know for certain that Gram will be at the door, in her little print farm dress and overlay apron. She will pretend she was not looking for me, but I always give several strong honks of the horn to announce my arrival, anyway!

I tenderly look forward to the all- engulfing hug Gram has waiting for me, and a kiss on the cheek.

Gram is a large lady with salt and pepper colored hair and soft green eyes, truly a farm lady from the past; the kind most ladies are disengaging themselves from this day and age. Most of the modern women, so I've been told by my "professional" customers, feel a need to "find" themselves, by leaving the farms and housewife segments and getting on with careers to help with family finances.

I can count on Gram having a new tight perm, so that all she has to do is run a comb through it on the way out the door. Her language can be a bit colorful, and her shotgun accuracy is legendary in the countryside. Also, she's probably one of the finest cooks and bakers around. She's let me know how happy she is to have me staying with her and her second husband Mack, the only Grandpa I've ever known.

Mack is a lean farmer, who besides farming and ranching also works for the county. He definitely loves this job, as he sees all parts of the county. On weekends if there are no demands from the animals, he will load Gram and me in the truck to go to the very ends of some road, opening grand sights far from the usual view. This countryside is yet primitive in many areas of the back hills. Only a few farms, mines, or stills pepper the atmosphere.

Gram's hug is wonderful as she takes my coat and sends me into the living room. I don't know what she is up to, but it must have something to do with dinner preparation. I am allowed to drift in thought.

Total disappointment is a new feeling to me, the hurt, the gut- wrenching stab of betrayal, the preoccupation with my mother's last conversation still with me. I know in my heart this is selfish, but Mom unfeelingly told me she wants a new start. AT WHAT? My mind questions.

Daughter of the Gorge

In the matter of weeks, after the loss of Daddy, she said she could no longer afford to keep their typical 1940's GI housing home. She seems so aloof, determined to lift from her heart a heavy burden.

Mom and I have always been close. I think this is why I hurt so much. Daddy came home from overseas so ill, we were told to expect death at nearly anytime. After all that, he's made it for sixteen years from that prediction, couldn't he keep on living? Does he have the right to destroy our expectations of a secure living mode?

I'm nearly twenty, no longer Gramma's baby girl Jamie, but here I am tired, lonely, and confused. What's happened to my life? I'd give anything to get this out of my mind. I barely remember the drive from Seattle to here, I've been so upset.

The weather matches my mood. Bad!

"Jamie, could you set the table? We'll have some dinner as soon as Mack is done in the barn. We have some new calves, and I'm certain you'll want to go up to the barn in the next few days and hug them up good. You'll love the new milk glasses I got at the dime store last week. They're green, my favorite color." Gram moves about in her kitchen in such a ballet of familiarity.

"Check out the new oilcloth on the table also. Actually I splurged!" Gram proudly announced. Oilcloth is something Mom hasn't used for years on her tables, always brightly patterned, and like a very soft linoleum material. Very flexible but feels a little oily. Anyway it is new, and Gram is very proud.

Gramma's splurge would have taken place in Camas. Her favorite kind of town. Clerks treat everyone as if they have known them all their lives. Bits and pieces of gossip drop here and there. Stopping first at Woolworth's the dime store, then of course Montgomery Wards (better known as Monkey Wards) with its creaking floorboards, and prim authoritive clerks. What she can't locate there she will order from the catalog.

Looking out the living room window, I'm brought back to where I really am. Across the driveway is a grouping of wild grapes. At one time they were a precious arbor, the starts brought over from the old country. Ever notice the little curls of vine that lie about grape leaves? Now leaves are bent with the rain, and they are dripping on one another until they bend with the weight, and the water falls to the ground where it becomes a tiny stream trickling along, searching for the driveway, joining others and becoming a rolling stream down into the pasture.

"Jamie, did you hear me?" asked Gram.

"I'm sorry, Gram, be right there!"

"Honey, don't think so much tonight. Tomorrow is another day, and we love your being with us. We'll talk in the morning if you wish. Just rest, and let's enjoy! The fresh milk is still in the skimming pans, so pour it into the pitcher. After skimming off the cream, you can put the cream in that bowl over there. Don't forget the butter, dear, it's in the cooling cupboard! The cream is so thick it hangs from the skimmer ladle. Tomorrow we will make new butter. Don't look for glasses that match, I think it's more colorful for each person to have their own!" There Stood Gram, her hands on her hips.

"Gram, you just told me you bought new glasses. Why aren't we using them?"

"They are just to look at for now. Christmas should be soon enough for their use." Gram's quite smug about this.

Grandma's meals feel good as well as smell good; she's a terrific cook. When you eat at her home everything is from scratch, fresh, and different to the taste buds. Tonight, I can tell its fried potatoes with onions, creamed tomatoes, home grown green beans, and homemade bread and jam. The milk and butter home grown and fresh! I'm lost in the wonder of this when...

A dramatic burst of the door, the slam of the screen, and the gust of air announce the entrance of Grandpa.

His red hunter's hat is soaking wet, as is the rest of him. His Italian black hair is still a shiny mop peeking out from the hat. He has beautiful teasing brown eyes, and a ready smile. He also smells of wet cow hide, hay, and cow pucky.

Anytime now Gram will send him right back to the back porch, to leave his boots, coat, and hat! This is tradition for the two of them. Sometimes he even manages the cold hands under the apron. That brings about a shout and some saltiness from the "Boss" as he lovingly calls his life partner.

Barbara Twibell

"Jamie, saw your car, checked to be sure the windows were up. Glad you got here before dark! This "ole" River Gorge is good at making up its own weather. You need any help with bags? Ah, I see you already have them in the house."

Mack is not the type for unnecessary small talk. He works hard and listens hard. He'll now wash up, change his duds and come back downstairs, grab the newspaper, and head for the living room. He always checks the heater, a four foot stove, with damper controls. Its only purpose is to heat. Gram keeps a tea kettle filled with water on top of the heater. Something about making humidity. Between the kitchen stove and the heater, it's very cozy.

Just before bedtime the doors to the rooms upstairs will be opened and the heat will flow wonderfully around the walls, and up the stairway to fill the bed rooms with heat for most of the night. The heat wears off later in the early morning hours, since the stove is banked, and then allowed to die out. The result of course is very cold mornings when we get up!

After all these years, there really isn't any difference to the room that has always been mine. It is easy to unpack and put my treasures where I can see them.

To its pioneer look, all credit must be given to the feeling that permeates the brown metal bed. Something I get only at Grandma's are these flannel sheets. They're much warmer than regular sheets, even though, a little rough on the toes. The sheets are always pink or green. Hearing that Mack has cleaned up and I am all unpacked, I rejoin everyone downstairs. We all chatter away through dinner and the evening until we're so tired we must go to bed.

3

I couldn't possibly survive this morning, if the quilt should slip below my nose. It may be early summer, but tell that to the rain and cold that accompanies it!

Across the room, one trunk acts as a table and there is a brown mirrored dressing table, covered with a runner. This dresser is on the same side of the room as the only window. I enjoy lying here thinking, and remembering how I have been trying to count hundreds of nail points for years. Trying to section them off square by square as to how many are in a section, times how many sections per square, then my eyes would close in sleep.

Since the rooms are unfinished compared to new homes, with no wallboard, shake nails are exposed; therefore, the challenge is to count each and every one of them!

All the windows in the upstairs area are smaller than in a modern home. There are a couple of rangy looking curtains nailed to the sides of my bedroom window. As one looks out, though, something strikes you. You're now seeing the most fabulous view in the world!

The pasture dropping away from Gram's home is dotted with various trees and fences. The whole panorama is outlined with luscious evergreen trees and rolling pastures. The little spring- fed creek coming from under the house meanders its way into the distance to the property line, surrounded at some height by blackberry bushes.

Daughter of the Gorge

Multnomah Falls, Horse Tail Falls and Oregon's Scenic Highway are in clear, everyday view.

It is always interesting to watch the traffic work its way along the river. At night one sees car lights twinkle like stars as they work around the scenic highway. It's so much fun to follow the lights in and out, up and down the hills.

To the pioneer, this was the Oregon they suffered to reach. Lewis and Clark and their party came down this same river. Just think in little over two hundred years we have gone from canoes to Grand River barges and airlines. There is not one thing in my view that is not incredible. To the right, the point called Cape Horn. If it had not been blasted for the Washington side of the Gorge Highway, this outcropping is said to have been larger than the "Rock of Gibraltar." Progress doesn't always know until it's too late though.

To the left is the flow of the mighty Columbia, back grounded by the Oregon Cascades. One can barely see the Beacon Rock, believed to be a volcanic core that the river washed the small mountain away from, leaving exposed the tall volcanic stem people by the thousands climb each year.

I know Gram is up! I can hear her! This is certain!!

She's been up a long time. There is a certain period of peace and quiet, then as Gram thinks her guest should be up, the radio is turned up, and the clatter of dishes ring like church bells in your head.

Barbara Twibell

The over- cheerful gab of the "Don McNeill Breakfast Hour", with the march around the kitchen that they encourage, is, at this hour, criminal! But, she marches, and she sings along. I can't help but giggle!

Why do crisp bacon, moist scrambled eggs and fluffy pancakes smell so good? Mom and I are lucky to have a bowl of Cheerios in the morning! Not at Gram's. It's the goods for breakfast and you better eat or she'll know you're sick or something.

NO! I will not get up yet...Just let me lie here and...count sharp shake nail endings. Daydream, forget I'm an adult, I'm Gram's girl!

There's no finish work in these rooms upstairs, except one bedroom Gram saves for special company. It is painted white, over thin ship lap. Arched in a barn shaped style. At the end of this room is a window about the size of one's kitchen sink. It closes from each end to the center. This room also is on the side of the house that is exposed to the entry gate to the farm. This gate is up the dirt road driveway and is about three football lengths from the house. A wire gate and hinge keep the property private.

Occasionally, a love struck local looking for a "petting spot" has opened the gate, and driven in a bit, and turned off the lights to his car. They've gotten comfortable, only to have the aforementioned window flung open and the blast of shotgun fire rip apart his intentions. Most of the time people leave in such a hurry that we have to go shut or repair that gate before the cattle find it open!

A room adjacent to this room actually has a raised floor, necessitating a person having to stoop over on entry. It is completely unfinished and again, has a small window looking out over the apple orchard. As I grew up, the scenery was altered by the growth of a fir tree. This room is a prized mess, and only Gramma knows its contents. There are round tubs, canneries, trunks, canning jars, out of date appliances, and various other clutter. There is an old dusty dress form in one corner Gram has an old jacket draped over. There are several cigar boxes near a ledge. These are full of pennies Gram and Mack are saving. Four canners are on the floor and are filled with hazel nuts. They are there to dry over the winter and be eaten later. Several wood poles are nailed horizontally on beams. These hold old coats, dresses, belts or anything that should be hung up. They might be needed someday, you know.

Gram thanks the family to not bother themselves with knowledge of the contents of any mysterious boxes.

"Jamie, breakfast is waiting you, and so is a beautiful day! It's only overcast! Gram can always see a better day. No sense crying over spilled milk, she would tell me. "Just clean it up and carry on!"

Gram and Grandpa's room is at the head of the stairs. No wall, as you come up the eight stairs there is the bed. There is no railing, and little dust rolls lie under the bed, here and there. Beside the bed is a dresser with mirror, and across one corner, a pole is nailed in to hang clothes on. This year they bought a nice piece of linoleum for under the bed.

Gram also made a new rag braided throw rug "to put their tootsies on."

I am not going to be able to ignore Gramma much longer. For me to get up entails a bit more than at home. There, we have an indoor toilet!!

Gram always says she can't understand why people want to poop in the house and eat outside. Just isn't sanitary. As opposed to the modern outdoor barbecue and inside bathrooms. Speaking of bathrooms, (baths) when I was younger, I was given a big round tub to bathe in. Now Gramma has the modern convenience of a fold- up rubber tub that is used on the back porch and when finished you simply tip it over, and empty it out onto the board floor where it seeps through to the ground.

"Jamie, this day is just gonna fly away, if you don't get out of that bed soon!"

This morning means dressing quickly, putting on shoes, getting down the stairs, (ever try running down stairs, keeping your knees together?) beating it out the kitchen door, falling over a half wet collie named Laddie, and beating it down the path into the "privy." Getting half undressed, and praying the Sears catalogue is there, in case the toilet paper holder is empty.

The "privy" is a two holer, not that I ever welcomed anyone to come in with me! A bucket of lime is always sitting on the floor with a cup inside. This is to be poured over the, Ah, contents when finished.

Topping the little out house are the most beautiful small wild roses you ever saw. I mean really covering the whole house with exception of the door... Guess what else? The "little" house leans backwards at enough of an angle to be a little uncomfortable.

Grampa says, "It has many good years left, and not to worry!"

In back of and to the side are the most robust and fertile plum trees one could ever pick from. Far larger than average- sized fruit purchased in a store. I never seemed to remember NOT to eat them too early, before being fully ripe.

Why do people over- indulge when they visit? I never eat such breakfasts at home.

There's nothing as tasty as hand cured, and hand carved bacon from a slab that's about eight by ten inches ... ummm so wonderful.

It seems that everything here is so homey. So personal. So private.

Gram doesn't even have hot water like we do. She heats her water in a copper boiler on the backside of her pride and joy, the wood stove. The cold water is from a gravity flow spring in the garden at the back of the house, and brought by gravity into the house to the kitchen sink. The spring is at the foot of the most beautiful tree. There is a small pool, deep and cool, with its own noisy resident frog. That part of the back yard being in the garden. The garden is about the size of the bottom floor of the house. One small section has a row of raspberries, and a row of black-cap raspberries. Another row is goose berries. Another corner has rhubarb plants. Mack then has the freedom to plant his garden his way!

Barbara Twibell

Remember the garden is at the back of the house, which is really the front because Gram says so. They only need one entry into their home.

She fills her "house milk bucket" from under the kitchen faucet, and swings it out over the sink staggering the few paces to the boiler sitting on top of the wood stove. The buckets of water are very heavy. Gram repeats this until the boiler is full. Use this bucket for anything else, and you better be ready to run!! I supposedly am raised in the modern mode of life. Yet, Gram is so careful how food is handled, and things washed completely that I think she is the more modern. Everything is fresh and healthy. This boiler is her hot water for whatever. The kitchen sink is one compartment. When she does dishes, she uses a couple of milk pans to wash in. Then rinses her dishes, and places them on her rack to air dry.

The front porch was never fully completed. So stands a beautiful glass paned door and screen about five feet off the ground with no stairs to it! A garden of over-crowded iris are stumbling over each other in vivid hues of lavender, purple, yellow and white, fighting for sunlight. When I was younger, I made auto roads in and around all the tubers. This kept me out of Gramma's hair for hours.

The kitchen cupboards are but boxed- in shelves, with pretty red gingham curtains on wire spring rods. There is a wood kitchen table and four round rimmed wooden chairs. A modern large refrigerator is in one corner. So, as you come into the house, the stairway upstairs is on your right

Daughter of the Gorge

with a sideboard next to it. Above the side board is a girly calendar Mack brought home from work. To the left are the kitchen table, cupboards and drain board. At the back wall are the wood stove, and the door to the dining room. There is no telephone. Neither Gram nor Mack can see the reason to have the nuisance brought into the home.

I cannot describe how I love and need this atmosphere, so unpretentious.

My daydreaming is interrupted by Gram asking me how I feel today.

"I had a great night's sleep Gramma, and I do feel better. Just being with you makes everything better.

I'll get over this Gram, I just have a hard time understanding why Mom couldn't let me know she needed help. She could have sold things we didn't really need, or I could have helped pay bills. She never let on. I was so happy. I thought Mom was, too." Talking about this was not easy.

"Jamie, Maurine and I talked a few weeks ago. Remember when I came up to your home for my last visit?"

"I didn't want to broach this subject last night. There are things you need to know... it was my suggestion you come be with me for the summer, or however long you want. Your mother needs time and space to see where she wants to go with her life now, now that your father's gone.

"Maurine married young; this you know. She was younger then, than you my dear. The man your mother fell in love with, was not the same man sent home to her from the Philippines. Your mother was left pregnant with you, and not enough money to raise you. Four years is a long time for a woman to be without a husband, and when he came home he could not be one. It was not in his heart, or body. This handsome virile man was left bitter, cruel, and crippled. Maurine was locked in a loveless marriage far too many years. The grief from your fathers' death most people would expect your mother to feel, is not there, only a release.

She loves you so much, Jamie. She will be all right. We'll just give her some time to repair, right?" Gram studies my face.

Wow, I never knew. The earliest I can remember, Mom and I together, we lived in North Bonneville, Washington. We lived in a small white house on Second Street. Mom saved very hard to buy a home with the money my dad sent from over seas. She wanted so to surprise him. It had only one bedroom, a small living room, a functional kitchen, and a wood-shed.

Mom took me to the stores. I remember there was kind-of a board walk we walked on. The stores were small, like dress shops, shoe repair, etc. We went for walks and she sang to me. She sang songs of Glenn Miller, she sang so pretty. I had not thought about these memories for a long time. Always there were the mountains! Always they shadowed us, encircled our lives. They might have been black with rain, or white with snow.

During the nights, my mother worked at the Sanitarium, or nursing home as they are called now. She would take me with her and bed me down in an extra bed. Mom always showed me pictures

Daughter of the Gorge

of this man and would say he was my daddy. Every night we would say a prayer for his safety while at war. I do remember a fire in Bonneville, though. We were so scared our house would burn. Everyone in town fought hard to kill the flames. And, they did!

My little mind had no concept of a "Daddy" or a "War."

"Your father kinda did a dirty to your momma, while overseas. He wrote to her that he had fallen in love with a Philippine girl and wanted a divorce. He hadn't even seen his baby daughter yet! Well, this really made your mamma sick, literally. But she did file for divorce as he requested, and things were going along fine, until, your father was sent home to die.

The doctors and his commanding officer felt he would not get better. They convinced your mamma to go to Spokane and see him in the hospital, feeling that seeing her and his daughter might turn things around." Gram looks so grave.

"Both your mom and dad seemed to feel in the long run it would be best to try to work out a marriage for their little girl, while he was alive. He was of course unable to bring that other woman back to the United States. I don't think it was ever mentioned again so as anyone would notice. My sweet Maurine was no longer herself after that."

Gram kind of looks so sad as she tells me all this.

"Gram, could this be why people thought my mother was so bitter about men?" Even I was surprised at her attitude towards conversations concerning men.

"Yes, Dear, she truly tried to live her wedding vows, but, it was never an easy life for her. You know though... Gotta give them credit, they pulled a life together for their daughter, now didn't they?"

I could tell this was the end of this subject.

"Enough now, Help me pick up the dishes, and I think I'll send you off to the chicken house to collect today's "Cackle berries" (Gram's words for chicken eggs) Gram is particular about her chickens, only Rhode Island Reds! And big beautiful brown eggs. The very best for cooking. When she was looking for a drumstick on a chicken it better look like a small club! Gram abhorred skinny chickens. Hers were always fat butted and singing!

The sun is coming out; I can feel the warmth starting to penetrate my coat. The grass is wet. I should have slipped my boots on. With the sun out, comes that weird steam off the field, kind of putting a ground fog all around. I can hear the cow bells tinkling, so I know the cows are on the upper pasture. The bells are so rhythmical. While cattle eat they swing their mouths along side to side clipping grass and then swallowing it. That's why there is a ding-a-ding, ding –a- ding rhythm. Some cow bells go "tink", some "clang, clang, some "dong, dong" depending on the size of the animal. All together, quite a remarkable chorus. Mack was careful to use a large bell on the bull, another size on the cows, and little ones on the babies. If a two year old was about to go to market, yet another size

Daughter of the Gorge

bell was used for it. Quite an easy way to know who is where! There were times in the past that Mack offered to set a bell on me!

Near a tall cedar tree on the way to the "hen pen," I pass a tall cone- shaped ant hill, about knee high... Each year during the growing up period I felt it my duty to destroy this work of art, with the appropriate sized branch, matching my growth.

When I was a "Wee One," there were times I couldn't run fast enough to beat out the angry worker ants. Nuff said?

As I became older and wiser, the branches became longer and stronger. The nest usually got flung galley west!!

Now that I am a young woman, the ants are finally safe to carry on. I'm really too old for such things... It's nice to be more mature. But, what if part of baby ant training depends on destruction, and training for rebuilding? There's the branch... the nest, YES!! No one's looking!!

Dirt paths have their own feel, muddy, slippery, dry, or overgrown. Today's jaunt to the chicken house means wet shoes and wet pant legs. Even if the sun comes out today, long field grass takes time to dry out. Gram's girl chickens she calls "ole Bitties" are careful to chorus out the cackles each morning, or they may grace the table Sunday! The boy chicken of course is the rooster, tall, bright red feathers, and proud of taking care of the girls. If he keeps a happy pen, it, may be a long time until he's Sunday dinner.

Got nine eggs this morning, nice clean brown ones. Other than one indignant chicken who squawked her eye balls out, the trip could be said to be a success. Breakfast was great, but Gram's lunches are a work in creativity. Soup, sandwich, piece of yellow cake, and Kool-Aid. Most of the time I'd beg for the grape flavor.

A great dinner was put on the table tonight, ham and beans, real farm-raised ham. Do up the dishes in the sink inside a tan-colored deep pan. Rinse the dishes under the tap and dry them right away. Then, more wood in stove, (living room) read the newspaper, Farmer's Almanac, have some hot chocolate, and Gramma says, "time to go to bed, Jamie, Mack has to get up for work at five a.m."

I NEVER GO TO BED until around eleven. You know dates, parties, and a life?

I HATE GOING TO BED EARLY!!

I mean, I don't have to get up at five o'clock. Who in their right mind does that?

No sense of any argument, I love these two people too much to be a brat. (On purpose)

This might be where I developed my need to read by flashlight every evening. Gram would be patient though, there was only a brown curtain across my doorway, separating their bedroom from mine. After awhile, Gramma would say sweetly, "Goodnight Jamie. You need your sleep."

Out would go the light!

4

"Jamie, would it be too much trouble for you to go to the store for some baking powder and some chocolate chips? Maybe pick up some snacks you enjoy. I don't know what young people like today. A box of those chocolate covered cherries too, if they have them." Gram's favorite.

"Wanna go too, Gram?"

"No, Honey, I must get to this ironing. It waits for no one, unless you want to do it for me."

"Is there anything else you need, Gram?"

"Be careful, but enjoy yourself. I'm not in a big hurry." With that I get a hug and a push off. "Scat!" she says.

Gram doesn't want to drive. Ever!! Mack told me he put her behind the wheel once, and was going to teach her. "This is the clutch. This is the brake. This is the gas," instructed Grampa Mack.

"Let this up slowly, while putting this in gear here, apply a little gas, and off we go"…It took the tractor to pull the truck out of the hog pen, and a dinner out in Camas that night for Grampa Mack to repair his marriage.

It's amazing how many miles of beautiful roads are in the Skamania county area. Not all of the roads are paved. There are many that have an oil base covering that crushed rock is poured onto and allowed to be worked into the oil, and then there are plain old dirt roads, many with deep ruts. When it rains they turn to brown mud. Most of the country roads are pretty curvy. Sometimes a person can almost choke in the dust and fear of

Barbara Twibell

corners and sheer drop offs. Travelers from out of state are heard to often say they can't stand to drive down so many roads that all they can see is a narrow path in the timber. Well, when you come out of those places you're met with the sight of your life, maybe a glorious canyon or blue, blue lake or little homestead.

5

"WHO THE HELL PARKED THAT DAMN BROKEN DOWN OLD BLUE CHRYSLER IN FRONT OF THE WATER HOSE? Some people must get their licenses from the Cracker Box Co. Hell Fred, I can't get my truck in there." Pacing with impatience, a man toward the front of the store was waving his arms.

I jumped, as reality pierced my brain. He's yelling about my car. It's me he's mad at, mad, this ape man is FURIOUS, and I'm the reason!

Fred calls out, "Anyone own the blue car?"

Silence...

"Great balls of fire, they don't have a brain either, and at least no one's spoken up."

"I'll move it, I'm so sorry," I reply. With great trepidation, I move up to the front of the store.

"Sorry's a damn waste of time, Honey," he sneers.

I began to feel the heat of embarrassment climb from my neck, on up to my face.

"Just a minute, just a cotton pickin' minute, I'm not stupid, nor am I unlicensed." Anger was flowing away from common sense.

The eyes I'm looking into are a flaming brown; they could not be any darker...

"AND, sir, you have the VILEST manners I've ever witnessed, or had the displeasure to hear. Couldn't you have just asked the violator to move their car?" I know I'm glaring at this despicable beast. His seething dark mood was enveloping my space.

"Wellll, Excuse oos me, little lady, how could I ask when I did not know who owned that pile of junk still sitting in the way of my truck?!!!!!"

This ape was now towering over me with obvious disgust, his shoulders broader than I'd noticed before. His hair was a soft brown, wild neck length, with a beautiful clean shine, part of which fell onto his forehead in a reckless fashion. In a glance, I couldn't help but see his jeans fit all too well, capping off a pair of black cowboy boots.

"I'm leaving, don't fritter yourself!" With this I jerked open the car door, slammed it shut, started the engine and left dust, as I crossed back over the Steel Bridge.

My car is not a piece of junk. It's a well-preserved Tank that runs very well on the straights. It's a soft blue, with mohair grey interior, pleasant dashboard, and lots of chrome. Anyone knows a Chrysler New Yorker is a fine car. Even if she is older.

Daddy wanted her for my safety. We paid three- hundred dollars! Buying this car for me probably was one of the best times Daddy and I ever shared together.

I needed a car, but of course, Mom felt I was entirely too young to own one. Daddy said the only way Mom would consent to me having a car was to go buy it!

Daddy had a friend who lived up in Lakewood, Washington, and wanted to sell "Tank," so we bought it. I looked for a station to buy gas, and as recommended, stopped at Twibell Brothers' Signal Station and loaded her up, with the best gas they

Daughter of the Gorge

had. Believe it or not, a nice man named Lynn serviced my fuel and said I "had a great buy". So "Tank" is not a hunk of junk. I said at that time I would not forget him, because he really was interested in my special day!

I'll never forget that first day or any of the details. When we drove "Tank" home and parked her, we anxiously waited until my mother noted it and realized the car was not going away!! As most parents, she found new freedom in not having to take me back and forth to work. In fact Mom drove less, and sent me out more!

Twenty nine cents a gallon for fuel in that "Tank." It is amazing how long it took for those errands.

Jump-up creek! Man, wake up Jamie, you've just driven off from the store without your purchases, and it's now half way home with no goods.

How in the world can I explain being gone so long, and bring home no groceries? The next closest store is at least fifteen miles the other direction. So, I look both ways, and I pop a U- turn and slowly mosey my way back. The store is now in sight, and that miserable "Big Red Truck" is gone. I must be more careful where I park this time, I park, and re-enter. To hear.

"Sorry lass," I'm greeted at the door by Fred. "I should have protected you a lot better. I had no idea you had a car of your own now." Fred leans out over his counter, using it for a counter balance for his stomach. "I figured you would be coming back soon." Fred nervously fidgets. "Lance is a little rambunctious sometimes; I'd like to apologize for him."

"Forget it Fred; he's a big boy, and, I noticed he has a big mouth! He can do his own apologizing."

"You up at your Grandparents? I mean visiting or something?"

"Yes, I think I'll spend the summer, probably the last I can get this kind of time off. Need to get away from city hassle."

"Lance never had a momma to smooth the edges. He's too much like his pa. He's foreman for his dad on their cattle ranch, down on the river bottom. Couple of months out of the year he does rodeo work... He's good too!! But, he usually comes back spitting nails. Takes longer to heal you know. He's a good boy."

Fred seems to be searching my face for some type of understanding.

"Well, he ruined my day. I can see why some horse would live to throw him."

On the way back to Grams, I can't help but think of the many summers Grampa Mack, with Gram and me, trotted off to the Steel Bridge Store. We'd crowd into their green pick up (Rig, Grampa called it) and drive through some of the richest farm lands in the world. Following a pretty creek bending here and there, meandering through pastures, woods, and parks, giving of itself, to whoever needed its pleasure. I always got lost in daydreams, and often fell asleep.

Who'd that big creep think he is? Still embarrassed, I tend to daydream on. It's difficult to

Daughter of the Gorge

not have your mind playback an unpleasant situation. Today definitely was unpleasant!

The Steel Bridge Store seemed such a hub of excitement. Everyone drove over to meet with neighbors and friends. We could buy candy, flour, pop, and cheese from a big wheel! This wheel of cheese was as big as a trailer tire around, and seemed about ten inches thick. Fred would always fill Gram's order, then, with the same huge knife, cut a piece for the "youngun". This must be where I got my love for "Sharp" Tillamook cheese.

Sometimes in the summer there would be a mass of people down on the Bridge Park for picnics. Once I remember being taken to a pioneer reunion. At that time in my young life I remember more that these people were very old. Some of the men had long beards. The ladies wore funny black heavy looking shoes. All were talking about their crops, or great grand children. I remember how neat I thought it was that they thought their children great. How I wish I could talk to these people now, and drain all the knowledge of the past I could get from them.

Such nice people. Gram says, "People here are always nice, unless they aren't!" Such wisdom!

I love, even now, to walk out to the center of the bridge and look over into the very clear deep moving water in which you can see the rocks. Great huge sturgeon seems to pause against the current, weaving back and forth showing off their size. Some must be as long as a person's leg.

It's deceiving how deep the water is under the bridge. So clear, and full of large and smaller rocks.

Here and there another kind of fish could be seen, but I don't know what kind. Fred is always reminding locale kids here not to jump off the bridge into the river. It looks so deep and inviting, it is just not the smartest thing to do. Too many people have been severely injured.

After rains, the forests are so beautiful. The clean pungent odor, the pine and fir smell stronger. Deep dark greens, and every other shade of green in the color spectrum. With dirt roads, everything near the roads gets a thick carpet of dust. Like, if you notice big blackberries next to the road you would not pick there since it's not worth it. You'd have to wash each and every berry thoroughly. But, they do let you know berries are ripe and somewhere along the way, they will be picking able. Hardly anyone cares if you're picking berries; just don't stray too far onto the farmers land. Maybe this is why farm houses are set back off main roads! You can see a tornado of dust behind a car or truck passing across a hill, and not even see a road.

Gram hates to dust and there is evidence of this fact. Though she's careful to keep up the places where someone might be "lookin." Her bedding and doilies are perfection! Her doilies are stiff with starch mixed just the way she wants it. By stiff I mean the edges are wavy all around a vase or whatnot on the table. Other beautiful doilies are on the arms of chairs and across the backs of couches. This makes for a very nice effect in homemaking.

As I get home and grab the groceries from the backseat of the car and head for the house, I can smell the most delicious scent of fresh baked bread and rolls. How Gramma gets pan rolls to stand uniformly six inches tall and so perfect, I just don't know. I love to break them open, put my nose a bit inside and drift away in the odor of yeast bread. I know this is not an accepted practice, but it is my roll, and I'm eating it!

After dinner Grampa Mack usually tells us about his day at work. Where they graded, or put in new culverts, or fixed pot holes or something, and the talk is exciting since this is how Gram gets her facts and gossip! I listen with one ear and enjoy also.

"Heard Jamie had a run-in with Lance Allison today!" Mack has that twinkle in his eye.

"Where in heaven's name did you hear that?" Gram huffed.

"Oh, I guess down at the Bridge Store," Grampa Mack smirked. "Ole Fred says our girl took nothing' off him, and rightly singed his proud feathers!" His eyes were boring into me, waiting.

"Jamie? You said nothing when you came home," Gram quizzed. "What happened? Did he go botherin' you?" Gram's face shows deep concern.

Mack's shows sheer delight, if I can read faces right!

Gram says, "That big Goliath does not need to pick on our Jamie. Mack, you just go speak to him."

"Hey guys, no big deal... I was the one in the wrong. I parked my car in the way of others, and he simply pointed out my error. If you will excuse me, I think I'll head up to bed." With that I give each a kiss and hug and head off to bed. If I'm not wrong I think I see disappointment in Grandpa's eyes, and concern in Gramma's.

While trying to go to sleep, I can't help but think that my relationships with men are altogether different than my girl friends. They are always in love, and I am always acquiring guys who change over to being big brothers.

Ted, My latest boyfriend was a sweet guy, and we had fun together, but he just was getting on my nerves. As soon as I knew I would be coming to the Gorge, I thought it a good time to break up. I find it's not an easy thing to do. I hate hurting people, so, it takes just the right time and words. I'd rehearsed this all quite carefully. We both love hamburgers, so we met to have lunch. After a little small talk, I swallow and get ready... Just then, Ted announced he has met a real fox, and knows how we are just friends and he goes on to tell me how she really rings his bells. Ted is so happy. There goes pride!

I'm not really into this "in love" thing. I want dearly to have a great marriage someday, and a couple of children, but I've just not found anyone whom I need to be with that much. Men at least the ones I have met seem so bossy and frightening to me. I love being able to talk about interesting things, go places, laugh, feel free. But it seems when I date fellas they seem to want to neck, kiss too much, and leave nearly no room to breathe. I'm not even sure I know them, and then they are pledging their undying love.

Guys ask a girl to go to the drive- in to see a movie, and then, they don't even want to watch the movie! Sometimes I go to the rest room so many times, or for refreshments, that these guys get all bent out of shape, and I never see them again. They asked for a movie, not for a petting match!

6

Today Gramma wants to iron, so she's given me the day to play! Said she had no need of my help. "Go have some fun." I don't suppose she gets tired of me just hanging around. Yesterday she had a bottle with a sprinkler attached to the end, and she sprinkled water on each garment and folded it in an oblong ball (navy style) then laid each garment in a basket for ironing today.

After leaving Gramma's, I decide to take Tank out exploring. There are many routes to the river. One of the first memories I come upon is where Toney and Mabel Chemento had their little Tavern/Restaurant. They were famous for their authentic Italian spaghetti. They have both died now, and the buildings have been torn down. They were such fun people. My parents once helped them out when they lost a trusted employee. Mom helped with the cooking, and I suppose Dad helped with the beer. On one of the walls was the first picture of Custer's Last Stand that I had ever seen. It was a brutal picture. I remember they had one of the first Studebakers (a car) that were in the county. It was a soft green. Actually I thought it a pretty weird looking car. Tony and Mabel were really proud of that ugly car.

The splendor of the countryside is causing me to want to explore every road down to the river. I've not had "Tank" very long, and I love the feeling of freedom of driving and making my own decisions. Daddy didn't live very long after our big car adventure. Owning a car has given me the delicious

Daughter of the Gorge

feeling of being adult! The price of fuel at twenty-nine cents a gallon is a bummer though. Not every day will I be able to cavort around as I plan to today.

I find myself wanting to rediscover things and places that others had shared with me. Could I find these on my own? Tank is a good car. So heavy that she fairly floats on the road.

Mom bought new tires and got a lube job for "her girl" before I left. Yesterday I got a small letter from Mom. She's very excited about the possibility she may have a buyer for our home. She said she was trimming down things that she really didn't need any more. Mom's decided to try to find a duplex, separated by a garage. If she can close on a deal, she says she wants to take a vacation, do what she hopes I am doing, just ramming around trying to figure out what comes next. Her letter sounded light and fun. There was no preaching as to what to do or not do. I about fainted when the enclosure dropped out of her letter, a one hundred dollar bill!! All mine to spend as I wish!! Gram sputtered on about sending cash in the mail.

Grampa Mack had said this Lance character's ranch was on the river bottom. I will, of course, see if I might find it.

Everything is so quiet; I wonder if people living here realize how beautiful it is? I'm certain they must! I'm the stranger here, not them! I can't fill my eyes enough! Everything is so fresh and healthy, cattle have a nice sheen, sheep are clean, horses look well loved and cared for, chickens and bunnies abound. Each little farm has its own history and little community sharing its past and future. One farm even has a pond that people have told me has large frogs. They raise them for frog legs (I wonder what they do with the rest of the frog?) Also they raise trout. This fascinates me! I really would love to stop by and ask to see all of this. They don't know me from sundown, so I'll not stop.

Another farm I'm passing has huge areas of raspberries and strawberries. A few years ago, I picked for the Mackey's. They were so kind to kids. Each year when the berry season was over they would have a picnic down at Beacon Rock State Park. I made enough money to buy my school clothes. One year I ate so many strawberries, if I had been weighed, they probably would not have paid me! I went home for dinner only to have Gramma proudly announce large homemade strawberry shortcakes for dessert. I just about got sick!! I choked it down, kissed Gram and told her how great dessert was. I remember I swore off strawberries for the rest of the season.

This road I've turned on now sure has a lot of pot holes. It's in terrible shape. I'll go to the end and turn around. I needn't ruin my tires or paint job just for curiosity's sake.

Oh Oh, there's not too much room to turn around in. Let's see, pull over to the edge, and swing the car around, back up, turn some more, and back up. I should be able to complete the turn now! I can do this, what the... What's this? I'm not able to steer... the car's slipping down and off to one side!

Daughter of the Gorge

Oh, man, what to do? I can't get my door open, no, it's moving, it's just so heavy since I have to get out on the uphill side. That done, I can see a jack will be of no help, so I get back in and I think if I steer the car back towards the road, at the same time putting a little gas to the effort, maybe I can drive along, and up out of this minor ditch! Yes, that's what I'll do…

Great! Brain left in the coat check!

Now I am in a mess, the car is defiantly stuck in the ditch. In fact it's laying to the right side in the ditch. I'll look in my purse, why I don't know. There certainly is no driver's manual in my purse.

"Schuss me," a male voice says, "may I be of help?" The hair on my arms stand up, I freeze. There's a note of sarcasm I immediately recognize. I turn, Oh no, it's him, all of him, and he's leaning against my car, with the whitest teeth showing through the biggest grin. Those big dark consuming eyes, the strong line of his jaw, his eyebrows, quirked in question.

I feel myself trembling as I try to come up with some answer that won't have me yelled at. "What are you doing here?" I rasp out. "You nearly scared the daylights out of me!" My insides rolling wherever insides roll.

"I think I could be asking you the same question, but, in answer, I was out on the back pastureland dropping off new fence posts for the repair of some high water damage, when I heard the unusual revving of an automobile engine. Figured some idiot got himself in a fix."

Lance straightens up and adjusts his rodeo buckle, and hitches his jacket a bit. His smile slowly becomes a smirk.

Oh pickles! Simmer down, Jamie. I think I could just deck this windbag. Heat is rising slowly to my ears, via my face! Looking past Lance, I now see a previously missed field gate, and a large red rig... door open and engine running.

"Well," repeats Lance, "do you need help or not? You're just lucky little lady that I was down here. Seems to me, at first choice, you should try to stay on the road. At second choice not be on THIS road! WELL?"

No one has ever talked to me this way, except a parent. And by gosh darn, he's not going to! I feel like I've been overexposed to a broiler.

"I DON'T NEED YOUR HELP! NOW OR EVER!" Is that me I just heard screaming?

"Okay!" With that Lance turns, heads for his rig, jumps up onto the seat, slams the truck in reverse and pops back through the gate. He then turns off the ignition, gets out, slams the door shut, goes back through the gate, closes it, and jumps up on the gate to seat himself across from me and just sits there.

I fidget, think, stew, fidget, and after several minutes realize it's getting a lot warmer in the car. In fact it's down right HOT! I need to do something, but what? I turn my head, and he's still perched there.

"Why don't you go away and leave me be?"

"Don't have to!" The male voice answers.

Daughter of the Gorge

"What right do you have bullying me this way? I'm driving on a county road, and where I go, or what happens to me is none of your business!"

"Sweetheart, I own this field, gate, road, and the ditch you seem to want to play in. YOU'RE TRESPASSING on private posted land, duly noted at the beginning this lane!" Now, he is turning his hat around, and round, in his hands cowboy fashion. That same smirk on his face.

It's unbearable; I can't take anymore of this! My back is killing me from sitting at this weird angle. I wrestle with my hips, feet, and arms to get the darn door reopened, and spring from the car. Phooey TANK, Grampa will come for you, I thought. I've worked up the courage to fulfill my new plan and without a word strike out at a brisk stride!!

"HEY, WHERE YA GOIN?" calls Lance.

"HOME, IF IT'S ANY OF YOUR BUSINESS!" Snuffs Jamie.

Lance was dumbfounded.

"YOU'RE A PRETTY BULL- HEADED GIRL. I WAS GOING TO HELP YOU!"

"FORGET IT!" I began my trek!

Lance had met many uppity girls in his twenty-six years. They were always whiney and lazy. God forbid, if you looked at anything else in passing! This bimbo, though, was like no other girl he'd met. She wanted nothing from him.

If he could figure out a woman, he probably would win a Pulitzer! There seems to be so much to this girl. She's marched out of sight with nary a backward glance. He really thinks she has every intention of walking all the way home.

Jumping off the fence, opening it, and pulling his Rig back through, Lance saw to it that he locked the gate, and then pulled up in front of the car. Her "prized hunk of junk," he chuckled. Moving with smooth efficiency Lance checked to see what gear the car was left in, and wanted to make certain the brake was not set. To his surprise the girl had left her keys and purse in the front seat. Boy, she must really have been upset!

Lance was glad he always carried the tow-line and gear in his rig it only took a minute to hook it up under the undercarriage, then gently pull the car out and up onto the road.

Deep inside Lance knew what he must do. That girl, in no way would accept a ride from him, but she would accept her own automobile to drive home. Looking at his wrist watch, Lance was amazed at the time that had passed. Nearly an hour. There was no reason to hurry... he wanted the venom of this rattler to dissipate before meeting up again!!

His insides tighten as he remembers her dark auburn hair bouncing along her shoulders and the sun burying itself deep into the strands, highlighting its freshness. The graceful swing of her small hips beating a cadence with her determination. She must be about five- foot- eight, and her long legs go all the way to heaven!

This was a great idea, thought Jamie. The fresh air, the brisk walk, and all the beauty of the Cascades at her pleasure. Why did it take so long

Daughter of the Gorge

to see the solution to that blow-hard? People don't walk as much as they should. It's been ages since I got out and felt the wind move against my skin, and felt the sun warming every cell! I feel so wonderful and so alive by this experience. I'm sure it will take at least four hours to get home. Gram won't be worried, though, because she knew I'd be gone most of the day. On the way I will enjoy nibbling on grass ends, and finding a few berries here and there along the route. Thirst will be my biggest challenge!

Do I remember this being such a slow and gentle rise all uphill? I know my pace is slowing; the heat makes every step seem heavier than it should. I'm so glad I am athletic. All I need to do is just keep marching along, one foot in front of the other!

I wish I had a bonnet; it is quite warm. Stopping to admire cute little bugs, and note very beautiful wild flowers gives me a break now and then.

"Yes sir, I showed him!!"I mumbled.

God, thought Lance, how those electric blue eyes snapped, when he pricked her anger! He caught himself thinking things about that girl he had no right to think. Besides, trying to caress that little hellcat would send a man to the doctor!!

Walking backwards changes the wear on my feet. I can now gaze across the river and watch the Multnomah Falls; careening over the edge of the hill to spill its way to the bottom in graceful fold over graceful fold. Some are deeper than others, lending the magical hypnotism of interest everyone has when gazing at them. Water just tumbles down, down, down. My eyes try to follow each fold all the way down only to have it melt out of sight. There are at least four falls in view, the latter the most spectacular. There, at the base of the falls is a beautiful huge stone and timber lodge. Gram and Mack took me there for lunch once. After lunch I busted up the trail behind the lodge for a closer look. You really can get wet!! Especially if the wind is blowing. From here we took the Oregon highway east, up to the Bridge of the Gods, and crossed over to the Washington side to travel back toward Vancouver.

This summer this is one of the trips I plan to remake. Maybe Gram will ride along with me!!

Moving his truck slowly along the way, with her car in tow, Lance was not in a hurry to find her. She needs to know the consequences of her rash actions. Otherwise known as temper. Actually, I guess I egged her on... I don't know why. I've been called a lot of things by women, but Bully was not one of them!! Surprised he's at the main highway, and no sight of that girl bothered him. Maybe she took a time in the bush...don't suppose she would accept a ride through hitch hiking? Since the war, this was a pretty acceptable way to travel, but not for a woman. Would be a lark, if any of his friends saw him roaming the country side with a car on the back, looking for a woman!

Two roads lead to the farm. If it were him, he would take the short cut, even if steeper. With the car in tow, there is not much choice, a decision must be made. I think that girl could be tired enough to make the same choice! This route is filled with

Daughter of the Gorge

curves, so there is no hot-Roding. The trick is to move slowly and smoothly.

Seeing a lone figure hunched over, and moving yet at a purposable pace, Lance knew this was his beaten little spitfire! Some of her steps looked a bit staggered. Yet, she was doing well for as long as she had been walking. Lance felt he would quietly slip up behind her, follow her for awhile, and pleasantly surprise her with the return of her car!

Hearing a car approach, Jamie moved to the side of the road so it could pass. She briefly considered begging a ride, but people are very kind here, and would insist on giving her lift clear to her grandmother's. Jamie knew she still had to come up with a story as to where her car was and why.

Why isn't this car going around me? Thought Jamie. I can get over only so far. Maybe it's afraid to pass in case another car comes around on the road at too fast a speed. I could really sit down at the side of the road...I could use a small rest...but, would I get up ever again? Jamie takes in the scene, she's so tired... I'll just move over and wave it on. As she turns, her eyes take in an unbelievable sight, a sight that causes her legs to fold underneath her. The pity party tears she had fought off for the last mile now burst in a torrent.

Lance's heart leaped when he saw Jamie fall. He stopped the truck immediately, and jumped to her aid. Reaching her, he scooped her onto his lap. "Ah, there now little darlin,' I never meant for this to hurt you. I'm sorry. You caught me so off guard. You were gone before I could straighten this whole thing out. Come on now, there's nothing to cry about! Your car was not hurt, and I have your keys here in my pocket. Your purse is safe on the front seat."

Jamie was past arguing, and plain exhausted out. His arms felt so strong; he smelled so clean, his hug so close and sincere. It had been so long since someone comforted her so warmly. BUT, still she hated him.

Squirming out of his arms and standing up, adjusting her blouse, she glared at Lance. "Thank you for bringing my car, and what else. Please unhook it and let me go home. I best not hear of this anywhere, and I don't want to see you ever again!!!"

Driving back to Gramma's was a tiring duty. There would be questions as to where she went today, and did she have fun?

I'm not one to like to lie, so I've made up my mind to avoid conversation as much as possible. Dinner is going to be fabulous as usual, but I'm not hungry, and tell Gramma I'm tired and am going on to bed. Saying my goodnights I drag myself upstairs, get into my night clothes, and disappear deep into the covers.

"What's wrong with Jamie tonight?" Mack asked. "Not like her to head for bed so early."

Gramma answered him with, "She said she ran into a little problem today. I've seen that problem look before, and if I were a betting woman, I would bet she ran into a HE, and I'm willing to guess which HE!" She couldn't help a little chuckle.

"Naw, that's reaching pretty far, Mommy. Maybe I should go ask her if she's O.K." Mack was starting to get up.

"Stay where you are. She was fine looking tonight, just a bit weary. She needs to sort out things for herself, Dear. Only one thing gets a woman's goat like that, and that is a man. I know the signs, believe me! She just doesn't know them!"

Jamie laid there in deep thought, why can't I hold my temper? Lance did offer to help me. It was my fault I was in that ditch, not his. I'm so stupid! Oh well, I can't change things now, and why worry about it? I won't get any sleep if I do worry.

7

Probably Gram has one of the nation's first daylight basements. It's fascinating to me that someone had the foresight to build this house to span a running ground spring. The air is always much cooler there in winter or summer. Rocks line the walls and shelves are built in to hold the canned goods. The rock lined walls leak moisture behind the shelves, adding to the dusky odor. Green moss tickles the wetter rocks.

Many quarts, pints, crocks, and gallon jars are stored in the dark, dank atmosphere. The underground spring leaps from the cave like setting, and gushes on through and under the house, to the outside where it becomes a creek. This creek flows on to be routed through the chicken yard. What a smart way to water chickens!

Gram is careful whom she sends to get anything, a person could slip. The dampness of the under side of the house means the family must be careful when walking in the main dining room. The floor is a little unsteady. We often wonder if we won't fall into the basement someday!

Part of the kitchen is over this area also, but, the floor seems to be stronger. The chances of it being cleaner was proven last Christmas dinner, when everyone was seated in the dining room, and I was helping Gram bring in the dishes filled with mouth-watering goodies. We were almost done, and Gram was scooping the gravy out of the skillet into a nice bowl. As she turned she hit her arm on something, and the gravy and bowl landed on the floor. She stood only a moment in hesitation grabbed a large spoon and started scooping gravy back into the bowl. I must have looked dumbfounded because she muttered with a pleading look on her face, "I just washed this damn floor this morning! This will be our secret, Jamie." A pleading look on her face. It was so much fun to watch everyone including my stuffy aunt, dive into Gramma's famous gravy and ask for more!

Gram's dining room is only used on holidays. This room is elegant compared to the rest of the living area. Its entry is off the kitchen. There is a beautiful cabinet that holds Gram's Blue Onion dishes she carried on the train from Missouri.

There are soup bowls and platters, things only seen at the special seasons. The door to the non-existent front porch is at the back of this room.

On one wall is another tall cabinet. To my surprise, one time when I was much younger, I discovered medical books inside. Both for humans and animals. Well, when Gram would go outside to hang up the wash, I would beat it to this cabinet, and check out the pictures of the male anatomy!!

I learned a lot about my body too. But, it was not nearly as interesting, as THOSE other pictures!!

Gram and my mother left Hale, Missouri when my mother was sixteen to make the long trek to the West. Gram was adventurous and had heard many stories about job availability.

At the age of thirty- four, my grandmother Pat was raising a daughter alone. In that day and age this was not acceptable. The townspeople always had something to say, and her daughter, (my mother), was chastised unmercifully in school. The best action for them would be to start new lives. My married but deserted grandmother picked up and left. "Life was not always fair," she taught, "but you can let life walk over you, or you can walk over life!" She reminded my mother that the Lord says, "Yea though you shall walk through the valleys... you shall get through, and you don't have to stay in the valleys!"

She told Mom she wanted to see the Pacific Ocean. Gram made the arrangements to take the train just a few days later.

The greatest thing my mother says she saw on that trip was the magnificent Mt. Hood when the conductor woke everyone up and said it was time to get ready for the stop in Portland. She fell in love with the Northwest right then and there!

They both got good jobs right off. Gram worked in the shipyard, and Mom got a job as a housekeeper/ nanny for a wealthy family in Portland.

One of the amazing things I've always enjoyed about my grandmother is her belief in freedom and relaxation. She hurries with her "chores" to be able to have time for herself, and me, if I'm staying with her. Today she fixed a picnic lunch and gathered a blanket for us to sit on, and a quart jar filled with grape Kool-Aid. Being from town, I don't always have the energy that she seems to have to cart all this to the hill in the pasture land. This is where she wants to go, though, and I follow.

Daughter of the Gorge

The lunch today consists of roast beef sandwiches, sliced beefsteak tomatoes, dill pickles, and potato salad. She will also have the latest LIFE magazine and yesterday's newspaper. We will read this and discuss current events, and laugh a lot. In the past she taught me to look for wild strawberries, blow a whistle using two grass blades, enjoy the beauty of tall fox glove plants, chase down different butterflies, and enjoy the scenery.

Gram always has time to talk to me. No question is stupid, no comment wrong. She treats me as an adult, and is so interested in my thoughts and ideas. I guess to be able to sit and converse as an equal is something I have with no other person.

"Gram, do you believe in God?" The question popped out before I could stop it.

"What?" Gram's head nearly swivels a complete turn. "Absolutely!" she exclaims. "Why on earth do you ask, dear?" Such warmth and concern trace her features.

"Well, you don't go to church." Feeling I may be on shaky ground, I drop my eyes, knowing I'm going to get an answer.

"Well, Honey, I figure there are different types of believers. Those who talk it, or those who walk it!" Gram's thoughtfully fingering the edge of the blanket. "We're pretty far from a church out here, and I never felt comfortable around those city folk and their Sunday clothes and phony smiles. They didn't know me, and I really didn't want to know them. All I have to do is see a little calf being born or a hatch of chickies or know the spring water is going to flow to believe.

You see those apple trees? Dead last winter, no leaves, those fox gloves, no flowers, but sure as taxes, in the summer they always return!! Too many things point to God, than not!" She had that satisfied look, the one that says, "That's that."

I asked Gram about dating. Was it possible in "her day", to have any fun, if there was anything to do?

"Lordy, Girl, there's nothing new under the sun! We actually had more time to know one another in my day! We went for county strolls, hay rides, made ice cream together, and no one had to drive. The horses knew the way home. Freed up the hands real good! Know what I mean?"

Gram pondered a moment then said, "I don't know if some of the new ways are good for children. It worries me they don't grow up slower. They miss the seasons of life. You know spring, summer, fall and winter. There's not enough spring... play, laughter, day dreams. Seems they're being hurried right on to summer. That can get them into the heat of things before their time!"

I reached out and picked a daisy, something else I've done for years, and started pulling off petals. "He loves me. He loves me not. He loves me, etc." We both laugh. Gram asks me if there is anyone special yet. Why does Lance spring to mind? Good grief. Too much sun!! "No Gram, I broke up with the last fellow I was dating. Well to be honest with you, he broke up with me!! It's pretty hard to date and get a career off and going!

Some of my girl friends are already married; one has a child. I tried to visit with her, but we had nothing in common, and I couldn't get away fast enough! I felt so out of place." I remembered clearly how I had hurried away, that action did make me feel bad.

Gram has turned over on to her back and is chewing on a blade of grass. I decide to do the same. Looking at the fluffy white cloud formations passing overhead eventually puts me to sleep.

Our evening was as relaxing as the day had been. Who decided we must be busy every minute? Who decided home is no longer the base to family life? Who decided to muck up everyone's lives?

8

Each day I am with Gramma and Grampa I fall into the easy swing of chores, expressed love from these beautiful people, and peace of mind. I seem to uncluttered each day things that used to drive me up walls. I don't even feel any walls!

Grampa Mack reached for his coat, then turned toward us, "Maybe we should eat lunch right away. Got a neighbor coming over in a little while. Wants to rent our upper pasture land for his horses, while they're mending fences. Told you about this didn't I, Mommy?" (A cute little nickname Mack used when he was dangerously close to being in trouble with the "Boss".)

"Actually Mack, you didn't. But you know farm affairs, and the extra cash won't hurt. There can always be a rainy day."

"Should be here by the time we finish lunch. You girls can come up and see a couple fine quarter horses unloaded." Mack then seated himself in his usual chair and waited for his lunch to be served.

In no time at all we had bacon, lettuce, and tomato sandwiches, ice tea, and a bowl of black cap raspberries covered with real cream sitting in front of us.

"Something great, Jamie, the owners are bringing all the gear for the horses. They need to be worked and were hoping you wouldn't mind a little riding this summer. Since you were just a little girl, you've been hounding me to buy a horse. This should get you off my back for awhile! Darn hay burners anyway!"

Daughter of the Gorge

"Oh, Mack, I love to ride. I'm not real good, but I'd love to take care of them!!" I feel like a fourteen year old girl again, barely able to contain my excitement.

Just about one o'clock we heard the sounds of a truck moving on loose gravel. "Come on Girls, get with it, and let's move it!! Meet you at the barn. Jamie, we'll need your help in case the cattle move into the area." An energized Mack jets out the door.

Gram called out that she would be along soon. It's hard to hurry on the path to the barn. Every time it rains, the path from the barn has more little streams running down the grooves, breaking loose rocks, and exposing them above the dirt to be tripped on. Being most capable of this act, I hurry toward the barn, but I am careful where I put my feet.

To my right is a small hazel nut grove, somewhere around eight or ten trees. I've climbed all over them! One summer I played in a branchy tree and daydreamed I was a pilot. I kind of had my feet on other branches to make the flaps, and used another branch drawn toward me as the control stick. This kept me busy for days!

I can see the horse trailer; it's nice. All white with red trim. Looks like a four stall rig. Very well taken care of, it's hooked up to a powerful looking red truck. Two men are pulling a horse out the gate of the trailer. The sun is in my eyes, but I'm certain I see Mack with the reins and another taller man whistling soft instructions to the horse. Oh man! Such a gorgeous animal. A light buckskin mare with dark tail and mane. Every hair is groomed. Mack brings her over to me to hold onto, as he returns to the trailer to receive the next horse from the man inside. This one's coal black with two white socks on his front legs. It has to be a HE just from his size. I would expect a flame of white from his nostril up between his eyes, but there is none. He is all black of face and body. His handler steps out of the shadows with him and accidentally knocks off his cream colored Stetson.

"Hello Jamie, like them? These are my babies. The buckskin you're holding is called Candy! This rowdy boy is Major. He's my rodeo horse." Pride is busting out all over his countenance. "He's a smart one, knows more than me!!

Mack, gotten? "Let's get Major through the gate and into the pasture! Candy will follow him anywhere. Glad you have that strand of electric wire along with the barbed." With such ease Lance steers Major where he wants him."

"Jamie, you gonna hold Candy all day or let her go?" I felt in a dream. Was all this happening? Candy was butting her beautiful head against my shoulder. I pulled her muzzle up to my face and let her nuzzle me.

We were made for each other. I was in love with a horse! I overheard Lance telling Mack that both horses would come to a single whistle. He would be leaving a snack bag. The horses always get a reward when they mind.

I took Candy to the gate, released her bridle and let her go. She crossed over to pass Lance and check out if she would get a reward. Sure enough, she got one plus a pat on her rump that sent her off to be with Major. They both turned to face us, and I hadn't seen anything so beautiful in a long time.

Mack helped Lance put the gate back up on the trailer.

"Thanks for helping us out. Unless a cougar passes through, I know there is no better place to leave my kids. Reckon they are spoiled, but they are well trained." Lance is busy putting things back in order.

"Jamie, how about going for a ride tomorrow? I don't have to work all day so how about going around this time? I'll bring the saddles and gear tomorrow." Lance is hurrying right along with his busy work.

I heard Gram slip up beside me and put her arm around my waist.

"Did you know about this?" I asked her.

"No. Mack, could we talk for a moment?" Mack and Gramma retired a few feet away.

"I knew you'd love Candy," he grinned. "She's wonderful, and better behaved than her owner." He steps closer. "I'd like to take you on a ride. I promise you'll love Candy. She, Major, and I could use a day off and some good company. Then I gotta go to work on those fences. Meanwhile hug Candy all you want, but be a little careful around Major. I'm the only one who rides him."

Mack and Gram return and Mack looks a little like paint had been poured out over his favorite truck. Gram looks satisfied with herself.

"Now Lance, if our Jamie doesn't want to go riding, I want that to be okay. All right? I don't want her doing anything she might be uncomfortable with." Mack is meek with his speech.

"Lance, I'll be ready, and thank you for the invitation. I know we'll each enjoy the horses. It's supposed to be warm and sunny." I give Lance a smile of happiness.

"Gram, didn't you say there were some new calves and barn kitties to see?" I note as we leave the two men standing side by side with that dumb look men can get. Not stupid, just that cute, dumbfounded look.

I don't know why I feel so good. It's been a good day, in fact a great day. The horses will be so much fun this summer. But, just maybe I feel good about seeing Lance again. Maybe I can keep my stupid temper under control. Lance seems so nice today, and so tall and handsome.

It's nice to be near someone like that. I feel like I could float.

"Lance would you like to come to the house for a glass of ice tea?" asks Mack.

"Thanks, but I need to get along home. Dad's sister Cleva is coming down for her annual visit to see if Dad and I are doing it right!! After Mom died Cle pretty well helped raise me. She checks out the house things now, and sees to it we get a decent home- cooked meal. I'm certain there would be words if I wasn't there." Lance steps into his truck and waves goodbye. Sticks his head out the cab and throws Mack a wave. "Thanks for the pasturing see you soon."

Daughter of the Gorge

Before we all leave the barn area. Gram opens the very large sliding door that travels on a track at the top. Gram wants us all to take another look at the kitties. She says the new baby kitties are in the last big feed bin. There are four large bins in a row. They are really big. Hold about eight hundred pounds of grain each. A different grain in each one. This grain is a special mix for the milk cows, range cattle, and calves.

Barns are dusty, very dusty. Cob webs form on timbers, and left over hay hangs on the walls. The windows are a testimony as to how they can look when not washed for seventy-five years. Barns have a special smell. Not annoying at all to those who have been around them.

This is a big barn, as barns go. It is as high as a three story business and as large around as the common J. C. Penney store. Five big sliding barn doors. Ten cow stations (where cows stand when they are milked.) Three holding pens for cattle brought in from auctions, or maybe housing a large bull and a huge center area for the year's hay collection. On the inside edges of the barn are two lanes, one on each side for cattle trucks to drive down or back into for unloading. Prevalent odors are dry hay, grain, and yes, manure. Since that is well- cleaned, a person can just pull up some hay and sit down! Gram sits on a bale and makes a large pocket between her knees, using her apron as a safe place for the new kitties.

Mack bends deep into the bin and digs out five cute kittens, preceded by their irate mother, who has screamed her way across the barn. They are so wiggly. Two are yellow tabbies, two gray, and one calico. I love the calico! We spend at least an hour playing with these babies with the sharp toe nails!

Our next stop is the calf pens. There are five calves. Three white faces (Herefords) and two Jerseys (little future milk cows.) New calves are so lovable. I can bend over and grasp a big armful of wiggle. They are fed not by their mother at this time, but have been trained to suckle from a special milk bucket with a long rubber teat protruding from the lower side. The mother now shares her milk with both humans and calves.

City people wonder what there is to do on a farm, miles from anyone, no restaurants, and no traffic. There is a peace, a belonging, a need that envelopes you from everywhere. There is always something that needs to be done, and something always needs your love. There is always SOMETHING to give your love to.

Daughter of the Gorge

9

I've never ridden such a beautiful animal! Her smooth gait, the proud toss of her mane, she knows she's some fine lady. We have been riding along, each of us in our own thoughts. The scenery is breathtaking. The man riding beside me is one with his horse. Which one looks more natural and at ease, I could not tell you. Lance has been the perfect companion since he came to the farm to get me. It didn't take him any time at all to have both animals saddled and ready. I barely beat him to the barn! I'm trying not to jabber; I really want this to go well. I steal a quick glance at Lance.

Lance seats himself a little more to the side. He wants a better look at his companion. He doesn't know which filly is more glorious. That indescribable hair floating over her shoulders, the bright eyes of anticipation, the beautiful even smile she rewarded him with when she turned in the saddle and caught him assessing her. Or his little lady horse? DUMB QUESTION.

"Lance, do you ever get tired of riding? I mean with the ranch work and your rodeo work, there must be so many hours in the saddle." (Ohhh did I just ask such a stupid question?)

"Naw, not at all," Lance grinned. "I love riding. It's more satisfying than driving past things too fast to notice them. I love to smell the trees, the different odors. I do enjoy a little of the pioneer spirit that riding can give. Did you know the average miles traveled by the pioneers were twenty miles a day?"

Jamie thought about that fact. "There are a lot of things I try to understand about those days. Like how did they clean themselves, their clothes? How did those women drag those heavy dresses all the way to Oregon? How did they keep from killing each other from the hardships? How did they keep from stinking?"

Lance was laughing now. "I once heard that the Indian women along the Columbia really smelled. A strong fish oil smell. When someone asked why they used so much oil, one of the "ladies" said that after a "lady" had the amount of children she wanted, and wanted to be bothered no more, she would let fleas infest her and she would use fish oil to smell worse. Then her lover would find someone else!"

We were both laughing so hard now that my sides began to ache!

Lance continued on, "I've many times wondered what it was like to be able to ride anywhere, no fences to worry about, no private property, you know, just go on forever in any direction!"

This sobered me just a bit. "You mean, you're interested in the pioneer days too? I've always been laughed at by my friends for going into the past again. It literally fascinates me, no matter what the story is or whom it's about. Someone in my past must have been a pioneer for me to care so much. I find myself looking at hills and rivers, and thinking of the wagons crossing them, dreading the dangers faced by the families.

It was so painful for them to travel from The Dalles to Portland. I can't help but think what

Daughter of the Gorge

price was paid to settle the West! To think we ARE the West!!

I, Jamie, am blabbering again!

Lance pulled up on Major, looked around, and headed across the open meadow. There was a nice full maple tree and a lot of shade. Getting down, he indicated for me to do the same. Taking both reins of each horse and leading them away, he dropped the reins to the ground. Lance then untied a rolled blanket from the saddle and a sack from a strap that had been tied out of my eyesight on the trip.

"Hungry? Aunt Cleva said a gentleman would never ask someone out and not feed her. Let's see what a gentleman fixes, since I have no idea what is in this sack!" With that he unrolled the blanket on the ground and began to dig into the sack.

"AHHA! What she does best!! Fried chicken, a couple dill pickles wrapped in wax paper, some of her famous potato salad, some carrot sticks, and two bottles of coke. Even a bottle opener! Waalha, two napkins! She never forgets the details."

I am amazed! A picnic dinner! His handsome face is so alive with joy. Joy of a little boy, not this tall, usually grumpy, (there I go, I'm not going there with these thoughts) very male man. When have I had such perfect fun? I remove my jacket and roll it up to sit on. Lance continues to set out our dinner, complete with paper plates and forks.

"I'm so glad Jamie, you said yes to coming with me. I need to get out of my rut. As Aunt Cle said, I can be a perfect bore."

"Or the perfect host" I return. I was feeling comfortable with this man. I don't know why we ever got off on the wrong foot as we did. Maybe we are a little alike? For as large a man as Lance is, he has a grace about him, and for the first time I can also see a sense of humor. This is the way of it, though, is it not? It takes time to get to know one another. He eats well! I mean he chews with his mouth closed, uses his napkin, and ate nearly all that was fixed for us. He has not gotten cross or acted like a teen- age boy. Perhaps I have been a little too picky about his manners.

Our dinner was over, and it was delicious. Lance stands, and softly whistles the horses back from their foraging. We fold the blanket; he reties it behind his saddle, and puts the dinner pack back on. He steps over to me, and offers me an assist up on Candy. I don't need help, but find I wish Lance to step closer to me. He checks my stirrups and lingers there a moment looking at me as if something else were on his mind, then abruptly steps away and swings easily up into the saddle of Major.

"We best get on back before your family sends out the sheriff."

"NO chance. Gram is probably glad to be rid of me for awhile! I think I can beat you back home though!!"

Lance's strong horse set aside that idea in short term, and we cantered along, the rest of the way saying little, and probably thinking much! To me the day was wonderful, even if it was short. Every time I glanced toward Lance's, way he laughed. Our time together a success, and another memory maker.

Daughter of the Gorge

There was no one at the barn when we got back, so, so much for worried folks! We watered the horses, brushed them down, gave them a generous portion of grain, and set them out to the pasture. Lance carried the saddles and gear into the barn, and hung them over the pole fashioned for that purpose. The bridles were whipped down and then hung up also. It was fun teamwork!

"Lance, can you come down to the house for some coffee? You told Gram you would!"

"Yes," he smiled. "I hoped you would ask. I have always enjoyed your grandparents. They have known me since I was knee high to a grasshopper, though not well! We would see each other at various Grange dinners."

Lance opened the large sliding barn door and stepped out, and down to the ground reaching out a hand back to me. Our fingers made contact, as Lance stepped forward and caught me to him in such a smooth move as to have me sliding against his whole manly frame. I barely noticed how strong he is, because at that same moment his mouth covered mine in the softest sweetest lingering kiss I had ever had. I don't remember coming out that door, but my feet were on the ground.

"Rather than walk the path down to the house, why don't I drive us around to the road and then in? I hate walking up hill if I don't have to." said Lance in a light- hearted way. He seems barely to note his previous actions. How can he be so cavalier?

Meeting us at the door was Gram. "Come on in kids. I made an apple pie and some fresh coffee.

Did you have a nice afternoon?" She was all excited!

"Had a great ride," volunteered Lance, pulling out a kitchen chair for me... I know how to pull out a chair...

"And you Jamie?"

I know, 'cause I can feel that my face has turned instant scarlet, nothing I say will be right. "Yes, we saw so many beautiful flowers, saw a couple of deer too, Gramma."

"How about the picnic dinner?" Lance smirked, in his easy way, goading me on.

"Oh, you've eaten already?" Gramma pauses, "Did you have enough?"

"Yes ma'am, But we're still hungry for that pie and coffee," Lance answered.

Hello, am I still part of this conversation? The two of them are going on as if I weren't here. Actually I'm probably not here. Did I dream Lance kissed me or did it happen? He does not seem changed by it...I know I am! I obediently pick up my fork and start to pick at my pie.

"Hi Lance! Hi Jamie! Great day for a ride, eh?" Entered Mack from somewhere outside. "I've been cleaning out the spring up by the barn!" Mack's eyes have that special twinkle. (The spring is just up the hill from the large barn door,) I think I can make reservations to die now. If he saw us, Gram will know soon!

The evening went well. Lance has so much to talk about, and that's right down Mack's lane! Anything to do about cattle or farming, and you've got Mack's undivided attention.

Daughter of the Gorge

    We all walked out to Lance's rig, and bid him goodnight. He said he would be back to make certain we were taking good care of his horses, and leaned out the window to tell me he has a few days of fence work he must get to. He backed out the drive, turned around, and headed out the lane. Why was I watching him all the way as he drove away?

10

I love waking up this way! Gram's doing her wash. She sets up the round tubs side by side on a couple of saw-horses. Behind those are her washing machine and wringer. By turning a lever, the wringer can swing around to be poised over the tubs, or be over the washer. The smell from her washing is incredible! Besides the wood smell from the woodstove on the back porch, there is the smell of hot water with soap in it, and the blueing stuff put in the final rinse water. The blueing is used to make whites whiter. Therefore for her to do a wash, Gram must build a fire in the cook stove, fill a copper cooker with water, and get it hot. This is a continuing chore to always have hot water.

When Gram is in full swing, she has clothes swishing back and forth in the washer while she is turning clothes in the first rinse water with a large long handled spoon looking tool. Then she dives in with her arms up to her elbows and feeds an article of clothing one at a time through the wringer into the second tub of rinse water. She swirls that around in the "bluing water", wrings it out, and then places it her basket. When the basket is half full, she hikes up the hill toward the barn a little ways, and then hangs the clothes out on a long line, strung from one tree to the other, over the path. She is very particular how things are to be hung. Gram gets totally beside herself if an unkind bird gets to her sheets. A more colorful language emits from her person. It means she must take in those sheets and wash them all over again.

Daughter of the Gorge

So, with my nose barely out of the blanket, and looking at Gramma's wind- up clock, it is only seven in the morning. Mack has had his breakfast, chores in the barn are done, and he's gone to work! Gramma's half done with hers! This is the smell I don't think I'll ever forget...the morning smell of the farm!!!

I know today are pancakes... I can smell that too!! Bacon or sausage, there is a choice today. I know I eat more when I'm at Gramma's. A lot more fruit. I don't seem to be putting on any weight, though. I'd guess that this morning there will be a large mixing bowl of apple sauce. The graven stein apples are just ripening and I know I saw Gram boiling up a pan of apples. She cheats and picks a few early and adds more sugar. There are times a spoonful can set your jaw on sour alert. That feeling that rings clear to your ears.

I'm right! On all bases, the breakfast is great! I think I'll do up the dishes and surprise Gram. She will not say no to me because she's too busy fighting dirt!

HONK, HONK, HONK,

"It's Mom! I shout at Gram, "I'd know that horn honk anywhere!" Gram closes off her machine, grabs a towel to wipe her arms, and heads for the porch door. I flip past her. After all, I am faster, and I know I can get to Mom before she gets completely out of the car.

It seems so long since I've seen her in person. Laddie, Grams gorgeous collie joins us from his sleep- state in the sun. He knows he should be barking, but his mind does not tell him why! He's ready though, running in circles, jumping for joy looking all about.

Sure enough, one long slender leg has just emerged from the car. I grab her before she is fully standing!

"Jamie, how wonderful you look, oh, how I've missed my girl!"

Burying myself in her arms, Mom finally is able to stand. I find myself surrounded by her Channel # 5 perfume. The smell is so familiar; it floats around her wherever she goes. Mom moves on to hug Gram, and mother and daughter walk arm in arm to the house. Mom just seems to know I'll follow with her purse!

Mack, as usual will bring in luggage later. I wonder how he does this all the time. Think he would ever say, "Bring it yourself!" Not Mack!

Gram turned to Mom, "You should have dropped us a line, Honey. I would have made up something special for dinner. Not that I can't of course". The joy I feel at being with Mom is reflected in Gram's face. She now has both her girls to fuss over! Meanwhile, Laddie has gone back to his place in the warm sun. He will choose when to get excited again!

I set Mom's purse on the floor next to the chair she always sits in when she visits Gramma. Isn't it weird how people plop down in certain chairs and lay claim to them?

The tea kettle is set up towards the front of the cook stove where the fire will have it dancing a jig soon. My mother is famous, to us, for having that cup of coffee as soon as she has landed. Gram's into instant coffee now. Mom hates it, but she won't say anything to hurt Gram's feelings.

"Maurine, you've messed with your hair," remarks Gram, her brows furrowed a little. Gram has such a way with words. So much for people's feelings. "In fact you dyed it!"

"Come on, Mom, people die, hair is colored!" My mother shoots me a HELP ME WITH THIS look. "I wanted a more defined color, something different. My own hair is rather dull."

Gram snorts back, "God thought it all right when he gave it to you. In fact you got it shaved off too! But never you mind now, I do think it will be all right."

My mother shifts in her chair, her shoulders stiffen a little, and she looks right straight on at Gramma. "Mom, I am a grown woman, and I want to feel good about myself. I felt ugly. Now I feel great. Renewed, changed!!" She looked at me, with a new understanding I've never seen before.

"Hey Mom, you look FAB. That style really moves and flows; there's an exciting balance! You would never let me do something like that to you though, would you? I like it!"

"Jamie, your father would not let me do this stupid girl- type things. You must remember, Darling, only his girlfriends got such privileges! He had me feeling old, out of step, out of style, and he verbally criticized any free thought I had. My marriage to your father took me away from me. I'm sorry dear. I know he's your father, but I forgot what I enjoyed, what I loved about life. I only truly had you to love. People wonder at my lack of mourning. If they only walked in the shoes of those they condemn."

Oh boy, this is deep. There is so much a child never understands about the people they love. Dad often ripped me apart and punished me frequently, but I just figured I deserved it! Well, I really think I did! But for Mom, that's different. She held the home together. She deserved better.

Now the tea kettle is going all over itself. Gram comes over to be near Mom. I know who is going to make the coffee. ME! There is a silence of understanding between these two women.

There are eight pale green mugs Gram got out of soap boxes. They are not attractive at all, but they certainly hold a good coffee and the hot chocolate that I'm fixing for Gram and me. Gram likes the small marshmallows sprinkled on top.

"Maurine," asks Gram, "did you get a perm in your hair? It looks so soft and natural."

"Yes, a chemical perm; a person need not be hooked up to that horrible machine any more! Remember that time you got your scalp seared off?" They both roll with combined laugher "Jamie had me convinced to try the new perms."

In Beauty School we had to learn to wrap these awful contraptions. Everyone hated the assignment. I think we had to do ten of them. Chemical permanents were easier and client friendly. They are more sophisticated and proven than the first ones. Hairdressers need to keep a close eye on the development of the curl. Girls who have problems are the ones who beat it back to the back room, and try to stuff some lunch down and lose track of how the perm is developing. I like to stand right there during the process. I believe it looks more professional. I specialize in correcting over- processed perms. Making a good extra income in this area. Oops, I'm daydreaming as my mentors continue to talk about my field of work!

Gram, turning more serious, asks Mom, "Honey, how long can you be with us?"

Mom acting a little cornered says, "I think just overnight, Mamma. If that's all right with you? I'm taking a few days' vacation, and this is kind of on my way. Uh, to Montana."

"Montana!" Gram and I shout in unison. "Why on earth so far? What is in Montana?"

"I really need to stay on my schedule, before I lose my nerve." Therefore I will leave tomorrow and return in a week or two. Maybe sooner, maybe later."

"Do we have to churn it out of you?" asks Gramma. "There is more to this than you are letting on. I could always tell when you were up to an adventure."

Mom blows softly into her coffee cup, as if to cool the already cooled coffee. I think she needs something to hang onto.

The silence carries on.

Finally, she looks up at Gramma, and there is a gleam in her eyes.

I've seen this look on my girlfriends' faces; about the time they were going to disclose a secret.

"Mamma, you remember when we came to the West?" We stopped at various towns you wanted to see. Sometimes staying awhile, while you earned more for our trip. Usually you worked at coffee houses, and I found work helping ladies who were expecting. These ladies were more than willing to pay someone to help with their washing and housekeeping. These were jobs we could leave at any duration, and still get on to Oregon." Remember, you said anyone can take a train west. I want to see what is in between. We had such fun together!" My mother fingering her cup continues." I have done something totally out of character for me. I made a stupid phone call, to someone I knew years ago, someone I met in Bozeman. I am going to meet with him. Please don't hit the ceiling on me Mom."

Gram looks as if she is going to speak, but settles back in her chair.

"Jamie always says, you can always ask "Information." That's what I did! I picked up the telephone, dialed long distance and asked for his number. He could have been dead or married; I did not care. Something in my loneliness kept me on that phone. I pretended to be doing a survey when he answered. I had met Monty, and we dated some; we were good friends in short time. I was so young, and frisky. I had no thoughts of settling down at my age, but Monty said he loved me. I probably laughed! After all we didn't have roots in his town; we were just playing for awhile. He wanted me to stay, and let you go on if that was what you wanted to do. Do you remember him now?" Mom glances at Gram.

Daughter of the Gorge

"Yes, I do, a fine young man, polite, handsome in that western way. I had no idea it had gone that far!" Gramma waited.

"It didn't! He was so nice, and I was carried away with being admired for the first time in my life by the opposite sex. You and I moved on, and Monty and I corresponded for quite awhile. One day I received a letter from him that said he was getting married. I never wrote back; by then I had met Jamie's father and he rather hurried me along, you know the war and all that stuff."

I think I've swallowed the gum I was chewing. This is my mother speaking? The original MOTHER SUPERIOR.! Romance? Love? MOM? All Mom does is can in the summer, quilt and sew in the winter, and keep close tabs on my dates!! Man, do I have questions, but I better keep my mouth shut. I want to hear more.

Continuing her story, Mom says, "When he answered the telephone, I got scared, but continued by asking if his wife were there, I was calling for a survey company. It was quiet for a moment, and then he said his wife died three years ago. She had been killed by a drunk driver. I felt so stupid; I mumbled how sorry I was and hung up. A couple of days later, I dialed him back and tearfully admitted the phony call, and how sorry I was to bother him. A conversation ensued and to make a story short, he wants to see me again. He now knows I lost my husband, he knows about Jamie, and I know about his daughter. We have a lot in common. He has called me every day. He still sounds so kind.

Jamie, could I have another cup of coffee?" My mother smiles sweetly as she extends her cup.

LORDY, I'm stampeded. I can hardly move! Mom wouldn't let me even talk to my friends on the phone. I could see them in school the next day! Kids are up to no good squeaking on the phone for hours!! Now she cooks up this long lost romance?

Gram is transfixed; her face reflects a mix of wonderment and concern.

"Maurine, Dear, could this be a little too soon?" Gram is choosing her words carefully. I mean, you hardly know this man! What must he think of you?"

Here we go! Boy, better get that coffee in a hurry. I can't miss this. It takes me little time to spring for the stove and the percolator. Forgetting a pot holder, I scream my anguish when I quickly release my hold on a very hot pot that will leave a red reminder those coffee pots on old wood stoves can burn deeply. My yelp of surprise is met with a warm hug from my mother, as she treats my hand. I don't know how mothers move so fast! I suddenly feel about six years old in her comforting embrace. I love it!

Love? My mother seems to be a more loving person than she used to be. For years now, I've nearly hated this harsh disciplinarian, this woman who had no warmth or time for me. Had she been hurt that deeply? All of a sudden she has this warmth, kindness, and she is so pretty. Her eyes have a sparkle I've never seen. She has a softer, lilting voice. Her eyebrows are sculptured, and her lipstick is painted by brush. Looking at her now, I can see she is a new person! Mom has on very high heels, the kind I never could wear. Mom has a new carriage to her walk; I believe it is called class! Class and confidence. If I didn't already love her, I think I would now for sure!

My hand wrapped in a dish towel, I'm led back to the couch. Mom moves to her chair. "Girls, I must do this. It seems right, and I can think of nothing else. Monty and I have stumbled through the years together on the telephone, these past weeks. I believe I am safe with this man.

He has arranged for me to room at his mother's. She is happy to have me as a guest. I have talked with her, also.

Jamie, I am so sorry. I have not asked you how you are doing." My mother asks. I think she wants to change the subject.

"Mostly just hanging loose with Gram and Mack," I reply. "Done some shopping, driving, and lots of talking!" I really don't know what to say.

"Ya, tell her about your picnic, your horseback riding" Gram has that evil little glint in her eyes again!

"Well, okay, Lance took me on a terrific picnic, and he boards two of the best looking quarter horses you ever looked at! Right here at Gram and Mack's. Candy is just special for me to ride. She's fantastic buckskin, sleek and gorgeous. You just got to…"

"LANCE?" My mother interrupts, "Lance who?" Suddenly, the old mother returned. The one I nearly hated.

"Lance is a good boy," Gram interjects, "knows his family well. Actually he is a rancher, cowboy if you will! He and your daughter are becoming acquainted. His Aunt Cleva fixed their picnic lunch!" Gram sits taller in her chair. Did I see defiance in her smirk?

My mother looks me straight in the eyes and says, "I'm glad you're making some new friends, Jamie. Just remember your manners, okay?"

Gram folds her arms over her chest and says, "Lance is a handsome man. He and his dad own some bottom land. Run a bunch of fine looking Herefords. Folks have been waiting for him to get hooked up, but he slides right out of the reins. The girls around here have tried. He likes Jamie. Least he's been leaning on our corral more than usual!"

"Man?" my mother asks. "Just how old is this Lance?"

"Will you two stop it?" I nearly shout. I feel like I'm surrounded by nuns. "I barely know this guy! Mom, this guy is an argumentative, bull headed, self-righteous, know- it- all. I don't like him in that sort of way. Know what I mean? He has just tried to be a friend."

Mom searches deep into my eyes, and a slow smile grows on her face. She rotates her chair to see Gramma better. "What new fancy work are you into?" she asks Gramma.

"A new tablecloth," says Gram, reaching for the pillow case beside her chair. This is where Gram keeps her most recent projects. This keeps "Fancy work" clean, in between work on times. Soon mother and daughter are chattering about sewing, and I deplore that subject!

A rush of cool air hits us, about the same time as the usual slam of the back door. Mack is back from the barn and his chores. He hangs up his denim jacket on a hook, and pops his bright red hunter's hat on the chair back, then proceeds to the cookie jar. Next he's off to the refrigerator for a cold glass of milk. By the time he enters the living room, he has all this plus the newspaper tucked under his chin.

"How long ya here for, Maurine? Been a spell since you were here. We sure enjoy the girl; she keeps us young! Are you guys warm enough? I could get some more wood. Well, this is enough for now. You're looking healthy, Maurine."

Mack is busy with his paper by the time anyone could respond, but of course he wasn't waiting for a response; his male conversation was complete.

Mack is a man happy in his home. Complete in his environment. Mack gets back up and hits the cookie jar again. He is a strong, lean man. He's on the thin side, and he eats all the time!!! A breakfast for Mack is a hot bowl of oatmeal, a cup of coffee, a glass of juice, and toast. Topped off with bacon and eggs, hash browns, and a doughnut! He raised the potatoes, the bacon, the milk, the butter, and Gram made the jam, and the bread. Only the flour, coffee and sugar and oats are store- bought. The chickens provided the eggs!

Following an easy evening of conversation, we all knew Mom would leave in the morning, with a

Barbara Twibell

bag of fixin's to eat on the road, and be sent off to her adventure.

11

After Mack had filled her radiator, checked her wipers, and kicked her tires, he would proclaim her little grey Plymouth coupe safe and ready for travel. Loaded with hugs, kisses, and great love, I watched my mother disappear around the hillside, waving energetically from her driver's side window.

Somehow I knew she would never be the same.

Waving goodbye to my mother again has left me a little empty. I really don't know what to do with the feelings I'm experiencing. I barely slept last night. No big deal, but I think after I do my self-imposed chores, I'll tell Gram I need the day off to meander the farm and enjoy the sun and nature.

Gram's has always been "Balm for my soul. There is absolutely nothing that compares with the scenery, history, or oneness with the land of Gram's beloved "cow farm."

Smells, textures, views, warmth. Today is perfect! As with so many in my few years, there are special feelings for the natural beauty of this home place. Living in the city affords no solitude; at least I could never find it! Perhaps not having a telephone or one of these new televisions has something to do with it! I can almost imagine the content of this land before it was settled. It's only been a hundred years! How can we have cars, trains, planes? In the space of twenty miles we've added thirty years of noise and lack of privacy to lives.

Rolling pastureland, wild berries, fruit trees, garden space, a mountain of tall timber, meadows, springs, so long untouched by so few. My heart just cries with abandoned joy on this land. My beloved Columbia River Gorge.

Lance shifted in the saddle. He looked each way. Having just searched the pastureland, and the extra forty, he was becoming concerned. Pat, Jamie's grandmother had said Jamie said she would be gone for the day. Jamie wanted to walk the farm. There is one heck of a lot of farm to walk!

Lance had been unable to let Jamie know he was taking the day off, and thought she might like a ride. This was as good; however, for he could surprise her.

He did hope it would be a pleasant surprise. They could ride double home!!

He had been unable to rid his mind of this girl. Plus, after finding her, he was invited to dinner. A guy can't beat that!

About the only place left to search was the mountain of timber. Mack only owned one side of the mountain, but it is the part that sets the farm in the view from Cape Horn.

An extraordinarily beautiful stand of second growth timber towers the sky-line above the main farm buildings. The first cut was done maybe seventy-five years before by Mack's father. At that Mack's father had the foresight to leave many old growth giants. Mountains like this are a haven for wildlife, with plenty of water from springs and creeks. Lance had no reason to have ever been in this forest; it was private property. Due to the mixture of terrain probably on this mountain, Lance figures this would be better on foot. So he drops the reins of Major, gives him a friendly cuff, and says "Stick around good buddy, I don't care to walk back!"

Venturing into this cropping of trees is a little like pushing aside heavy deep green stage curtains. Tree limbs caressing the land. The evergreen scent almost stings the nostril. The ground under his boots is a springy carpet of many years' fallen needles. Branches interact with one another to close off any view inside or out. Even a hard rain would not likely reach the ground under the umbrella protection of these guard trees. Lance had timber on the bottom land, but neither as thick nor untouched as this. Lance removed his hat out of respect to an invisible power.

Lance breathed deeply the musky smell of mushrooms and moss. The moss such a rich green, too pure for a painter's brush, so fine as to look like tatting. The ground so spongy his boots were leaving depressions. Ground water was so prolific; Lance needed to pay attention to where he was walking. Little springs appeared from nowhere, only to disappear back to nowhere. When had he ever walked in such beauty? Sun rays through the trees, looking like walkways to heaven, like a holy garden.

Lance fell back against a large rock outcropping as if hit by a howitzer, the wind knocked from his lungs. Legs feeling like rubber. His head pounding, from the sight before him.

Completely free, innocent, and absorbed with appreciation of natural beauty reposed Jamie. Her feet in the spring, her hair still dripping water down her athletic body. Sun rays dancing in her hair as it lay on her creamy shoulders. Jamie was sweetly encouraging a grey bunny to eat some watercress from her fingers. Her soft laughter wove through the solitude. This little meadow could have been some private holy place reserved for Indian maiden right out folklore. The pond is an area, which is not much larger than a tennis court. Anyone would want to escape to this beauty.

Lance felt incomparable heat in his body and a tightening of muscle. The perfect intruder. Never in his twenty six years, had he seen anything so fabulously private or shockingly beautiful.

Jamie was clad not even with a wrist watch. Her clothes were neatly stacked nearby. This was not the first time. This was her place.

The bunny knew her. It bounced all around her. The bunny reflected no fear of this woman. Lance choked back the fear he could ruin this. He could not keep from looking. The firm perfect breasts. The long slender legs reaching all the way to heaven. One more minute and he would hate himself, so with sweat moving over his forehead, he quietly exited this unreal world. He would hate himself for leaving.

Leaping into the saddle was a mistake! His body was hard as steel. This was not going to be a comfortable ride back to the barn! Lance was to find himself, pondering what he had been privileged to witness. He felt this must truly be how God designed things to be. Innocent, clean, and beautiful. "I'm never going to recover from this," grumbled Lance to himself. "I best brush down major, give him some feed, then, I'm headed home."

Mack finishing up at the barn, yells over to Lance, as he heads for his truck, "Ya leavin, Son?"

"Ya, sorry I forgot I had a chore due to be done after all. I couldn't locate Jamie. Please give her my regards. I'll be checking in with her soon. Great day for a ride though!"

Stretching in the meadow sunbeams and finger styling my hair as it dries is so relaxing.

Ever since Gram felt I was old enough to enjoy the acreage without a chaperone, I have come to my pool. There have not always been convenient times to be here. The weather has to be fairly warm, and no chores to do, like helping Gram with canning. So a time like today is a treasure. It is easy to drift off in time, and feel how Indian maidens once enjoyed this very place. Maybe even birthed their babies in such a spot. Maybe even Indian weddings happened here, unknown to the modern world when it comes to enjoying this kind of getaway to nature. At least to my modern world.

The rush of work, obligations, and time frames left me a mess sometimes, even when I was in school. With dating (without in my case) this was stress! Let alone schooling, with all the tests. Yes, my discovery of this special pool is my greatest secret. Neighbors are not close, by any means, and not prone to snoop on someone else's property. Therefore I secretly shed the bonds of today, and go native.

The musky odor from the moss, the blend of fir and cedar, wild flowers, and the hum of bees never

Barbara Twibell

gets tiring. And each year there are more sweet little bunnies born. I can persuade them to check me out as a friend. They come so close; they come to my hands or legs, or even hop up into my lap. They are so trusting. Once in awhile a female deer and fawns or fawn will wander within eyesight. They take my breath away. How very graceful they are in their suspicious movement. A mother skunk and four babies have just waddled nearby; I did not move or make a noise.

It is so great to just meditate, to be one with the surroundings. Feeling like that is hard to do in Seattle!

Popping my hair into a pony tail, I grab up my clothes and jump back into them, and wave a temporary adios to my spring pond. I will be back! When again I need your comfort!

12

Both Gram and I are thrilled when we reach the mail box and find a letter from my mother. Yes, a Montana returns address. The walk to the mailboxes was a long walk. The boxes were placed at an intersection of four corners, almost a mile from the house. If we felt like a walk on a sunny day, we'd go. If not, Mack would bring it in. I loved the walk primarily because of the glorious fox glove plants. They are favorites of mine. Depending on various times of the year, we sometimes ate wild strawberries, blackberries, salmon berries or different kinds of apples, prunes, or pears along the way. Gram has always enjoyed teaching me survival techniques, trail marking and track reading. As if I would ever need this in an apartment or at work! This is the fun of being here. We both hesitate to open the letter. Do we want to know what is going on in my mother's life?

Gram and I decide to carry the letter back to apple orchard near the house, and lie down in the grass and read it there. Just a few feet away is an old flat bed hay wagon used during hay season to throw the hay up on and carry it to the Barn. Besides we don't want the neighbors to see our reactions, if there were to be any! The nearest neighbor could not see us for a very long period once we left the mail boxes. I figure this is a carry back to Gram's past and her worrying about what neighbors are making up.

"Dear Ones, (that's a start) so you can relax, all is well! (How did she guess?) The trip was tedious and fraught with my own worry, as to if I should be coming to Montana. (Her worry!) I've not enjoyed myself so much in years! Montana is so large! The scenery much as in the Gorge. So dramatic and wild. I have even seen an Indian chief. (Come on Mom, get to it) Monty is adorable, (what?) He and his family have made me feel so welcome. (I bet)

Monty built a log cabin with a stone fireplace and a flagstone walkway. (She's a goner.) There is a beautiful view of a valley and river (oh, no) and lovely pines. Monty's mother and daughter are attentive and sweet. I did not know such a family exists. (Thanks- what are we?) I know this will surprise you, but I am going to stay on awhile. They have assured me of my welcome, and Monty has so much to share with me yet. (I'll bet) Suffice to say I'm having a great vacation, and think of you often. I will write again soon! Love you both bunches!!"

"Gram, she's a goner! I'll be lucky if I ever see her again!" Knowing I feel a small twinge of jealousy concerning someone else's daughter, this will be hard to swallow. How can anyone fall for someone so quickly? Bet his daughter doesn't want my mom any more than I want a dad! Hey, I'm just a little ahead of things aren't I?"

Honey, I have waited too long for your mother to sound like a girl again! Do not worry! There is always room for love. True love just moves over and makes room for more. Your mother has always loved you. It is about time someone loves her! Besides us, that is." Gram grabs the top of a tall sprout of grass and chews on it.

Daughter of the Gorge

We both lie back on the grass and just let the puffy white clouds pass over us. The sun warmly baking into our skin, caressing us into our afternoon nap.

The evening went pretty much as usual, some talk about what was going on in the world of politics and local gossip. I'm pretty tired for some reason, and beg off to go to bed early for me.

13

"Jamie, Jamie! Hurry and get dressed please. Some of the cattle are out!" The call of the wild! Usually a neighbor or passerby would drive down to the house to let us know the cows were out and going heavens know where, at a pace faster than normal. A gentle, lazy cow could instantly turn into an eager teenager with the keys to the car. An animal that could not see an open barn door could recognize a middle fence line down or a gate left open from five acres away.

It was our "duty" to run out and recognize where the bells or bell was going.

Cows move along gathering mouthfuls of grass along the roadside, moving here or there, ambling, until they notice someone coming up on their side trying to turn them toward home. Then they gather unheard of speed. My gramma's language changed dramatically when she ran across uneven ground, with wild blackberry vines and hidden mole holes in the field. She did; however, teach her granddaughter how to herd. Come around from the front and turn the beast back to a homebound track.

Jumping fences, tripping over logs, sliding into blackberry bushes, running until I could barely breathe encouraged me to THINK in the same language. Cows have a neat run. They throw their feet out to the sides and their udder swings back and forth as if in great need of a bra! Just about the time you get them to the gate, they note it and run on by! Whoever is behind them has to hoof it

Daughter of the Gorge

across a corner to head them off again, sometimes stepping into surprise cow pies. Anyone who mentions "stepping" into cow pies is not totally honest, a lot of the time it is a "slide across" the pie, trying to gain balance on that trip! Threats of a hamburger future, and all parties getting exhausted, finally means the cows being led back to home field.

Cows are sweet animals. So curious. I know one time I was working on a fence up by the road, and there was not a cow in sight. I decided I wanted to put fence staples where some had popped out, permitting barb wire to loosen enough to tempt calves or cows to make their escapes.

Anyway, here I was, bent over thoroughly engrossed in my job. When suddenly I jump in surprise. Right behind me, with big brown eyes, long eyelashes, and so sweet a face, was one of our cows! It's amazing how quiet these animals can be when it suits their fancy. They always fit that big wet, cold nose right between a shirt and slacks on the bare skin.

Gram is closing in on my position. By now, I know she is tired. Running after animals is hard work. The fear of actually losing one is very real. If a cow gets into the wilderness, a cougar could have her for dinner, much less the damage that could be done to her body, (udder or legs) that might cause her to bleed to death before she is found.

We're done now; the cattle are back in their own home pasture. They didn't even say thank you. Talk about appreciation!

Barbara Twibell

"Jamie, look what I have!" Deep in the pocket she had formed in her apron are four beautiful red strawberries. They are wild, but large for being wild.

"Gram, these are great! I'm starved after all our running." I grab two.

"Those dang cows are not worth their salt lick." Gram plops down in the grass. "I'm not fit enough to be shagging my fanny all over the forty! Jamie, you're so much help to us. We love the time you're here, always. It might have killed me to do this by myself. Guess if I were a cow fastened up all the time, I might look for greener grass too. As it is, the exercise probably is good for my ole bones. Sometimes I hurt so badly in the back I could sit down to cry. But then, who would hear me and care? The cows might care, but they can't help!"

"Gram," I ask, do you get lonely on the farm? You go days without seeing anyone. Don't you miss people?"

I find a blade of grass to chew on, just the tip end.

Thoughtfully she answers.

"I keep so busy with my work that one day fades into another. Between all of those animals, the every day chores, and the natural beauty here, I just don't miss any of the fuss of the world. If people would greet one another as happily as animals

When they see you, or leave off their moaning about their troubles and picking ya

Apart, maybe I might miss them. Everyone has troubles; it's how you carry them that matters.

Some just feed off the misery, and don't move on. They don't let people forget, cause they can't. I left Missouri cause of that. Years ago. No, I don't miss people! I do miss my kids. I wish you were closer, but I think all parents feel that way. When I think how I just picked up and left my family, I guess I have no place to wail. That is why we treasure the time we have with you, Dear. You fill up my bones with joy!"

Mack is a good eater, that's established. I know few who relish the smell of food in the manner he does! Mack is a person who truly enjoys the privilege of eating a meal prepared for him. He comes in from outside and always checks the steaming pots and pans, and Gram always chuckles.

"Tonight we are having homemade chili, and crackers. It has been cooking most of the day. No, the beef in the chili is not the runaway cows." Mack has not heard about our run away day yet! Gram carefully taught me her secret recipe. The onions must be Walla Walla Sweets, diced small, mashed tomatoes, (skinned) one large or more clove of garlic, fresh ground beef, one cup sausage(mildly fried and drained) and beef fried mildly, check over red beans, (boiled soft beforehand), and add all the ingredients after draining. Salt and pepper to taste. Add hot pepper to taste. Nothing of Gram's is ever measured if it is something she fixes often. If it is a new recipe, then she will add a touch of something to improve it.

"Boy this is driving me crazy," says Mack. "Smells so darn good!" Mack then went into his daily rundown of his activities.

Barbara Twibell

"We worked hard today moving a slide area. We didn't know this road was closed! Guess no one was back there in a spell. Back behind the fish hatchery. Damn nice country. Should have left it closed. We spotted a bear! This bear a big one was walking along like he owned the whole world. A damn new worker, wanted to poach him. He's some mouthy guy. Got him a high school diploma and can't smell his own stink." Mack rests his big hands under his suspenders. His frayed jeans leg bottoms now show about four inches above the boot tops.

Mack loves his work, whether it's farming or county. He loves the men he works with also. He goes on and on in animated description of the day's activities, and Gram listens. It's neat to witness their mutual respect.

While Gram fills Mack in on our exciting day and sets all the dinner things out that she wants on the dinner table. I wander into the living room and flick through the J.C. Penney catalog. I really don't need anything, but it is something to do while they chatter on about this and that. I am now called to dinner and it tastes so good, I eat too much! There are some times of the year that certain foods hit the spot. I have always had a fondness for chili. Then what does Gram do, but surprise us with a piece of fresh apple pie! My mother and grandmother are the best cooks. Each mother down through the generations has made cooking fun. Each strives to please the taste buds of any person. Though I have little time to cook fancy or tasty for one person, me. I can cook and love too.

Daughter of the Gorge

She smiles at Mack and continues with her story. "We had a fun day, took a walk, picked some fruit, and just had a good time together."

WHAT? Hey, what about the cows? Those weren't rainbows I was slipping in! I thought to myself! Come on Gram, we could really milk this one. (Pardon the pun) Gram smiles that "leave it be" look, and I slip into the living room again to listen to the radio. I feel like a little girl. Contrary to another time when I was a lot younger and I was visiting Gram, when I came to realize I was growing up! I had spent the evening devouring the Penney's catalogue, when I noticed how the models looked in the clothes that were of my size. They had breasts! So did I. They had nice hair. They looked almost grown up. Did I? I raced up the stairs, took off my clothes, down to my panties and bra, and did the model pose. I did look like them! Never again could my mom make me believe I was just her little girl. I was older than that!

14

It's a wonderful, sunny warm morning, and there are those nails above my head stabbing into my view. Where did I leave off last time? Count them up!

I can hear Gram coming up the stairs. Gram usually does not do stairs except when she has to. Gram injured her back and limits the times she goes up and down the stairs in a day. My curiosity is pricked!

"Jamie Darlin', are you awake? Fine, I was sure you would be! I have a plan for us today. If you're willing! (I know by the way she started this I'm in trouble) I want you to help me tear down the back porch today. Hurry along and put on some older clothes and shoes. We must finish this before Mack gets home tonight. I've got it all figured out, and we have time to finish. Are you game to help me?"

As I get dressed I wonder about my grandmother's sanity for the first time. Does Mack know about this plan? I can't afford to lose my happy home yet, so there are no options!

At breakfast, a large one, as if for a field hand, Gram goes on to tell me she wants a new porch. Mack has promised one, but he hasn't found the time to tear down the old one. He will get to it someday though…It has to come down, lumber stacked, and nails removed. Not an easy task. Gram has it all planned out. I grab down a board hand it to her; she will remove the nails, and stack the wood. She is too large to be on the roof, but I am not!

I don't know about this, but I will do it. Gram doesn't ask for much, and she is convinced this is a good project.

The job moves quickly. Gram says we have to be careful about picking up the nails, so the cattle don't swallow them. The roofing took the least amount of time. The cross members and beams the longest. They were really nailed in. This house was built by farmer standards, so it was built very strongly.

If I weren't having so much fun and feeling naughty, I'd probably be hurting. Gram insists everything be neat, piled, and swept. She only tells me now, that I might like to take a drive about the time Mack comes home, because he will be mighty surprised when he steps up onto the back porch that is not there.

Surprisingly Mack had little to say. That he was surprised would be an understatement.

I guess we're going to Camas tomorrow. Mack has to pick up some two-by-fours, a new screen door, some roofing material, and nails. Seems we're going to build a new closed-in back porch! He has a mess of old windows in the barn that can be re-used on the new porch. Gram won! Mack wasn't even mad at her. He was concerned about one of us getting hurt on our adventure. Mack says if I'm strong enough to tear something down, then he supposes I'm strong enough to help put up the new.

15

The usual way that Mack and Gram drive to Camas or Washougal, is to take the Washougal River Road. They rarely go the main highway. Sometimes they turn off and go up over Mt. Pleasant. The views are incredible. The Cascade mountain range and its valleys open up for full inspection. A gorgeous mountain in the distance is called Mt. St. Helens; it is as perfect a cone as any in the world. The evening sun sits on it and makes it look like a strawberry ice cream cone. Some say it is a volcano and could erupt again someday. There are old paintings by trappers of an eruption way back in the early settlement times. As of now it is fabulous, and on a clear day one can turn around and see Mt. Adams and maybe even Mt. Rainier. These are all Washington state mountains. Mt. Hood, the closest mountain to us is on the Oregon side of the river. Any route chosen is a delight.

Camas is a mill city. There is a very large imposing paper mill, which all roads seem to lead to. There are two main streets that are lined with stores. The main highway winds its way just to the outside of the main street. There are some well known cafes and bars. The usual dress shops, stationery stores and five-and-dime on the corner. Camas High School has so much spirit! They have a great marching band. Most what they are known for is a tough football team. Camas and Washougal High Schools are hard to beat. I know for certain that these players work hard all year and a little sporting was right up their alley. Well, I'm

Daughter of the Gorge

daydreaming again. We are stopping at the Copeland lumber for the things Mack needs for the porch.

The sun is out and it's mighty warm to be hammering all these nails. All the animals are under shade trees, looking over at us as if we've lost our minds. No one should be working in this weather. This is super hard work, but I'm enjoying it ever so much. Working with Mack and Gram is natural and easy.

"That's cute!" barked Lance.

I about fall off the roof from fright! I never heard Lance's truck pull into the farm.

"What are YOU doing here? Are you so dumb you can't see someone could fall from this roof?" I must look a fright, and I don't appreciate a person sneaking up on me.

"Well, since it's not your face I saw first, I just said, "that's cute". Lance has that put down tone to his voice. "I came over to see my horses, and to pay Mack for the first month's rent. Seeing you was optional." Lance ran his fingers through his hair, leaving little pattern lines in his hair. Frowning he continued, "I'm never sure how I might find you!"

"What do you mean by that? I explode. Lance can cause me to feel like an idiot with just a look sometimes. Then he smiles, and I know he is just loves getting my goat, and I jump for it each time.

As much as he infuriates me, he pleases me. I find I'm intrigued by something about him. He is so blasted manly. So authoritative. (Bossy?) So strong. So handsome. Why am I even thinking these things? He just thinks I'm a kid, and I know nothing.

"Mack, I the have time to give you a hand. Jamie can get off the roof that way and get cleaned up and we can go ride for awhile before it goes dark. I'm sure I can work faster than she can!"

"I look just fine anytime I ride your horse!" I spit back. There he goes bossing me around and telling me to clean up before I ride. As if I wouldn't.

"Why are you telling me what to do? I don't need prompting."

"First of all, Sweetie, you do look cute. Told you that... But, you can't ride safely with those cut-offs; you'll burn your legs. Plus, you might not be safe with that blouse tied in that knot under your... umm, A shirt of some kind might be better."

Oh, who does he think he is? I don't think I ever want a man! Is that Gram and Mack laughing with Lance?

Gram senses my thoughts and hurriedly adds, "Honey, we're laughing with you, not at you!"(Funny, I'm not laughing).

I decide I'd rather ride than win this one, but Lance will get a piece of my mind one day about his take control attitude.

I wonder what Lance meant by safety surrounding my blouse. I just don't understand the arrogance of men. Reminds me of my tennis partner in high school. He wanted me for doubles because I was quick and strong. Then he would proceed to boss me the whole game. He just knew he was the best, and he wasn't. Neither was I!

Daughter of the Gorge

"Now children, it's too warm to fuss. Come on with you!" Gram scolded.

I had burst out, without remembering Mack was up on the roof with me, and Gram on the ground handing us whatever Mack called for. I felt like a jerk.

Gram decided it was time for an ice tea break. So, I should come down anyway!

"Come on, and please join us, Lance!"

We all enter the house. It is considerably cooler than the roof. I take my leave and go upstairs to change. When did I get all those black streaks on my face? I can barely believe the picture I make. I look like a coal miner! My hands are black on the insides. Oh pickles, how awful I must look to Lance! I change, but now must pass behind them after getting downstairs, and get to the kitchen sink to wash my face. This is the first time I remember missing that bathroom that Gram doesn't have!

I can remember brushing my hair back with my hand all the time, but didn't realize I was painting my face at the same time I was nailing down the roofing paper. I grab up a wash cloth, and make my way to the kitchen, quietly dampen the cloth, and slip out onto the back porch to madly scrub my face and neck. Leaving the cloth hidden on a nail, I casually move my way back to the kitchen sink to thoroughly wash my hands and arms. As I finally get to the table take up my ice tea and get a second breath, Lance and Mack stand up to leave. "We ain't got much to go girl. You be with your grandma, and Lance and I will finish up."

Barbara Twibell

"Lance, when I'm done here, I'll call the horses over and start saddling them." For this, I don't wait for an answer; he is already out the door.

I'm questioning to myself if my mother might not be riding horses in MONTANA at this very moment!

Major is such a magnificence! I wonder if he knows this. He is probably as conceited as his master. I am now hanging in mid air determined I'll get his bit into his beautiful mouth. He seems to know my height well enough to pull up his head at my every attempt. His soft eyes convey no ill trust, just giving this girl the brush off. In it goes. Now to pull the harness on over the ears, Bingo!! Success! Major knows, and I know he allowed this gift to me. He had all the strength to fling me far west had he wanted to. In drawing his face down, I could bury my cheeks to his muzzle. Horses are so soft and smell differently from other farm animals. It's not an unpleasant odor; it goes well with leather. Major, of course, must keep an eye toward Candy. Loving is fine, just don't monopolize his time. Other than the saddle being heavy, Major took it very well. The blanket under the saddle is a deep green Indian design. Too bad to cover it!

Moving on to do up Candy. She is a lady and desires all the loving! If I never got the bit in, she'd not care. Everything is so easy with her. Her darker ears look so becoming with her tan coat. Her eye lashes any woman would die for! I have loved caring for these two beauties; they seem like my babies, too. They definitely have a master, and their eyes are alert for him.

Daughter of the Gorge

I tie the reins around the fence rail loosely, and let them play at waiting.

Lance whistles and I awake! I do not remember slipping away after sitting down under the apple tree. It was so shady and peaceful.

"Caught ya napping!" Lance bends to lend me a hand up. "Didn't think that roofing would take so long. We won't have such a long ride, but it should be nice. It stays light until ten o'clock. So we have about four hours to enjoy!" With a tap of his heel, Lance moves Major off in the lead. Like two robots we girls follow in their tracks. After passing through and closing the pasture gate, Candy and I move up beside Lance and Major. Both sit as one. I remember then that horse and master know and trust one another explicitly. Rodeo work requires practice and trust.

"Lance," I ask, "what type of rodeo work do you compete in?"

"I settled on bulls, and calf roping," he answered confidently. "When Dad's health is on the better side, I compete more often. This has been a slack year for me. He has not enjoyed good spirits this last couple of months. I don't want to leave Dad to all the summer work when he's not fit as usual."

"Oh. When I first met you... at the store, Fred told me you did rodeo work. He said that was why you were so angry with me." Did I just broach this subject?

"Rude, I was. Sorry. I had just had my butt kicked off by the last bull I rode. Then when I got home, I found my father ill. He had let me go, not saying a thing about not being well. I was ticked, and you got kicked. I've since told Dad that I got hurt some, and needed to take it easy for a season. He believed me too easily!"

I have trouble believing, that I, Jamie am riding along, not in a dream like when I go to sleep. This is really happening. There is a real live, story book dream guy riding beside me, sharing his thoughts. I mean, I love Zane Grey books; I always have. The lost girl, the cowboy, the horse, the wide prairie...

"Hey! Lookout! That's an intersection! Where are your brains? Do you want to get hit by a car? People are not on the lookout for horseback riders. Aren't you paying attention?" Lance really can scowl.

Darn, in trouble again! Candy dances a little, because I pull back sharply on her reins.

"I'm sorry; I was just lost in thought." I wonder to myself, if this will be enough to change his mood. I just don't seem to be able to not botch up with this human. Maybe I should quit trying.

"I guess other than you not listening to me, there is no harm done. I just can't replace you or these horses that easily." Lance has a look of great concern.

"Lance, I didn't mean to do something so stupid. I was just wondering how I could be out on this perfect day, these wonderful animals, and such a neat guy, and, I was too listening about your father's illness, and your pretending to be hurt." If I could for once, not feel like an idiot when I am around this man. Maybe this is the problem. He's a MAN, and I feel like a little girl. He's much too old for me!

"I think we will stop up ahead and take a moment to enjoy the scenery. Let the horses forage for a bit." They love this deep green grass, and there is quite a patch in the meadow up ahead. Lance gives Major a bit of heel, and we all gallop, I notice Candy is the follower not about to be left behind.

Lance leaps from the saddle and comes back to assist me. I am not a great rider, so I probably show the need for help. But, in my dreams, I am awfully good! At riding that is!

"Jamie, let's sit here. Come closer. I don't bite! I'm not a mean guy. I'm just not used to caring about someone's welfare. At least not a female someone! Therefore, I guess I get grumpy, or something. I come off barking at you when barking is not what I mean to be doing." Lance does that thing again, the running his hand through his hair. I like it!

"Dad and I put up with each other; there is no one else to please. So, we lose the social skills necessary for lasting friendships. I apologize! Will you forgive this ole grouch?"

Lance leans close towards me, seeking my answer. I can barely keep from choking with laughter, his intense forthrightness totally unknown to me. My mother once told me that my father never apologized for anything...ever. I feel numb, what do I do? This hunk is apologizing to me. Lance is leaning closer; his eyes are so incredible. He has a slight five o'clock shadow. He's closer; his smile is so perfect. His body is turning into mine; he is definitely closer!

"Yes!" I murmur from full soft lip coverage, stifling any further comment. His lips press me back gently, as his arm reaches behind my back giving me such secure support. There is this added dimension, a wonderful floating feeling. He deepens the kiss. I've never felt so warm and electric before. Somehow in the matter of seconds, he has fully enveloped my body, my mind. I am vaguely aware of the progress he has made, but I can't put a stop to the warmth I now harbor. The kiss goes on...Never have I been kissed so warmly, or thoroughly. There is no threat; I feel no fear with this man. I feel protected and special. I feel I am certainly kissing him in return as I've kissed no one. He is not grappling, he is not rough, and he is not taking "advantage" of me. He has the advantage!

Are my arms around his neck, are my hands playing with the curls of the nape of his neck? Am I even here?

Lance pulls slowly away and smiles down on me. "My gawd, what a way to spend the evening."

I'm a complete hussy! I've not lost the ability to think before. I have always been in control, and I certainly don't feel that way now!

"Jamie, I think we should talk about when you're going to come over and meet Dad and Aunt Cleva. I would like to have you come to dinner. Think Saturday would be okay? I'd like to show you some of my life. Be smart to come while Aunt

Daughter of the Gorge

Cle is at the house; you'll be fed a whole lot better. Okay?"

"I'd love to. Why did you kiss me like that?" I asked in a dazed fashion, trying not to show there was any effect on me! I still can't think!

"Cause it was time, and I wanted to." Lance got the horses, and we rode on in light discussions about rodeo work or fun, and how to pick great horses.

Lance thought nothing of what just happened to me. Do men not feel just swept away as a lady gets from a kiss like that? I'm afraid to let my imagination carry any thoughts at all. They all seem high schoolish.

All the while Lance is telling Gram and Mack about our ride, my mind wanders. This ride was special for me. But, to a man, it was probably nothing. Never! In all my experience (like none) had I felt like this, and it is frightening. I need to drop this thinking it's too mind boggling. Yes, I'll not think of it again!

Lance tells Gram he's coming for me Saturday. He didn't even ask Gram for her permission. I always ask about going somewhere. Why does he command response?

My feelings are confused. I like the attention of Lance, but it bothers me. He can take over my life in this childhood setting. I am independent and do not need complications, like the transfer of powers! When I get the chance I will set him straight.

16

The mornings on the Gorge are crispy even in the summer. This necessitates time lying in bed enjoying the tranquility of the moment. I'm noting where the sun hits the floor, and how long it takes to travel over to a certain copper boiler. Listening to the robins chirp, I'm thinking my mother is probably listening to the same sounds. I am wondering if she misses me, as I miss her. Has Monty kissed her? Did she feel like I do now? I feel so fluttery inside and so happy. I wish we could talk about this.

One of the mysteries I wonder about when I lie in bed looking up at those darn nails is…When you want a roof not to leak; how come putting a thousand little holes in the roof keeps you dry? Does our roof at home have all these little nails in it? Why aren't they rusting? Why does it seem important to count them? Maybe this is why they are covered with sheetrock in my old home. These nails have become old friends to me! Always there for me to notice or count.

Gram's floors upstairs are a bit dusty. I notice dust balls skipping along if there is any type of movement of air. Of course, there are not many; they are just skipping here and there as if playing with your eyesight, daring you to tell their hiding places to the owner of the house. The larger part of the floor has a portion of linoleum, but that does not cover the whole floor. Copper cookers with lids and a couple of trunks are along the walls with various other "treasures". The dust does not seem

Daughter of the Gorge

to matter here. At home dust could ruin a whole day. Better do it right, or do it again. I honestly don't know when Gram dusts. I know she HATES housework. But, again it seems okay! Her home seems clean. It has LOVE! It makes memories. I wonder, as I lay here thinking, if something has happened to families and the time moms have for them. When did it become so important for homes to be so sterile? For homes to be cleaned on weekends instead of playing as a family, as Gram finds time to do.

Gram is always fussing around fixing something, doing these projects on her own. Accomplishing so much without flurry, and I know she washes the floor. Her mop and bucket are wrestled with weekly. I just never have been aware of the production we city people put into it!

Gram notices so much more of life than people I work with. She takes time each day to "smell the roses." She works so hard the way she has to accomplish her tasks, but she seems to have more time to enjoy nature and her home than I've noticed other ladies doing. Including my mother. You see, Jamie, you can lie here all day and think of dust balls and nail endings!

The wait for Lance to come get me for dinner is nerve wracking. I bathed today in the round tub, and I don't want to do that again!! So all day everyone has seen to it I don't do anything to get soiled! I've done my hair in the soft waves Gram suggested, her hovering over my every curl...like who is the hairdresser here? I have changed clothes four times. "Must look just right for Aunt Cleva."

If I hear that one more time...

I have finally chosen a sea green skirt and blouse, with a matching sleeveless print sweater and white pumps. If we examine the horse collection, white pumps will do all right! Sure! I honestly think something more durable should be worn just in case I am escorted through horse barns, but Gramma insisted wearing what was proper. She reminded me Lance has seen me wearing nothing but jeans.

Lance pulls up to the house, honks lightly, and comes to the door. He's wearing tan slacks, brown cowboy boots (shined) and a soft blue crisp shirt, with a dark brown leather jacket. Everything fits him as if it were tailor made. I've only noticed the State Patrol ever wearing shirts that fit like this! If I could drool over a pretty picture...

"Do I need a jacket?" I ask, still admiring Lance's tailored good looks.

"Naw, I'll keep you warm!" Lance seems pretty pleased with himself.

"I'll get one just in case," as I walk to the closet and pull my short brown jacket out and put it over my arm. Now, I'm pleased with myself.

Lance is giving me the weirdest look over. I don't think there is an inch of me not scrutinized. I am not used to being checked out this closely. I would feel much put out if I didn't know that I secretly had been checking him out also. It is his knowing smirk that annoys me!

Lance chuckles and asks, "Is there a time I must bring Jamie home, or is she a big girl now?"

Daughter of the Gorge

I find myself stuttering a response, "I beg your pardon? I'm quite able to look out for myself, and I'll let you know when I wish to be brought home, or maybe I should drive my own car!"

GADS, here I go again. Why does he do this to me? I can feel the heat rising in my face.

"I'm sorry," mutters Lance, "I thought that would be funny." He glances at Gram, but she's not about to help bail him out! She does, however, give me a glance that says, please behave! Hold your tongue.

"We'll be seeing you then," Lance says to my grandparents. "If you're ready, we'll be on our way." His hand gently, but firmly steers me out the door by the arm.

"Bye Gramma," I mew, "I won't be too late."

Lance aids me up into his pickup and closes the door.

The jaunt to Lance's home only takes about a half hour, but our time together already is fun. I tease him about the fact I didn't know big trucks could smell so pretty. He laughed and said it took considerable time to clean up the cab to make it habitable for a lady. He added, "A very pretty lady." He also announced he had to drive into Washougal to get a hair cut and fuel his rig.

Haircut? Ugh-huh, his hair is beautiful! The kind a woman dreams of dallying her hands in! His profile is so manly, so strong. He smells so good. Old Spice does it to me!! I can't believe how my mind and eyes enjoy resting on this man. It seems so easy to fantasize about being with him.

"Jamie, if you don't quit looking at me, I'll not be able to take you to my place, we'll just park instead!"

"I'm not looking at you! I'm looking at the scenery out your window. Gee whiz!"

We have curved around a forest- lined gravel road and turned off to the left, past some cattle shoots and then driven up a dirt lane winding around a huge long barn and some sheds housing tractors and various farming equipment. To the right of that, I now notice a green stained clapboard home, with a full screened- in porch. The house seems to have a chimney, which would be for a fireplace. Looks like it might be made from river rock. It is a surprisingly large house.

I notice a fine looking pole fence, as we were coming to the house. The fence, though shorter, also frames the front yard.

A huge maple tree demands my attention between the house and the barn. The lane here at the house becomes a circular drive. Lance parks and says, "This is it! This is my home. Welcome, Friend!"

"Oh Lance, this is incredibly beautiful! How you must have loved growing up here!" Every space is filled with beauty. Flower beds stuffed with every imaginable color, texture and type, sprinkled with a hoe, watering jug, or bumble bee! Some spaces in the garden looking as if the implement used was just absent- mindedly dropped when the day got cooler or the telephone rang. Do they even have a telephone?

Daughter of the Gorge

On the porch are four overstuffed big armed chairs. So inviting! Nearby is an antique wide-topped table covered with a homemade checker set. The pieces are as large as the palm of my hand.

"Dad made those. He can be pretty clever with a piece of wood, don't you think? He got to cussing one day when he kept dropping the smaller game pieces and kept having to bend down to pick them up. He had me laughing up a storm! Dad's not real keen on being laughed at. Now he never drops one!! He'll challenge you to a game before the evening is done!" As Lance reached for the doorknob, the door swept open, and before us was a very attractive woman, I'd guess, in her early seventies. A warm smile worked her laugh lines!

"I could hear you coming from the time you drove up, Lance! Taking you quite a spell to come to the front door! Thought you might be needing some assistance! Come in, Girl, your feet need to move to make progress!"

If I had been ill at ease when coming to the door, that was instantly erased on the spot! She evidently enjoyed life.

Lance lunged forward and grabbed his aunt Cleva in a big hug. "It's been so long since I've seen you! Probably a whole hour!! Is it now your practice to greet me each time, at the door as I return?" Obviously a little dig here.

"Auntie, this is Jamie. No need for introductions; you each have heard me speak of the other! Other than a lie here and there, all is true!"

"Jamie, how nice to make your acquaintance," said Aunt Cleva extending her hand forward. "We both have quite an evening ahead of us. These boys rarely entertain guests, so we'll see where their manners are this visit. Go on with you Boy, I will let you know when dinner is ready."

As I moved further into the room, Lance took my jacket from me. I couldn't help being drawn to a huge fireplace made from river rock, it being the center of one wall, flanked on each side by bookcases made from rotary cut two by twelve's vertically standing with various sized areas for books and knickknacks. Never had I seen such a rough, yet beautiful fireplace. The opening was large enough for an eight year old to stand in! An upright grand piano sat crosswise in one corner, with a conversation center made of two rockers and two sofas. Of course a fire crackled in the fireplace.

"Gonna burn us clear out, he is. This is summer. Don't need any fire for a girl!" A slender but strong, slightly graying man with a cane came bursting out of the hallway. "Son, I ah, think we can let this burn down a bit, maybe find a damper piece ah while we have dinner, don't you think, Son? I'll just do that! Didn't hear ya come in!"

"Jamie, this man with his foot in his mouth, is my dad, Burt Allison. You see, there is a definite family trait running here!" Both handsome men look bemused with one another.

"Glad to meet you all grown up! I met you when you were just a little girl, along with your mother in North Bonneville." His smile sincere, he knows he is forgiven. Lance takes my arm, and gently guides me to a sofa. The three of us settle into easy conversation about the house, how Burt built it with the aid of his wife and friends, and a lot of back- breaking labor. The river rock actually came from the Washougal River. This surprised me. I would have thought the Columbia. Burt said he preferred this rock. They hauled it a long way!

Aunt Cleva joined us after a little while and asked the usual date type questions families ask, leaving one on guard and feeling as if one had just taken a geometry test. I found a little giggle inside myself thinking how much fun it would be, to be able to ask coy questions in return, to the mother types, who are certain you are not good enough for their little "Darlin's."

Like, did you know your son can be a jerk sometimes? Did you teach your son to paw all over a woman, or was he born a pervert? Did you know your sweet son demands favors for the meal he bought you? Why did we break up? Oh, if I could only have told a couple uppity mothers the real story about "their" sons!

Lance is nothing like some of those dates, though.

"Jamie? Are you in there?"

Lance has just caught me daydreaming again. One of the better things I do!

"I'm sorry, I just spun out for a bit; something triggered a memory. How discourteous of me. I'm really so embarrassed!"

"Wouldn't be the first time Lance lost a lady's attention!" remarked Lance's father with a satisfied smirk. He gets up and moves to a chair more broken down, and apparently more suited to

Barbara Twibell

his fancy. In minutes Burt is engrossed in his Washington Farmers magazine.

With that, Aunt Cleva laughingly asked us to join her in the dining room; dinner would be served. There was an easy kinship between the three. One could see their sincere love. There were digs, denials, joking. Most of all, a wonderful pot roast! The gentlemen have made many offers to have "Cle" move in with them. On a regular basis. Tonight came another offer, when the peach pie made its appearance.

"Never! A woman can stand you two only so long! I have my own home and social life!" Cleva passes around the platters of food again satisfied she has been courted properly for her devotion to her brother and nephew. "I'm not about to give up my independence to suit the two of you!"

Lance and I volunteered for cleaning up after dinner. The others retired to the living room to set up a Pinochle table; they feel certain they can beat us.

I feel so much warmth in this home. I miss a dad and woman atmosphere. Joy is what was missing from my parents' home. They just moved around each other, not with each other. I had never identified this before. This is sobering to me. I would work hard not to have this feeling in my home someday.

SNAP! The dish towel nipping my behind jerked my mind to reality! Lance had scooted a bit back from me and was preparing the dish towel for another assault. SNAP! Darn, that stung!

Daughter of the Gorge

"Stop that! Can't you find something else to do? I don't have a towel! You don't play fair! Maybe I should throw some water on you…"

"If you want Aunt Cle to come through that door to protect you, you might, or you could pay me to leave you alone!"

Lance steps closer. Raising the towel higher and over my head, coming to rest around my neck, pulling me closer and closer until I was melted against his form. He had worked me to the counter, but not forcibly. Tenderly brushing his lips across mine, I felt myself being lifted until seated.

His smell so clean, lips so soft, plundering, nipping, deepening as I found myself swooning into feelings so engrossing, I scarcely heard Aunt Cleva calling if we were about done. They were now set up to play games.

"Not nearly," mumbled Lance against my ear.

"Be there in a bit," I rasped. "We're almost done."

"No, we aren't," Lance moved quickly to unseat me and went out the back door.

Where all the dishes belonged, I didn't know others I could guess. What on earth possesses Lance? I must redirect where this is going. He is so sure of himself, obviously he's had young ladies here before, and they aren't here now. I'll not be caught in this trap!! Working in a beauty salon, I'd seen what happens to girls who become willy-nilly. He's not Willy, and I'm not nilly!

One last look around the relatively modern kitchen left me convinced it was in spic and span order. No telling where Lance stomped off, maybe

Barbara Twibell

he needed something from his car. That being, I readied myself to reenter the living room.

"Game time! Come on, Girl, and get your beating!" Burt was ready to beat me into the ground, the excitement showed in his eyes. Do I tell Burt now that he has picked a game I know nothing about? "Catch the cards, read them, and weep girl! Lance and you be partners, Cle and I will soak ya!"

Lance entered the kitchen and came through the doorway. He paused a moment and noted where he was to sit. Across from the most intriguing girl-woman he had ever met. She was totally naive about her effect on a man. She sat with cards in her hands that were all askew and a very big frown on her face. Didn't anyone besides him notice she was about to bite through her lip?

"It's your bid, Lance," Burt blurted.

Lance smiled and held his cards closer to his chest. "Three hundred." Lance knew he was going to love this!

Cleva studied her cards thoroughly. "Three twenty."

Everyone was looking at Cleva. With expectation, "Well," said Lance grinning ear to ear, "what's your bet, Jamie?"

Jamie felt the room closing in on her, what to do? Maybe she could bluff this along, and learn as they go. What is she supposed to see? No matter how long she looked at her cards they still didn't mean anything to her.

"Three eighty!" A satisfied smug smile danced on Jamie's face.

"I pass," said Burt.

Daughter of the Gorge

"It's all yours, Honey. I pass too," said Lance as he stretched back in his chair.

"I also pass," stated Cleva. "What do you call?"

They were all looking at me again.

"I don't understand what you mean," Jamie muttered. She helplessly looked to Lance.

"Just pick a suit, the cards you have the most of!" He leaned closer into the table.

"Oh, of course! How dense of me! Nines!"

With that, Lance rocked off his chair in gales of laughter!

Burt just stared. "Sweet girl, you've never played Pinochle, have you?"

Cleva chuckled and reached out to console a beet red young lady who got caught in her bluff!!

Jamie could just die! These were virtual strangers, and she had just do-dooed on herself!!

"Put down all your cards, Fellas. We are going to teach this brave girl a game she will enjoy the rest of her life!"

I could not remember a warmer feeling than what flowed over me, with such kindness. Usually I am used to being made the fool. Now it was laughter, and the promise I would learn. Everyone agreed on that!

Lance just looked at me admiringly and gave me a wink!

The evening ended with the usual "Thank you'd," and a round of hugs from the seniors. Jamie had her invitation to come back any time with or without Lance. "He's a scoundrel anyway, Child! You pass along a greeting to your grandparents for us! Get her on home safely,

Lance." His Aunt Cleva is a jewel. I can see why the guys miss her when she decides to go back home.

Lance gives his thank you's, as do I. We step outside to the most beautiful evening I've ever noticed before. The moon is so full that the Cascades are like large dark warriors standing guard over the river, looming high on each side. The frogs are doing a jolly good chorus, and peacefulness reigns as an umbrella.

The truck cab is cold, and I begin to shiver. Lance draws a blanket out from behind the seat and wraps me snugly in it, pulling me gently to him. As we leave his home the moon shines through the tree limbs, touching objects making them a bewitching scenario of guesswork. How many little beady eyes look out from the dark at us?

We pass in view of a hay wagon and in the shadows are a couple of standing cows. My mind races to the fact that less than a hundred fifty years ago this could have been a camp out area for traveling pioneers. Why, Indians might have been watching their movements from the top of Rooster Rock. An Indian maiden perhaps might have been enjoying this same moon with her handsome young warrior. How much could that moon tell us?

"Okay, where are you? You haven't said a word since we left the house!"

Lance looks perturbed. "Are you going to tell me where you were? I'm certainly not used to you being so quiet!"

"I'm sorry. Tonight has been so perfect, and the moon's so beautiful I slipped into the past and was wondering how many pioneers looked to this same moon to find peace from their travels or promise for their futures. The history of this area just does something to me. I feel it, dream it. I think of it as if someone in the past begs to be remembered. Silly isn't it?"

"No, I feel it often, too. When I work the fields for hay and mend the fences, sometimes I feel someone is standing behind me, seeing to it I do it right. Someone cleared the land and suffered the weather, dug the wells, and trapped the game. Then other times I feel like tearing the fences down. They don't belong here. Some warrior is letting me know I would be freer without them," Lance professed.

We have stopped now, and I have returned to reality that I am not home, but parked at the top of the Cape Horn view area. It is not a large area to park and cars certainly pass by, but it is the most remarkable lookout on a full moon evening.

"From here we've always been able to see Gram's houselights. Sometimes we'd even blink our headlights to them." I snuggle a little more.

"You will also note, you can see my place's lights from here," Lance points out to me. "Before the dams were put in, so I've been told, my great-great Grampa could ride across the river to get supplies down Portland way. The sandbars are ever changing and drier years lead to some good rides." A pensive Lance continues,

"Just think Jamie, Lewis and Clark came by here as did Dr. McLaughlin and the Missionaries, canoes, ferries, paddle boats, and fur traders.

People who wanted new starts. They all looked at the same water falls, rivers, hills, and Mt. Hood. We are a part of that legacy, Jamie. We both are. You are the first woman I've been with who is remotely interested in the life as it surrounds us. You are so different from other girls, and, you don't even know it!" Lance dreams on.

"Is this something I should change? I ask.

"Absolutely not! Change nothing except that temper!" Lance traced his finger over my face slowly, studiously, smiling as he looked into my eyes. He carefully moved stray stands of hair curling about my neck and placed a warm kiss to my lips, then my neck. Then back to my lips, tugging gently with my lower lip. He moved to hold me closer. Just closer, and so dearly. "Jamie, what do you dream of for yourself? You dream for others, but what do you want?"

"What do you mean?" I ask. (No one has ever asked me what I think! I was raised to anticipate others' needs, and moods.) "I really don't know how to answer your question." I feel a little uneasy. "I guess the next step for me is to go back to work. I never intended to be at Gram's this long. But I love them so and find it difficult to think of finding an apartment and a new job. I don't think I want to go back to the past. I don't even want to think yet!" I actually feel a slight stab of fear, with just the thought of going back to the rat race of the city. "The better jobs are in larger cities or larger towns. Then on the other hand, I would like to go to college if I could secure a scholarship. I'm a tad lost as to my future, aren't I?"

Daughter of the Gorge

"Why would you ask?" I felt curious as to why Lance would have an interest in what I planned to do with my future. Perhaps he feels I'm a leech at my grandmother's. I find myself wondering if I'm not!

"Well, it's about time I take you home! Can't have you out too late, can I?"

Lance slips the truck onto the highway and homeward bound he moves. Move he must, for his memories also include a beautiful young woman by a pool. It is not the moonlight in her hair now, but the very picture of her body that is very visible to him in his brain. The girl at the pool... What is he to do?

I felt the evening was over too soon. I think I might like being with this man. But why do men take you home just when they are becoming pleasant to be with? Oh well, this has happened before. About the time I think someone really likes me, it is time to take me home. You know, don't call me, I'll call you!

"Goodnight Jamie. Tonight was special. I know Aunt Cleva and Dad had a great time, as did I. I'll walk you to the door, and I will be seeing you soon. I have to be gone for a few days. Be a good girl okay?" A quick kiss, and he was driving quietly back up the lane, through the gate and out of sight. I could hear his rig for minutes rolling down the gravel country road.

Coming home from a date I find is a lot different than from home. At Gram's I need to steel myself for the hike to the outhouse before I go to bed. The very shadows from the moon that an hour ago was so romantic have now turned into goblins all the way to the little house on the hill. The tilty one.

I don't have a flashlight and its dark in here. Ever think some animal might be down under there just waiting to make a grab? Where's the paper? Of course-I knock it off while looking for it.

OH GOSH! I hear breathing; it's getting closer. A TWIG! OH NO! Is there a bear out there or a cougar? (Here kitties, kitties) I must get out of here! The last thing I need is to be found on the pot, trapped, DEAD. I can just read the obituary notice now.

Time to make a surprise break for the house. If I run fast enough, "IT" may not realize what went by, before I make it to the house. THIS IS IT, NOW...

I am to the back porch in record time, breathing hard, scared spit less, when I realize from the corner of my eye memory, I just blitzed by a cow!! I just ran the four-forty because of a cow that couldn't sleep!

It's so like Gram to leave a glass of milk and a couple of ginger cookies out for me. I turn out the lights and creep up the stairs, pull the curtain aside and make ready for bed in the dark. It would be chilly on regular sheets, but my bed has pink flannel sheets.

The window is letting in the moonlight, and as I lie here, I can see the cars come around Cape Horn! A few moments ago I was on that bend of the highway!

"Goodnight, Jamie," says Gram.

"Goodnight, Gram," I sigh. Should have realized she wouldn't be asleep until I was safely home!

17

If I would ever die of memories, I just know one of them would be waking up to the more pronounced scents and sounds around the farm. No where else in my life can I identify so much. As for Gram, nothing will improve her lack of singing ability! So profound is the difference in voices between her and my mother. My mother has a fantastic voice, and one rarely hears her sing, while cooking or just fooling around. Gram, on the other hand, bellows in a bovine voice, and enjoys it thoroughly. Usually the same collection of well-known hymns, "The Old Rugged Cross," "Jesus Loves Me," "In the Garden, and old pops like "On Top of Old Smokey," "White Christmas" and a few others. What ones she does not know the words to, she makes up. Sometimes those words would burn preacher's feathers. Head held back, chest thrust out, and hands and arms extended, she was in concert with only the chickens and cows to hear.

My grandmother is up at the crack of dawn, starts her baking, washing, soap making, whatever and is well underway before I get up. My mother, on the other hand never gets up until at least noon. Then she dresses, gets her coffee, and lights up a cigarette and smoking several more before she gets on with her day. Mom never goes to bed before midnight or later, doing her work long after I usually have hit the bed. Gram's in bed by eight!

Gram heats and hauls her water; mom turns a faucet. Gram whips her food up with a bowl and spoon, never spilling over the side any contents;

Daughter of the Gorge

Mom flips a button on her Mixmaster. Mom vacuums, Gramma sweeps. Gramma churns her butter, and Mom makes margarine by popping a yellow food color bubble inside a plastic bag, and squeezing it until golden and mixed. Mom has the new home; Gramma the broken farm house. Mom buys from the store, and Gramma works hours in a large garden. Mom has the indoor bathroom; Gramma the outhouse.

Why have I always found happiness here rather than at my mother's?

Did the war remove so much from people's lives? I truly wish my mother could be happier. I also wish she would answer our combined letters to her more often.

It is time to rise. I cannot lie in bed much longer, or this will give Gram the permission she needs to attack her lazy granddaughter!

There is something about stretching the toes out under the sheets that feels sooo good. Unless the foot starts to cramp as mine is now!

"Hi Gram! It's such a neat day isn't it?" My plate of breakfast is ready for me. All I need to do is wash my face and hands. It always bothers me a little that washing is out in the open. But, there is no wash basin in the outhouse, is there?

"Hello yourself, Sweets! A good morning to you! Would you like orange juice or apple juice this morning?"

"Apple please! Ummm, this bacon looks so wonderful. You cut it so thick Gram, I could use it for house siding. The way Mom and I have bacon, you can't get just one strip at a time, three or four sticks together!"

"Did you enjoy your evening, Dear? Those are real nice people, though we don't know them closely. They are there for others if needed, and that's what is important, you know." Gram is wiping her freshly washed hands on her apron.

"You were a little later than we expected, but it was still a decent hour. I wasn't worried, but well, I guess I was a little." She smiles and winks.

"We took a little drive after dinner and cards. It was such fun, Gramma. I learned a game called Pinochle. Such an odd name for a game, and certainly difficult to learn. I think I was the sacrificial lamb. Anyway, it was a super night. Gram, Thank you for letting me goes."

"Land sakes, Child, You're a woman grown! You needn't have asked us at all. It was kind and thoughtful of you to do so. We appreciated your trust." Her smile and manner are genuine, and I choke back a feeling of overwhelming love when I realize this is the first time someone pointed out I am a woman.

Until now, I may have anticipated that knowledge, and never realized it.

It rings consequential to me that a few years back I discovered I was getting breasts when I got tangled in a cow stanchion. The pinch hurt and that brought on realization that my body was changing! Then one evening while I was looking through a Penney's catalog I noticed my school dress size. It was then that I really saw how tall and grown looking these girls was. I was a teenager looking like the girls in the catalog! Talk about a protected existence. My mother did not want me to grow up. Isn't it funny until then I had no concept of where I was in lives growth chart.

I'm wondering at this point, if I need that catalog again! Maybe it could tell me how to grow up gracefully.

"I don't feel like a woman grown, Gramma. I don't know exactly what I am. I still feel like a little girl, even when I was working. I just did my job, and went day to day." My thoughts are drifting over my few years, compared to hers.

Gram pulls her chair out from the table, and sits across from me. She searches my eyes, no, my very soul. She is listening, as no one else can!

"Gram, don't you suppose I should go job hunting? I'm not very grown up, if I'm hiding out here! (My chest is tightening up just saying these words.) I mean I love it here, but won't your friends begin to wonder about me?"

"Honey, as if it mattered to this old bird, what anyone thought when it comes to you! Why Mack and I bust with pride and love, where it comes to our Jamie.

When a birdie is hurt, you take it in. You care for it, love it. Then when it's time for that birdie to fly, it will. All of its own accord. You're our love, that's why your mother and I wanted you here. To get stronger. To be happier. To belong to yourself! You're not to worry about what's not there! Now, there will be no more of that subject."

"Gram, when a guy, I mean, when he holds you, and you start to feel sort of weird, I mean it's nice, but."

"Lance a bit smitten I bet!" Her eyes were all twinkly. "I had a feeling you two might be teaming up!"

"But Gram, we're not teaming up...on he contrary, he's older, and more experienced. I think he's just being kind, like he is doing what is expected. Only I don't expect it! He can infuriate me in moments! He's controlling, he's stubborn, too good looking for a girl like me to keep up with! I don't want to be his hobby piece!"

Gram fidgets a little, "Has he, ah, made you feel like you're of little meaning to him?"

"No, no not at all. He makes me feel special, but Gram, that's me. What have I got that is any different from any other girl? Why should he have any interest in me?"

"Probably because you infuriate him. You're stubborn, sassy, cute, adventurous, pure, and more than worth looking over! Give him and yourself a break! I think he will be a good friend! If he has not tried to bed you..."

"GRAM!"

"As I was saying...He might be good for you!" Gram resolutely voiced.

"Gram, these pancakes filled with blueberries are so wonderful!" I watch Gram as she shuffles about in the kitchen, putting things away in the refrigerator, the pantry, and back on various shelves. Her dish towel is on a rack just behind the wood stove. She takes out a slightly battered pan,

Daughter of the Gorge

places it in the sink and that is how the dishes get done. A modern rinser, or dish drainer is sitting on the counter top. Gram is an artist when it comes to stacking a dish drainer. A fly would need a road map if he found her dishes. When she is done she covers them with a clean towel.

My observations of Gram are purely selfish. I love her so much, and I don't want to forget her way of life. I realize she is an every day joy, and a link to the past that so intrigues my soul.

At home, when it's time to take out the table scraps and vegetable peelings, it seems such a chore. I have to find a sack, then wrap the stuff in waxed paper, put it in the sack, and take it out and place it in the garbage just so, making sure the sack does not break. We can't attract the flies, you know! Gram just steps out the back door, throws the scraps to Laddie, and the peelings go over the fence to the chickens that work her garden every day for worms.

She always wears her print apron, with a Kleenex inside her pocket. If she really gets to flying around the kitchen, she will use the bottom of her apron, caught up in her hands, to carry a hot dish. Or I will catch her wiping her hands with it. She has done these things enough years; she is a ballet of motion to watch.

Today I decide to help Gramma with a chore I enjoy doing, and she grumbles over. Gram would like me to be on this perpetual vacation, but I really need to be doing something to feel I'm earning my keep. Therefore today I will clean out her cook stoves and wood heater. I have gathered the big ungainly bucket she uses just for this chore. If one held her arms out and touched her finger tips together that is about how big the opening is on this bucket. I've gathered the stove crank and the little shovel to dip out the ashes. The stove has cooled off, and the embers are almost out. There is a compartment on the left hand front that opens under the fire bin, and the wood lies upon a grate. There is a fitting here that I connect the crank and rotate it vigorously back and forth until all the ashes and wood particles fall into the ash pan. Now comes the part where I must be most careful. If I move too swiftly, there will be ash all over the kitchen, and I know how Gramma hates to dust! I carefully spoon out all the ash and lay each layer in the bucket. I remember to do this slowly and carefully. Success! Clean air! Now I wipe the whole stove down with a damp cloth, and take a big wad of wax paper to the whole stove and grill area to shine it up! I move on to the wood heater in the living room and carefully add its ashes to the bucket. Now I place a damp towel over the bucket top to keep the ashes from flying out as I move through the house and then outdoors. The ashes are then placed on the ash pile Mack has established in the east corner of the garden. When done, I spray with the garden hose lightly; to firm the ashes and make sure they are completely fire-free. Gramma takes as good of her stove as we do our cars.

After mopping over the two floors where I worked, I feel great! Big job done and Gram is so pleased with my work that I get that huge hug from

Daughter of the Gorge

her that I love so much. Gram can make me feel like the most precious person ever. Now, I must have a piece of chocolate cake and a big glass of milk for the work I've done for her. Something about grandparents make you want to work for them. No matter how you manage to get the job done, it is good enough for them. If the job is re-done, it is not in your presence or re-done as an angry putdown.

It is time to share the rest of the day with Candy. Gram has her fancy work out, and this is something I don't have in common with her. Her chores are caught up, and she is perfectly happy to spend a couple of hours making little connected holes out of string!

She also seems to know my need to be outside. I don't do inside really well; I much prefer outside work, or checking out birds and flowers. This afternoon I just want to walk with Candy. I don't even think I'll ride her. Candy is always ready for an adventure. Leaving Gram, and calling out to Laddie the collie, off I go.

Anyone who thinks a horse does not like to walk along with you as a best friend, has not had one to experience this with. I am so grateful to walk among the wild carrot, fox glove, mountain hollyhock, and the great camas lilies. I stoop to check closer the tiger lily, one of my favorites. The blue flag and yellow flag lilies, oh, so many glorious wild flowers are attended by the most energetic fat little black and yellow bees. The meadow lark's song is one of the prettiest one could listen to. An occasional gold finch dips in front of my eyesight.

Robins and blue jays abound at various periods. Wild strawberries crawl along the pastureland, overlain by wild blackberry tendrils. All the berry family grows abundantly in this area. The sky is such a blue. Big puffy white clouds are rolling leisurely overhead leaving no threat of rain in their path.

The rag weed, late goldenrod, pink fleabane, field mint, rough bull weed, deer brush, and cow vetch are all flowers and weeds Gram taught me to love. As I walk along, the fragrance from these flowers is as desirable as can be found. There are too many kinds of grasses for me to know. I know I pull out ragweed and tansy as I walk along. I've enjoyed humming and singing several tunes. I love to whistle. I can do that here. In Seattle if you whistle while walking along, someone might look at you as if you're nuts. People are losing this mode of entertainment.

Candy is wanting some grass and water. She strains to reach out to particular clumps of green vegetation. I know I don't have far to go to find just what she wants. The fields just beyond the Cape Horn Grade School have ample supply for her. I will enjoy a break myself.

The three of us cross over and make ourselves at home. In the distance, cow bells ring in pasture lands. An occasional truck or car moves along a nearby hillside. The wind carries the laughter of children freed from having to be in school.

Laddie is frolicking around the underbrush and plowing headfirst through the grassland. By the time he swings back around to me, his coat will be pock marked with grass burrs. I hope he does not locate a porcupine like he did last year. That took minor surgery at the vet's to remove over seventy quills in his mouth and muzzle. He particularly likes to corner a skunk. This really gets him into trouble with Gram.

Having a horse to love is more than I ever dreamed would be possible. I have always wanted one. But impossible for a city girl. Mack had thought to buy one, but I'm not here to care for a horse as I would have to be. Such luck. She needed to have some care this summer, and I get to have the privilege to be that person!

I wonder what Lance is doing out of town? I must admit I miss his company and banter. I'm certain Candy misses him also.

If nothing is organized for tomorrow, I think I will drive into Vancouver and see how the job market is for hairdressers. Give me some time to check what rent is there also. I don't think I want to mention this too seriously to Gram yet. I really don't wish to mention it to me, either! If Mom were to ask me, though, I could answer honestly that I have been looking.

Candy seems well pleased with her break, and Laddie is within whistling distance, so I think it is time to head back to the farm. The walk was great, but I will cheat and ride Candy bareback if she does not mind. It truly is better sight seeing from the top of a horse! We walk along, and Laddie catches up with us. He quietly jogs along with the horse, not even lifting his head to see where he is going.

Barbara Twibell

To me it seems like we eat, do some chores, eat, do some chores then eat and go to bed. Each day is filled with some glorious activity, yet, we eat!

It's no surprise then that I'm at the table again. Stew is the main dish, with homemade rolls. Wow! Will I ever be able to cook like this?

"Gram, I think I'll go to Vancouver tomorrow. Do you want to come along?"

I knew she wouldn't. She enjoys her home, and to leave it means to have to gussy up. Girdle and nylons (rolled of course) is not her cup of tea, unless she must see a doctor.

Seeing the doctor or going shopping means the works. A nice dark dress, nylons, black shoes, one inch square heels, gloves, and a little box hat. She would have started early to be ready. She would wax her "whiskers," pluck her eyebrows, run a wet comb through her hair, and look forever for matching earrings. She only gussies up four or five times a year, but in her mind trips to Vancouver or Portland demands this type of dress code.

18

I have left the house with a matching skirt and sweater and cream colored pumps. Gramma knows I will be too late for dinner tonight. I've told her I'd get something out at one of the cafes on my outing.

I've chosen to make the trip along the main highway today. Sunny and warm is the forecast. Its funny how people raised in Washington will still look up when they go outside just in case they might need an umbrella.

It's such a peaceful drive, no billboards, not too much traffic, and little noise. Farms stretch out to the right with pastureland curling over the hill out of sight. On the left hand side are various types of trees, brush, blackberry vines, downed logs, and the occasional ravines and stolen views of the Columbia River. The highway dips and curves and swings around to nearly meet itself by the next curve. Across from this point I can see the beautiful Crown Point, a concrete domed lookout on a mountain ledge overlooking the Gorge from the Oregon side. This lookout is just off the Oregon Scenic Highway. Coming off the hills into Washougal the area flattens out in front of me, and it is easy to see the sand and treed islands out in the river that make navigation tricky on the Columbia River.

Washougal is famous for the Pendleton Woolen Mills. I have two of their reversible permanent pleated skirts. The skirts are actually made to wear on either side, and they are gorgeous. Pendleton

Barbara Twibell

puts together the most wonderful plaids. A store selling their irregular stock is connected to the mill and can be a source of many good outfits at greatly reduced prices.

Stopping at a small white gas station with a wooden roof out over the gas pumps will give me a chance to visit with some really kind people. They have many small repair items for cars for the passing motorists as well as a well- stocked candy shelf for people like me. The elderly couple has converted the rear of the station that used to be where major repairs and lube and oil jobs were done into a home. They are so sweet, and each time I have come in whether with my grandparents or just by myself, they insist on giving me a candy bar. Now, I wonder if modern stations as I have near home aren't missing the boat, so to say, by not giving of themselves with a small bit of kindness! Definitely I'm going to fuel up with this couple, rather than go down the road a ways and be treated indifferently.

Crossing over the Washougal River Bridge, there is a large wooden building with lots of cars parked out front. This is the skating rink, and I remember one year our family helped put sand bags all around it during the Vanport Flood. The water was so high, it was frightening. Flooding is so unpredictable; there is absolutely no guarantee the water will not just keep coming and cover all around us, to keep us from being able to reach safety. Everyone was scared to death.

The Vanport flood did terrible damage to the Vancouver/ Portland area. My father had been a

Daughter of the Gorge

district manager for "The Oregonian" in Vancouver, and it was his job to get the newspapers to his carriers all through Battleground, Woodland, and parts in-between. Nearly every road we went down, we got turned back to go another route. One girl rode her horse around her route, since she could not ride her bike. Even in the mud, her customers got their newspaper. This was such an adventure trying to get the newspapers to everyone.

In the small town of LaCenter I remember falling on the ground. I was jerked up by my arm and bawled out because the cut I acquired would probably become infected from the germs in the mud of the flood waters. It did! At twenty I still carry that scar on my knee. So many homes were surrounded by water. Many people stood on the dykes and watched their cattle try to make it to dry land. Sadness still comes over me when these memories are dug up.

My biggest disappointment was that Jantzen Beach, my favorite amusement park, was under water. Half of downtown Vancouver and Ft. Vancouver were swamped water. My memories just flood back as I drive on my way into Vancouver.

Passing through Camas, the paper mill smell sometimes is overwhelming. Mack once told me to hush-up when I was complaining about the smell. I was told that's the smell of jobs. My first lesson in economics. The mill, Mack had said, was the major employer of the people in this region. Many families were second generation employees. Camas is a really pretty town. It meanders along the

Barbara Twibell

highway, curving around the mill. The residential area lies from the river to the flanks of the hill behind the business area. They boast of some great parks with lots of trees and play room.

As a really small child, in the late 1940's, we lived on East Ninth Street in Vancouver. This was the home my parents bought after my dad was able to hold a semi solid job. Many afternoons I would ride my bike around the block and probably drive the local dogs nuts with playing cards stolen from my mother's cribbage deck clothes pinned to struts of my bike fenders clattering as the loose ends struck the spinning spokes.

It was great to stand at the entry to Ft. Vancouver and watch the soldiers march on the parade field, a sight that has long since faded into history as the military has left the fort. There are fabulous old officers homes still standing along tree-lined lanes. As I drive by today, I understand that there are plans to excavate the old original Hudson Bay Company Fort Vancouver of the early 1800's.

I'm now driving past Harney Grade School. The school I attended. Somehow it just is not the same; the trees don't look as big, the school looks smaller, and so does the playground. The last year I was there we had a big earthquake. My lunch was knocked out of my hands; milk and sandwich went flying. We were all marched outside away from the school to stand and watch it sway and pop bricks. The earthquake did quite a bit of damage. If I remember, the auditorium was condemned. It had such a big stage and seating like a theater. We had a big May Days Festival with a real May Pole. I don't know who did all the work, but long lines of yellow, blue, and green ropes hung from this high pole. Each child was given the chance to walk around the pole braiding the lines. Why did this have to disappear as a tradition?

Downtown Vancouver is changing and I really don't know if I want to find work here. I don't see any large salons. I think I'll just drive around and see how the apartment areas look. Well, my heart's not in this search. I can't believe how late it has gotten, and it is time for me to do a turn about and head back to Gram's. It is surprising how far away her home seems to me at this point. In fact, it seems worlds away. I can see the huge wooden frame of the roller coaster across the river on the Oregon side at Jantzen Beach. How exciting it is when coming off the bridge and there is Jantzen Beach! Someone told Mack they might tear that down and build a big motel. Such a shame if they ever even think of it.

I like taking the lower river road in Vancouver. It goes under the Interstate Bridge and runs along past the deserted shipyards. A lot of ships were made during the war. Now just skeleton remains and concrete walls are all that is left to tell of an active past. There are many terrific plans for new highways along here, and some general juicing up of this part of town.

For all my bravery at going out to job hunt today, I would have to say it's been a total flop. My heart is not in leaving the Gorge, for going back into the real world. The memories and observations have been wonderful and fulfilling;

another time might be better to look for employment. I really don't care to make a hasty decision and find I'm not happy where I would be working.

Why I let Lance gets me upset about my future I cannot fathom. I don't need him to remind me I will soon have to find work. Maybe after my mother makes up her mind where she will be, it will help me in my decision making.

Speaking of Mother, I tend to wonder more all the time when is she coming home? We don't hear often enough from her. I'm not much better at letter writing either, so we deserve each other!

Man! I can't believe I am at Gram's gate. I drove straight through, without stopping at the One-Stop Café in Camas. I had every intention of having something to eat there. I can't believe I did this!

"Hi everyone! I'm home!" How warm this seems to my soul, as I sling my purse into a chair.

"Jamie, did you eat dinner out?" asked Gram.

"Believe it or not, Gram, I even forgot to eat lunch! Maybe I can fix something from the fridge."

"We had roast beef tonight and there are plenty of potatoes and gravy to warm up with the green beans that were left over, and I will fix something else for Mack's lunch tomorrow. Eat what you need. You must be famished." Gram started to lay her fancy work aside. It takes Gram more effort to get up from her chair than she is comfortable with.

A couple of years ago, Gram was making her bed and stepped back too far and fell down the stairway. There is a window at the bottom of those stairs, and she went right out through it onto the back porch floor. There was no one around to help her until Mack got home. Needless to say, both were really upset. I think she hurt her back badly, but she just laid low for awhile with her remedies, and got back to her work. She just hasn't gotten around quite as well since then. Mack gets the broom when he says he can't believe she fit through the window!

As I slice the roast beef and put it into a skillet, Gram gives her disgruntled grunt. I had no idea she was right behind me!

"Land sakes, Child, why are you dumping the potatoes and gravy and meat all together? Looks more like something a bum would put together for himself." Gram is standing there with her thumbs hooked in the arm holes of her apron.

"Feel sorry for the fella you ever marry if you're just gonna dump and fry." Her head shakes back and forth.

"Gram, I'll never marry, and this is for me. Fixed my way. No one else has to eat it. I love it this way, honest!" I can't help eggin' her on a little.

"S'pose you're going to put catsup on top of that mess? You can't live without catsup." Gram still disapproves of my dinner.

I laugh with her as I look for the dinner plate to roll my meal into. The steam is ascending with the most fabulous odor; I've made a meal fit for a king! Leftovers can be better than the original meal in my mind. I've always been able to dump food together and be quite content. It probably comes from eating whatever Mom was able to provide for us while Daddy was overseas. Many a night we would have homemade toast and warm milk with a pat of butter on top for dinner. Often we also had homemade bread covered with gravy. My mother said every woman worth her salt could make good gravy. I grew up with making do with what was on hand. Mom could look in an empty cupboard and come up with a wonderful, filling meal. Gram is maybe even better. Here on the farm there is so much food walking around or growing. How wonderful to walk out the door and pick berries, plums, apples, grapes, goose berries, raspberries, lettuce, carrots, corn, everything!

If I'm able to do anything different here, it seems to be thinking! I have so much time to reflect back through my times with Gram. I don't believe I ever thought so much at home. There was no time.

"Jamie, you're off somewhere again!" Gram scrunches her chair back a little.

"I was just thinking about how good a cook you are, Gram. Who did you learn from?" Another fork-full reaches my lips.

"Child, each girl learns in her mother's kitchen! My mother learned from hers, and so forth back. Girls didn't have careers like your generation seems to have to have. We helped out with the cooking and chores as we grew up. Then one day we'd set up housekeeping on our own. Marry up and have children, then teach them the ways. There are the basics; from that you add flourish!" Smiling, Gram tells me she enjoys them fancy

Daughter of the Gorge

"Good Housekeeping" magazines. There are some very good recipes.

"Do you ever think of having a telephone, Gram? I mean, I just wondered."

"Nope, don't see that I need one. Besides we don't have the lines out here yet. Maybe they will be here in a couple of years. I really don't think I want that noise around. If people want to see me, they can just come over and visit. I want to be looking at them when they're talking to me!" Gram draws herself up and smiles.

"Seen Lance lately?" brought up Gram.

"No I haven't. He's busy out of town. He has more important things to do than checkup on me."

"Oh," grumbled Gram.

I'm finished with my dinner now and wash my plate and glass out. I dry the items and put the dish towel back to dry on the rack behind the wood stove.

"If you'll excuse me, Gram, I think I'll go up to bed. It's been a long day." I start for the stairway. "Gram, thanks for being you! I love you so much!"

"You too, Darling. Sleep tight! I'll be coming up stairs pretty soon."

Barbara Twibell

19

"I got a letter from your mom yesterday, Jamie. I didn't mention it last night because you were to tired to be going into another discussion. Do you want to read it now?"

"Wow! Of course I do! What does she have to say for herself? Is she coming home soon?"

"Here, Honey, you'll want to read for yourself. She's doing well." Gram hands me the letter and goes into the living room humming to herself.

I've read and re-read her letter about three times. I've read between each letter of each word. It still has the same results. Mom is coming home in a week, and she is bringing Monty with her. She can't wait for us to meet him. She KNOWS we will just love him. Has she lost her mind? If she brings him here, how will she ever get rid of him? Boy, mothers teach one thing and do others. She sounds so delirious; my mother, the very same person I read every joke in the "Reader's Digest" to, and she didn't laugh once. Her whole letter sounds as if she is laughing the entire letter!

They plan to leave very early Friday morning, and drive straight through to be here late Friday night. They will drive Monty's truck of course. How will she get her car here, or back here? I hate the way I'm feeling. Shoot, I don't know how I'm feeling.

"Gram!" I yell. "What does this letter mean?"

"It means your mother will be here in a week to see us, that's what it means!" Gram responds from the living room. Continuing on, "I believe we best get some baking done, and figure which old hens aren't laying as good as they could be!"

This is Saturday morning. I think I'll leave Gram and Mack to a day by themselves. It's only an excuse, but right now I need time to myself. They understood when I said I needed to get away to think of the changes evolving in my mother's life and maybe in mine. I feel like a spoiled brat in some ways and like a helpless little chick in other ways.

After changing into a red plaid blouse and blue jeans and a red kerchief around my neck, I slip on my cowboy boots and put the car in gear. I wave back at the dearest couple on earth. They are so understanding of the space and grow-up time I need. This is not a waste of time, though. Gram gave me her shopping list to fill.

Turning onto the main highway I decide to go east, perhaps up to North Bonneville. I love the easy curving highway with the tall evergreen trees guarding the roadside. The mixed ferns and maple trees of shadowing greens. Large hulking rocks covered with deep green moss peek out in various places just asking where you think they rolled from, or were they tossed here by an ancient volcanic eruption?

One of my favorite homes is ahead. It is a rock house. It has a peaked roof and a large bay window. This house has haunted my dreams for years. There is something so natural about it, yet there is a coldness its image eludes. I wish I knew the floor plan, because it must have a fireplace. Homes have always had personalities to me. Some are happy homes, some sad, some gracious, others unkempt. Some cozy, others cold. My favorite choice would be a log home. There are so few.

I seem to really like the things most people can't wait to get rid of. Pioneers lived in log houses and probably got sick of them. I love wood stoves; they're now going out the door for new electric stoves. Quiet ranches, horses...on and on!

The walls of the Gorge are about four-thousand feet high covered with dense second growth timber. Mountains peer from distances in the background. The Gorge is the only clear, clean cut pass from eastern Washington and Oregon to the western coast. The wide, deep, amazing Columbia River cuts right through it. The rock formations, slide areas, volcanic caves, ice caves, waterfalls, and lakes take my breath away. Every mile is different. Long tunnels allow the highway to cut through mountains without destroying the graceful pitch to the riverbank. I wish today I could drive clear to Goldendale, but today will be shorter for I already feel better than an hour ago. I've climbed Beacon Rock maybe four times in my life. It sticks up in the scenery like a giant upside down thimble. Many barges and ships have made their graves at the base of this volcanic plug. It's quite a worthwhile climb to the top. I can sit there for hours and look around. Unfortunately the wind and wind chill have sent me running back to the car today!

North Bonneville is known for the Bonneville Dam and power plant. This little town was established for the workers on the Dam site. I always picture Bonneville like the palm of my hand with the fingers being the mountains beside the river, and the space between the thumb and forefinger the passage of the Columbia River with Bonneville tucked under the thumb. The setting is majestic and awe inspiring. The main street is covered on each side with small businesses, cafes, gas stations, and a grocery store. This is one of my homes. Many childhood memories are here.

The grade school had a high metal slide other small children and I enjoyed playing on. One afternoon I finally managed to get to the top. After all I was only three, so this was quite an accomplishment. When I stood up to look around and prepare to sit down and slide, an older boy crowded past me and knocked me off the top. The children ran and got my mother who nearly died when she found me knocked out cold. I don't know how we got to the doctor, and I don't remember the trip. I was, however, miserable all night because he told my mother not to let me sleep. She had to make me stay awake with any number of means at her disposal. Isn't it fun to run around in the past, looking for the places we lived?

Memories of my mother's hard work to keep me safe and secure, walking over the areas we shared, has just woke me up to my mother's time and need.

It's her time and her business. I am now ready to welcome her friend, as I should have in the first place. Forgive me, Mom, for being so selfish!

Guess I best get Gram's list filled. This day has passed so quickly and has been such a delight.

Flour, sugar, yeast, baking powder, Coke-a-cola, bananas, oranges, Spam, mayonnaise, hot dogs, and buns, Oh, and a bag of marshmallows pretty well completes my grocery list of Gram's.

"Yes, that's it, thank you very much." I smile. "I used to live here, during the war; about fifteen years ago. I was just a little girl then." I wait for the checker to respond.

"That's nice; do come back again." The clerk begins to ring up the next person.

Well, see if I share with you again, I think as I turn to leave the store.

Tank holds a great trunk load. I could have bought out the store and still had room left, so these few things had to be placed just right so they wouldn't spread all over on the way home. As I slam the trunk lid in place, a movement across the street catches my eye.

A shiny red rig, with a handsome hunk helping a cute blonde female type person into the front seat. He's laughing as he closes the door, and bounds around to the driver's side and jumps in. She moves over nearer him as he starts the rig up and drives down the highway. Headed west. Headed home. LANCE!

20

"Honey, is everything all right?" Leaning with one hand on the kitchen table, Gram looks quite concerned. "I was happy to get the groceries; Lord knows I was short on some items really important, when I want to cook up a storm. You look a might peeked tonight. I know your momma coming with her friend probably upset you, but it is not the end of the world!"

"Gram, it has nothing to do with that. I'm okay in that situation; I have come to understand a lot this summer. I am happy for Mom. I miss her, though."

"You've barely said boo this morning. You passed over dinner as if you'd just eaten with the Vanderbilt's. When you don't eat, I know something is wrong! Ah, I just figured it out. You've not heard from Lance for awhile. You will Darlin, soon as he gets home! I should have thought of that sooner!" Gram turns back to the tea kettle that is jumping with steam demanding attention before spilling out onto the cook stove.

"I don't care to hear from him again, and I haven't missed him. You've misjudged our relationship... there is not one?" Jamie grabbed her milk glass and slugged it down in one large gulp.

"Gram is there anything I can help you with this morning? I thought if not, I would like to go to the barn and play with the cats. They have grown into such special little beauties. I want to make them a couple of yarn balls to play with."

Barbara Twibell

I knew playing with the cats would help lift this sullen, heavy, unknown feeling from her heart. She had no reason to be angry with Lance just because he had a girlfriend. After all, who do I think I am? Men might kiss, even well, someone other than a girlfriend. She thought he was a friend...why then this awful guts wrenching misery? Come on, Girl...get over it...there is no "it" to get over. Did I honestly think there was something else to this friendship? How stupid of me! Come on... Have some fun!

After a couple of hours of playing with the cats and making pull toys for them, and treating my wounds from their sharp little toenails, I turn to a game or sport I have always enjoyed when the barn is as full of hay as it is now. I love to climb the high built in ladder that goes up on one side of the barn. The hay is dropped on the barn floor until it makes a huge mountain of dry hay high in the mid section of the barn. This is accomplished after flat-bed wagons are driven through the drive-through in the barn and a huge fork like affair is dropped into the hay, and it lifts it high and carries it over to the drop point. A complicated grouping of ropes and pulleys do what man would have to pitch-fork weeks to accomplish. There is enough hay put away to feed the whole herd for the winter, into spring! When I first watched this done, Mack used a borrowed tray of horses. Now a pickup hauls the wagons.

This mountainousness mass is wonderful to leap into from the ladder! The weight of my body makes the hay split aside to allow a free slide back down to the floor.

Repeated trips ensure that dust will be flying through my hair and sticking to every piece of clothing. I don't care, though. The adrenalin high I get from the free fall into the hay is worth it! It's been a couple of years since I have been able to do this, one of my favorite rainy day games. There has to be a great harvest of hay to last so long, or to be this large to start with. The cats will now take a week to find, for I'm pretty certain I have scared them over to the next farm. I love the smell of fresh hay. The main thing I must do when I do this jumping is to set aside all pitch forks, for obvious reasons!

"GERONIMO!" I screech. The flight through the air, the landing and slide onto the floor...so much fun...except I am now looking at a pair of crisp pressed slacks and shiny black cowboy boots.

"Interesting." Lance steps back and offers me his hand, as a help up off the dusty floor. His lip is curled in a half smile.

"What are you doing here?" I sputter.

"Your grandmother told me you were up in the barn, playing with the cats. Since I came here to see you, she sent me on up. You're not carrying any cats in your pockets I hope?"

I don't want to answer Lance. It would do nothing to change the circumstances. I feel found out, and for some reason betrayed. This is my family home, and if I want to play in the hay I should be able to, without feeling guilty. What right does Lance have to make me feel like an idiot? I cannot help it, and I start to cry a little.

"I didn't expect to hurt you, Jamie. You look like you're having such a good time! Takes a lot of nerve to jump from that high!" Lance slips his hands into his pockets and leans against a beam. "I missed you, and I just got home a couple of days ago and well, this was the first I could come over."

By now I think I've picked most of the hay from my clothes, but I know hay is in my hair. I cannot help think I look like the straw man from "The Wizard of Oz."

"You missed me, and you came right over. Is that right?" I feel the steam starting to rise around my neck. "You hurried right over? I think not! Don't play me for a fool, Lance."

"What are you talking about?" Lance starts toward me.

"I saw you with your girlfriend in North Bonneville yesterday. From the way you helped her into your truck, laughing up a storm, you sure looked like you missed me." Now I'm in control again! Feeling a little foxy, I await his answer.

"You saw what?" Lance reaches out and grasped my arm, none too gently. "What you saw, Missy was a rodeo barrel rider I had just picked up from the bus stop. I can look really happy when I'm about to a make three-thousand dollar horse sale. A barrel rider only buys the best. I have the best. She picked out her horse, and Dad left this morning with her and her horse for Utah. You know what, Spit-fire? You're jealous!" Lance tips

Daughter of the Gorge

back his head and gives a good ol' fashioned belly laugh.

Lance nearly collapses when I give him a deadly aimed kick to his ankle. He falls forward, but not before he has his hands on me, dragging me down on the barn floor with him.

"Damn, that hurts, you little hellion! What's got into you? Hold still! You're like a damn bar of soap!" Lance now joins the club of dusty clothes.

"You can quit your cussing. I don't abide in that. Let go! I want up now!"

"You don't abide? You don't approve of a man letting you know you're acting like an idiot? You're lucky I don't use a few other well known cuss words. I know a lady doesn't like cussing...but you're no lady, at least not right now." Lance still has a good hold on me.

"That does it! Get out of my way. Go home. Leave me alone!" I feel so miserable now, but I will not let Lance have the upper hand.

"Leave you alone? Easy, but I had hoped to have some fun today, and I'm not leaving before I do." Lance knew he was headed for trouble, but since he was already in trouble what did he have to lose?

I try to get another kick in. My struggles are for naught, for the moose has me pinned. His hands are in my hair, and he's tilting my head back at no lack of pain. Some of my hair is caught in his watch.

"You deserve a spanking for your behavior! I'll let that go for this time. Think twice from now on before you accuse me of being with another woman.

I can't handle the one I've got now. But I will. Yes, by God I will!" Lance dipped his face down and took my lips, my eyes, nose, cheeks, neck...

The world is wonderful; I can't remember why I'm angry. I'm floating somewhere between the clouds and heaven. The repeated kissing, deep, slow tugging, the caresses, strong and warm, caring...

"Fomp" My backside slams the floor.

"Tell your gram I'll not be able to join her for dinner. I was looking forward to being with her again. I'll be going now, and leaving you alone."

The door of the barn opened and closed before I could catch up with what had just happened. The sound of a nearby truck engine starting, and gears being rung through grated my nerves. He loves his truck, and this is not how he would normally treat it.

Oh dear, I've done it again! The path back down to the house seems rockier than usual.

My heart is heavier than I knew ones heart could be and still be in one's chest. This man infuriates me in a flash. Yet, when he holds me or talks to me, I have never felt so loved. Loved?

"Gram, I'm a mess. I've hurt Lance's feelings and I didn't mean to. He just embarrassed me, and I lost my temper." I stumble into the kitchen where Gram is cooking.

"There, there." Gram sets aside what she is working on, and enfolds me in her arms as if I were again ten years old. "Just what has happened, and where is Lance?"

"Well, you sent him to the barn to find me, and he did. I made a complete idiot of myself, jumping around in the hay like a little kid might. Sliding down the hay, I was having such fun, Gram, and then I slid right into his feet. There he was big as life, and I didn't know he was there. I just wanted to die." I backed away from Gram, and looked at her face. Her face only showed concern.

"Did he laugh at you?" Gram asked.

"No, he just said, 'That's interesting.' He didn't say anything that was that bad. I know I overreacted. I got angry and essentially told him to go away and leave me alone." I hung my head. "He told me to tell you he wouldn't be here for dinner. He was so angry, Gram, and by then I didn't know what to say."

"Is that all that happened? Are you sure you've told me everything?" Gram prodded.

"Nooo, ah, he kissed me rather thoroughly before he stomped off. How could he do that when he was so mad?" I sniffed.

"Jamie, you were the one mad, not Lance. Sounds to me like he just found a way to shut you up." Gram chuckles as if she knew a secret. "Why don't you change clothes, fuss your hair up a bit, and drive over to Lance's home and apologize properly for your behavior? We can wait dinner for you. I'm a firm believer in being honest with a person and asking forgiveness for something misunderstood. You both will be able to sleep better tonight. Especially if you wish to remain friends. Men don't think women know how to say they're sorry. Be a good lesson for each of you." Gram swings back to the stove. "Put some perfume on too. You don't want to smell like the barn. Go on with you now. Don't stay long..." Gram swooshes her arm toward me.

"Thank you for helping me, Gram. This will make me feel better, and not so much a louse."

It is far from being dark yet, and it is so pretty. I drive with my windows down because I want to feel the fresh air. I feel much better about seeing Lance again. I really don't like being a tyrant. I've never cared how relationships ended before; they just came to a mutual close. I know I don't want this one to close. I have enjoyed his company much more than anyone else's that I can remember. One thing bothers me about what Lance said to me. The part about not being able to handle the girl he has. What did he mean? Does he mean me?

I see Lance's truck parked at their house. I pull up and take a deep breath. Now is not the time to chicken out. Stepping from the car, I notice the most beautiful circle of California poppies. Such a brilliant orange. Someone has been busy with flower beds. The porch looks so inviting for sitting and drinking lemonade. Some Indian design throws rest on the rockers. A quilt is thrown over the large overstuffed couch. Well, it's time to knock on the door and get on with this.

What will I say? Hello, can Lance come out to play? I'm sorry I made a mistake. Wrong house see you later.

My heart drops, for its Lance who opens the door.

"Hello..."

"AH, you've come to see the horses. Good. Aunt Cleva, we're out to look at the horses. It's Jamie. We'll be back soon." Lance reaches back and grabs his Stetson. His hand reaches my elbow and guides me off the porch toward his barn. His pace is brisk, and we're not talking. As we enter the barn, Lance spins toward me...

"I'm so sorry," I blurt out. "I was way out of control. I didn't want you to find me that way. I mean playing like a kid. Please forgive me?" I start to cry. This is not easy.

"Hey, don't cry. There is no reason. Of course you're forgiven. I had a chance to think too, and I know I would have felt the same if I'd been caught writing in the snow! Neither one of us would have been wrong; we just would have felt captured."

Lance held me close in his embrace, his right hand running through my hair. "Jamie, I promise to never hurt you, not deliberately. Will you believe me? I love being with you and wish we could spend more time together. We'll have to work on that if that is all right with you! Let's go look at some of our best horses now, so you can act like that's what you did come here for."

Lance's laugh is infectious, and I feel myself loosening up ready to continue on without the tears. I hate to cry.

We walk on through the barn and out to a side corral where Lance steps up onto the fence and whistles. I can't say any horse came to him, but the attention span of each horse definitely changed to include Lance in their view. The natural curiosity made them want to come nearer.

"Oh, they are such pretty babies! They are so perfect. What is that one with the spots all over its rump?" I can't get enough looking.

"That's an Appaloosa. Favorite of the Nez Perce Indians. Great horse. Mostly I raise Quarter horses. Best for cattle work, rodeo work. Tempra, the girl you saw me with, bought a big black, with four white socks. She wanted something for show and strength. She will have her hands full in training him the next couple of years." There he goes running those hands through his hair.

"Lance, thank you. I think I should head home now. Gram is waiting dinner for me, and I told her I would not be gone long. Thank you again for being such a good friend. Please have patience with me! I promise to get better." By now it is easier for me to laugh.

"You're welcome. I probably will be over on Saturday. I want to meet your mom. She is expected then, isn't she?" Lance is moving me back toward the car.

"Okay, but you will be bored. We girls can really get gabby. See you then. It is good to be friends!" After feeling so bad, I suddenly feel so good!

He is still watching me as I look back in the rear view mirror.

Gram was right. I do feel better.

Daughter of the Gorge

21

I'm amazed at the preparation Gram has gone into getting ready for my mother's visit. She has sent Mack off to the food lockers in Washougal for sausage and hamburger, steaks, and a roast. Mack is also supposed to bring back some French bread and olives. So, I can guess at the menu to be one night of roast beef, one of spaghetti and French bread, and finally one night of steak. I think perhaps I'll stay around for this!

I know we've churned enough butter to grease a cow; I've peeled apples until my hands hurt. There will be enough 'vittles' to feed Washougal!

The floors have been swept, and then mopped twice. I have been given the job to wash the windows inside and out. Earlier I was beating the living room rag throw rug on the garden fence out beyond the back door. This carpet is all braided, and it is made from dress and shirt remnants. In a shrill voice I was kindly reminded about not letting the dust come back inside the house. If I ever wondered if Gram cleaned house, I won't ask again. I can see now she works and fusses for hours before anyone comes.

All the extra fruit jars on the drain board have been carried to the fruit room under the house. The cook stove will be cleaned tomorrow and polished with wax paper.

I have just been asked by Gramma to scythe the back yard area. There is no such thing as a mower at Gram's. The yard is just clumps of field grass and various weeds. They are all green colored though, so when cut it can sort of resemble a managed yard. Her favorites that I must be sure to go around are giant pink poppies. Frankly I think they are ugly and smell worse. Not far from them are my favorites the fox glove. Gram has a hedge of purple and white lilacs that run down one side of the house, the side that could face the out house if not for their height. Mack taught me how to swing the scythe with smooth rhythmic motions right to left. Everything Mack uses is sharp and in good repair. The size of the area that needs to be done is the size of three driveways. I'll go ahead and cut down to the outhouse and around the drive coming into the house. I know Gramma; she will want everything to look as good as it can.

Gram and Mack have no illusions; their home is old fashioned compared with the real housing and ranching world. They would tell anyone, "It's paid for."

Chores done, I re-enter the house to find Gram winded.

"I just made up the spare room for Maurine and put a new quilt I just finished on the bed. Looks real inviting. Her friend can sleep on the couch downstairs."

"Gram, he can have my room. I don't mind." I volunteer.

"He has no need to come upstairs. I don't want him seeing the unfinished rooms; ain't none of his business." She pulled her apron around in a hitch that usually meant discussion was closed. From the looks of things, I would guess Gram has hidden quite a few things so that everything looked tidier.

Daughter of the Gorge

"Jamie, how about you digging some potatoes from the garden for me? I want to get as much done ahead as I can. I think I'll have you get enough to use at breakfast time and dinner. Dig plenty!" Gram surges ahead with her other details.

The yard's ready, food preparation is on schedule, and all we have to do is waiting. Poor Mack gets his head bit off if he forgets and wears his boots into the house. Gram is not about to have her floors dirty now!

22

I can't stand waiting one more minute. This whole day has been a bummer. I know it will be late when they arrive. I've looked at and reread each and every magazine in the entire house. I know Gram has emptied out the fresh coffee twice. For someone who has worked so hard, Gram is determined to look as if she has all the time in the world and she is always ready for company.

Beep, beepity, beep...

"They're here! Come on Gram, they're here!" I shout, as I spring for the door. Never leave someone to get out of a car and find the door by herself. That just never happens in this family! If we know you are coming, better stand back and prepared to be met with enthusiasm.

"Oh, Mom, I've missed you so much." I have missed her more than I realized. I can barely believe my excitement.

"Honey, I've missed you too. Give me a big hug!" Mom smells so good.

As everyone reaches the door, Gram welcomes Mom with a big wide hug. "Sweetie, you look fine! Come on in, Jamie, let everyone in!"

"Mom," says my mother, "I want you to meet Monty and his daughter Louise."

Monty's daughter Louise? I think. What is she doing here? Monty is enough to take in; he is plumb handsome. I can see why my mother stuck around in Montana. But as I search to get a clearer view of Louise, she is uh, stylish (probably snooty).

Daughter of the Gorge

She is tall, slender, and blonde. She smiles and extends her hand.

"Hello, you must be Jamie. I'm pleased to meet you." Louise smiles again.

"Ya right. I mean, yes, me too. Mom wrote that Monty has a daughter. I guess that's you." (Man Jamie, act like an idiot!)

My focus returns to Mom. She's looking at Monty. He looks like a movie star or one of those cigarette men in the commercials. He has the most beautiful white hair and square jawed outdoor look. My thoughts are broken by Gram's voice saying, "Come sit. Make yourselves at home. I have made some homemade doughnuts and coffee."

Mack stands and shows Monty a seat near the fire. We girls work around the kitchen getting coffee for everyone. My mother puts her arm around Louise and says,

"Louise has had a big part of making me feel welcome at Monty's home. I just know you girls are close enough in age to become good buddies. Louise will start school this September at the University of Idaho. Isn't that great?"

"What are you studying?" I ask, almost choking on my politeness.

"I haven't made that choice yet. I have many interests. Daddy says there is no hurry." Louise smiles again.

I'm thinking if she gives me that phony smile once more time...

"Mom! What is that...? On your finger? Is that what it looks like?" I gasp.

"Yes, isn't it wonderful? I know what a surprise this is. But I love being engaged! Monty asked just as we were deciding on what time to leave. I'm so happy," gushes Mom. Monty asked me and I knew I wanted to say yes, so I did! There was no time to let you know. We wanted to get married with our family with us, so we decided to marry while we are here for a few days. That's why we convinced Louise to come along with us." Mom puts her arm through Monty's, and they look at each other with total dedication.

"We will go to Stevenson and get our license, and the girls and I can go shopping for a dress for my wedding." Happiness is written all over Mom's face.

The ring Mom shows us is gorgeous. No one has to be brilliant, pardon my pun, to know Monty spent money on Mommy. Gosh, I cannot believe this has happened so fast. I just cannot fathom this is my mother. I also wish she'd quit squeezing Louise's hand. I am her daughter. Only I should be squeezed by her.

"Jamie, Darling, how wonderful you look. I'm counting on you standing up for me as my maid of honor. How fun for you since you missed the first time around. And, also, we're waiting to take our honeymoon until little later. Soon as Louise goes off to college, Monty is taking me to London. I can't wait. Remember how fascinated I've always been with castles and all that goes with the medieval stuff? Perhaps Queen Elizabeth will find time to have tea with us, if we give her a little notice."

This humor coming from my mother?

Monty comes over to me, and puts his arm around my shoulder.

"We expect you to come see us, anytime you wish. We have a spare room. I feel as if I know you already, listening to your mom brag about you. I'm extremely fortunate to have met such a great lady as your mother. Maybe I should have waited to ask you for your mom's hand, but once I bought the ring, I just could not wait. Will you forgive me, Jamie? I care a lot for your mom. I didn't think they made them like her anymore. She brings so much fun and joy into my heart," Monty brags.

"I intend to take good care of her, Jamie, and we are going next week to have legal papers made up so all parties are cared for if I should die. We will be a family in every way as far as I'm concerned."

"Well, I don't know what to say, Monty. To pretend I'm not surprised would be lying, but I have only one wish, and that's to see Mom happy."

Louise spoke up, "Aren't we lucky to get to have each other as sisters? I was so surprised when Daddy told me." A miserable smile on her face.

"Would you girls have another doughnut and pass them on?" Gram offered.

"No thank you," said Louise, "I must watch my figure."

I was already part way through my doughnut. This girl is too perfect. I know I don't like her already. If her slacks were any tighter, I would know if she shaved her legs! This western look in clothes has always looked great to me until now.

Barbara Twibell

Being my mother's only child leaves me with no experience of suddenly sharing her with someone else. Maybe Louise feels the same way about me. She's probably a nice person; I'm just not sure I want to know whether she is or not.

"We figure we aren't getting any younger, and it is time to start our new lives together," states Mom as she moves closer to Monty.

Monty smiles and adds, "We enjoy so many of the same things, and your mom sure loves the ranch and all of the animals. I honestly think we can make a family. You girls are young adults, but you still might need a home base to come running to if you feel you need it. I plan to offer that. My home is your home too."

"Yes, we love each of you girls, and I for one intend to build good strong love bonds between all of us, but if you have trouble with this, know that we love each other, and we, Monty and I, will have a home," Mom states strongly.

"What are you thinking? You are much too quiet!" asks Maurine of my Gramma. Gram has been listening with rapt attention while these two justify their love to the rest of us.

"Mack and I are very happy for you, Dear. There isn't anything we could add, but our best wishes. We are certainly happy you have found each other and are going ahead with your lives. I have felt Maurine is too young to spend her remaining life alone. Isn't that right, Mack?"

"Yup, pass the doughnuts back to me, will ya?"

"Thank you guys. I've never been this happy before, except when Jamie was born. I want to feel this happy a lot more of my life." With this said Maurine yawns.

"Say Mack, I'd like to lay a bed roll up in your barn with my daughter. Kind-of promised her an old fashioned dad and daughter outing. Maurine said you had plenty of hay, and she didn't think you would mind," questioned Monty as he throws a glance at Louise.

Louise grabs up her stuff and looks so thrilled to be with her dad. I could tell at this point their relationship is real. The kind every girl dreams of. Gramma had nothing to worry about concerning the spare bedroom, did she?

"Sounds like fun to me. Drive us up to the barn in your pickup and we all will get there faster. Besides, you can get back here in a hurry in the morning when the pancakes start to turn on the griddle." Mack gestures toward the back door. All three are ready to leave in a hail of chatter about barn mice, bats, or any other varmints in the barn.

"Tomorrow promises to be a big day." My mother laughs. "Best we all hit the bedrooms. Goodnight, Monty." She wraps her arms around his neck and gives him a chaste kiss on the cheek. "Goodnight, Louise, have fun tonight." She then comes over to me and throws her arms around me and hugs me, oh, so tight. She steps back, and then comes at me for a big kiss on the mouth.

"There my good girl, how very much I love you!"

"Good night, Mom and Mack, see you in the morning!" With a light step she heads up the stairway to her room.

Barbara Twibell

I'm still standing here wondering just what all has happened to me. Gram is starting to pick up the various dishes left around and heads back into the kitchen. I guess I'll help her pick up, and I will head for bed too.

23

Sure enough pancakes! Oh boy, they smell so good! I can't believe it! My mother is up too. The woman who never sees light until noon! She must have picked up some new life changing habits in Montana. They are chattering like a couple of magpies. Another female voice, no, it can't be. Louise! How long have I been in bed? I feel a pang of jealousy.

Dressing in one of my best casual outfits- dark brown slacks, a gold blouse, and my brown polished cowboy boots, I decide to leave my hair down today. A little more sophisticated look perhaps. A second glance in the mirror, and I feel ready to meet Miss Perfect and the new day.

"Well, good morning, Lazy Bones," says my mother as she comes over to hug me. She steps back with motherly pride, and a big smile on her face.

"Finally up?" remarks Louise. "I was wondering how long you sleep. Dad and I have been watching Mack feed the cows."

Of course you're up, I think to myself. No one could sleep when lights are tossed on in the barn and the cows are brought in for milking, buckets are banging, huge doors are moved open, and cows are arguing over whose place is whose.

"I had some reading to catch up on. I didn't feel I had to run right down here! Gram lets me know when breakfast is ready. She is determined I have a vacation this summer." Boy, I hate having to explain myself to a stranger.

Gram brushes by me. And says under her breath, "Good return, dear and good morning!"

I make my run to the privy and decide to go check on eggs for Gramma. I hate letting anyone know that is where I had to go, so I'll add to the trip and not give Louise anything to grab onto. The hens have not all laid yet, so my smart idea will have to be replayed later in the day. The hens tolerate the intrusion with a few squawks of displeasure. I have seven beautiful, smooth, warm brown eggs to take to the kitchen.

The morning grass has such deep dew that my boots are completely wet. A couple of brushes on the back of my slacks with the boot toes and all looks polished again.

"Thanks for remembering the eggs," says Gram with that knowing twinkle in her eyes.

It's funny how some days go along in neutral, and then a day comes along that someone throws it into passing gear, and you just try to keep up. Today is a passing gear day. I feel as if I'm on a roller coaster I can't get off. I certainly don't care to spend a day shopping. But today is Mom's day, and even Gram is getting "gussied up."

Gram is wearing a deep, dark blue dress with white trim. Lipstick, perfume, and costume jewelry top off her going- to- town clothes. She thinks we girls are way out of order wearing slacks. She sports her fashionably rolled nylons with her black one inch cube heels. A comb run through wet hair, and she is ready to go.

The marriage license was gotten with Gram and Mack as the witnesses. We all jumped in our cars

Daughter of the Gorge

and left Stevenson and headed back to Camas for our shopping. It was time to look for a new frock at Farrell and Eddy's on Main Street for my mother. I had to admit it was fun. Even Louise got into the opinions. Mom chose a soft pink and white seersucker dress with a white matching belt. She looked so marvelously young in it. Monty kept teasing Mom about what color dress he should be buying.

Louise and I each found new dresses. I bought a new purse, too. I haven't done much shopping while at Gram's since I'm not earning anything right now. Here I am thinking again that I need to get serious about finding work.

It has really been fun shopping at Farrell and Eddy's store. We must have worn the sidewalks down another inch buzzing back and forth through the stores.

"Let's all go to lunch. I'm buying," declares Monty, "and I'm really hungry. In fact so hungry my stomach thinks my throat's been cut."

Everyone's laughing and nearly all of us ordered hamburgers. The food and my lemonade are beyond description! The Ideal Corner, how great!! How can a hunk of beef, the works, and good goop make...

"Hey, hi there everyone!" A beautifully familiar voice booms out. "I thought that was your rig, Mack, and seeing the Montana plates, I figured that had to be Jamie's mom all the way from Montana." Lance looks incredible. He had dressed with care. No one would convince me differently. He wanted to find us, and he had.

Louise, sitting next to me utters, "Wow, what a hunk! He could put his boots next to mine anytime." A poke to my elbow was her exclamation mark.

Even hearing such a comment from her made my stomach curl in repulsion. This is a friend of mine, not a hunk of beef in a show case. Lance is good looking, but why should she take such notice?

Mack, standing up, (you knew he was about to introduce Lance,) was interrupted by none other than Monty.

"Lance Mason, I can't believe my eyes! Folks, this here man are one of the foremost rodeo riders around! Damn, boy, come sit down. You're lookin' so good!

"I remember you got busted up a little helping Joe Finch when that bull up and turned in his stall, just about the time of release. Ole' Lance here just jumped over between the pens, reached under Joe's arms and pulled him free. I was in the announcer's box, and everyone thought Joe would be a goner. Tore up your arms and back a little if I remember right."

Lance extends his hand... "Mr.?"

"Carpenter, Monty Carpenter, and this is my daughter Louise. She was much younger when we met before. The years pass too fast, don't they?" Excitement abounds in Monty's facial features.

"Well, I'll be; it's a small world isn't it? Hello, Louise, nice to be meeting you. Did you folks have a good trip over?" Lance clasps Louise's hand.

"Lance," Gram punctures the conversation, "this is my daughter Maurine. Jamie's mother.

We're in Camas today celebrating. Maurine came home engaged to this fine fella and will be marrying him on Tuesday."

"Glad for Ya, Ma'am. Jamie has been pretty anxious for your visit!"

"I told Jamie I'd be over today, but thanks to the note on the door, I decided to see if I could find the group here. Town's not that big that I can't locate a pickup."

I see my mother look over at Gram and ask her a question. Gram gives an affirmative nod and smiles at me.

"I've always wanted to ask questions about rodeo riders," says Louise. "Isn't that dangerous work?" She bats her eyelashes, and leans in toward Lance as if totally captivated by his conversation.

"Of course it's dangerous. What a stupid question Louise!" I pat the space next to me, to make room for Lance to sit.

"Hi Jamie, you look great to these eyes," Lance whispers.

"Lance," says Monty, "you have a river bottom ranch Mack tells me. Does that hold anything unusual from a regular ranch place?"

"Water is there, and plenty. You just don't need it to cover your place. Flooding has to be watched each spring. Mack brings his cattle down to enjoy the grass in the summer, and sometimes I need to bring mine up to his place when it floods. I don't believe there is anything much more beautiful than the river-bottom." Lance then gives the waitress his order.

Barbara Twibell

"He raises the most fantastic horses too, Monty. They are wanted by everyone who needs a great quarter horse," I chirp in, feeling a little left out of conversation.

"They're some of the best all right," Lance concurs.

"While we're here, could you show me your horses?" mews Louise? I just love pretty horses." Looking at no one else at the table, she takes a slow sip of her Coke.

"Of course, I'd be pleasured to. How about riding back with me today? It's a perfect day to ride the bottom land." Lance is looking closely at Louise, trying to size up her interest in horses.

Hello, am I even here? Louise is making about the fastest time in the West that I have ever seen. And ole' Dumb Dumb is falling all over himself for her attentions. How can he do this to me? Doesn't he know how this hurts to be ignored and outclassed? Why should I care? We're just friends aren't we? I don't care. Absolutely not. I don't need his conversation or rapt attention.

"I'll be in the truck, Gramma, when you are ready to go. I think I'm tired of shopping and everything else." I'm not going to sit here one more minute and listen to this goblety goop.

When I left, Lance didn't seem to notice. His head was bent forward closely listening to little Miss Muffet.

When we got home, I headed out to the field. I just wanted to reflect. I found a big rock and sat down to feel sorry for myself. My mother has gotten her life together, and here sit I. I just want to cry. I've had this problem before with so- called girlfriends. When I find someone who I think is great, the next thing I know my girlfriend is going steady with that guy. I'm not certain, but I think someone is sneaking up on me...

"Honey," says Mom, "I think you need to talk. You left that restaurant before you finished lunch and that's just not you. Come on, Honey. This is what we moms are for, you know. You are my special and only girl. You always will be my only girl. Louise is Monty's daughter and I care for her. But not as I care for my own flesh and blood." Mom sits down beside me and leans her head next to mine and puts her arm around me.

"When we got home just now, Mom said she thought you might feel over- whelmed with meeting the Carpenters and evidently the sharing of Lance.

"Speaking of Lance, he's quite the man. I think... You think more of him than you've realized on your own. Woman to woman, Dear, don't let some other woman tread on your man. I honestly think he's too smart for Louise and is just being nice to her. Or he may see if he can make you jealous. He's man enough to use Miss Louise to his advantage, too. He may feel this is one way to shake you up a little."

"What are you saying, Mom?" I sniff.

"If you don't want some other woman getting your man, let him know what he means to you. Smile, be kind, and don't start barking. Let it seem you know Louise could mean nothing. Be yourself and don't pout. You are the only one who knows if he means more than a friend to you. If you find he does, there are ways you can signal this to him. You'll know!"

At this moment, my mother is closer to me than she has ever been. Never has she taken the time to show she cares for me as she is at this moment. I'm a grown girl, but her arm around me feels so fabulous. Could being in love have made my mother this much more loving? She has always been available to talk to, but not this revealing. She rarely had anything good to say about the male species, I'm probably lucky she even told me such a thing as a man existed!

"Thanks for coming out, Mom. I did need someone. I miss you sometimes something awful. I try to be grown up. Then sometimes I don't want that responsibility either. I have to be honest with you, Mom. This is all happening so fast that I feel I'll not be able to keep up with you. You will be so far away." I catch the choke in my voice.

"There's no reason you can't come visit, or maybe even find work near us. Have you thought of that? They do have beauty salons in Montana!"

"How you figure men, Mom?" I ask, changing the conversation.

"The same way they try to figure us women. They don't. If you enjoy someone and feel safe with him and trust him and feel better with him than without, I would say that is a good relationship!" That's how I feel about Monty. I know I love him." Patting me on the back, Mom stands up, stretches and leaves to return to the house.

"Stay out and enjoy the day, Honey," she says as her voice fades away.

Daughter of the Gorge

The cow bells ringing in the background and the small yellow bees humming as they dance around the flower tops, the brush of a breeze in the nearby apple trees create a symphony to my ears. The sounds heard in a farm field combined with a warm sun can be more healing than any other place a person can dream of.

Once in awhile if I listen very closely, I can hear a distant tugboat horn. Barges carrying things up river and then back, day after day. At night, car lights look like fireflies dipping in and around corners on the scenic highway on the Oregon side. Cars also of course come around the cape. It's just a longer string of lights on the distant hills that catch my attention. I like to pick a car and try to follow it up the gorge toward Bonneville.

The air is changing, and it is not as warm as when I first came out. A lot was accomplished today. Mom and Monty got their marriage license, and now having to wait the three days. Mom checked with her old friend Don Brown in Bonneville, and he said he would be thrilled to perform their marriage on Tuesday afternoon. He has the most beautiful front yard. If there is no rain, it would be a great place for a wedding. Small as it will be!

Mr. and Mrs. Monty Carpenter! Maurine Carpenter! I like it. I think I can get ready for a wedding!

I'm not going to worry about Lance. Louise lives in Montana...I live one heck of a lot closer!

"Wasn't today fun?" my mother questioned all of us after were all came home for the night. She and Monty just beam. They look so comfortable together.

"Sure was strange you knew our Lance. I just can't believe he's that well known. He leads a pretty quiet profile around here," Mack contemplates. He pushes his big calloused hands up under his red suspenders.

"Put that boy in the rodeo, Mack, and you have someone to root for. He's not easily thrown off. Doesn't liquor up and girl-chase like some. Has his fun, but heads home right after, I have been told." Monty seems to be talking with real pride and knowledge on the subject.

"His pa isn't too good, and he has to run the ranch pretty much most of the time Monty. The horses he's invested in need close care too. I board his favorites here. Tomorrow you should take a look. He'll probably show you himself since it's the weekend." Placing another log on the fire, Mack leans back in his favorite chair.

"So, what you got up there in Montana?" questions Mack.

"I got cattle too, six hundred head of black Angus. Give or take fifty or so to rustlers and varmints. Human and animal. Our winters can get bad, so we try to lie in as much hay as we can. Got a couple of ground silos and a beer company sell their leftover mash to me. The cattle really love that! That is stored in a pit silo.

"My first wife and I built our log home. She always wanted one; nothing else would do. Well, for the hot and cold weather we get, that house does fine. It has four bedrooms. It was too bad Katy didn't get much time in our home. Damn cancer. Terrible loss to us. She was such a happy woman. Since she died, I gave up ever being happy again. Then along came Maurine!

"We've been alone long enough! Maurine here brings the happy smells back in the house and the laughter. Pat, you sure taught her to cook! Yes sir, we're pretty glad to be bringing her into our family." Monty gives my mother a little friendly poke.

"Knock, knock, anyone home? We're done with the showing off horses now. Any coffee around?" Lance calls as he opens the door. He moves so Louise can crowd past him in her excitement.

"Ya, Dad, you should have come. What fun, such a great place! Horses all over. Cattle too, but not as many as we have," Louise proclaims as she sweeps into the living room. She strikes a stance that demands attention with her eyes glued to Lance.

Lance carries on, coming into the house reaching for his coffee that Gram had gotten for him.

"Move over, Jamie, do you want me to sit on the floor?" His grin, as our family might say, is as wide as a wave on a slop bucket. He looks at me with so much energy. He was just out with another woman and…Gram is throwing me that shut up look, and so is my mother.

"I'm glad you came back over tonight, Lance It was so fun having you locates us in Camas today. Such a surprise!" I soften my voice more than I want and gaze into his glorious eyes.

"I wanted to surprise you! Wanted to ask you to go to Portland with me tomorrow. Can you do that? Maybe you want to be with your mom, and I shouldn't ask, but …"

"She'd love to go," says my mother. "I can have a small list of things for her to get me if that is okay with you."

"She needs to get out more," pipes up my grandmother.

"I'd like to go. Can I? I've never been to Portland," Louise interrupts.

"I need you here with me, Daughter. There are some preparations I need your help with. Some announcements need to be written to our friends, and you write a whole lot better than your poor old Dad!" Monty gives a quick wink to Maurine.

"In answer to your invitation, Lance, when shall I be ready? What is the dress code for the day?" Feeling happy inside, I walk Lance out to his car.

For the first time I readily walk into Lance's embrace. I feel so secure in his arms and so warm. His arms tighten about me. I can hear his heart beat right next to my ear…

"I'll see you about nine in the morning. Be sure and bring a light jacket. The mornings take awhile to heat up. In fact, have you noticed the hills keep the sun out? That is why the dew is so heavy some mornings." Lance has not let go of me.

"Yes, I noted that long ago when I picked strawberries across from Cape Horn School. My hands were so cold I wanted to cry. But, being I was the city slicker here, I thought I'd better be brave and not be a softy!" I shiver just remembering. Or is it from being held so closely?

"Are you cold now?" His voice is so soft, and his mouth is tickling my ear. He nuzzles a slow kiss on my cheek waiting for my answer.

"No, not at all. I just shivered when you did that."

"When I did what, Jamie?" Lance pulls me ever so close to his frame.

"When you do, you know whatever you're doing. I like it, but it makes me feel funny. Like I'm warm, but chilling too, and there are Goosebumps on my arms." I'm rewarded for looking up into his eyes, because he stops any further comments from my mouth, by taking charge with his.

"Time for you to go in! I don't want you to catch a chill now, do I?" Lance steps away from me and I nearly fold up! My knees feel like rubber.

"I'll be looking forward to tomorrow." The red truck rocks and rolls up over the hill to the gate and disappears out of sight. I can still hear the muffler system way into the distance.

As I turn to go back to the house, I look up into the sky. I don't ever remember the stars being so clear and beautiful. My body will not release the new feelings Lance stirred in me. I feel as floaty-so light as a feather. I have not felt the sensations I feel ever before in my life.

When I opened the door, it was to look at eight sets of eyes staring at me. Only Louise was looking at a magazine with faked concentration, since she was holding it upside down!

Barbara Twibell

Wanting to keep tonight to myself, I said, "Goodnight everyone. I don't know about you, but this has been a very busy day, and I'm tired.

24

"I had some interesting news from my father last night," Lance opens our conversation on the way to Portland. It nearly blew my mind. Sometimes I wish Dad wouldn't bring such earth-shattering news in the middle of the night. I find I can't sleep after digesting it."

Not wanting to butt in, but wanting to be of help if I could, I ask, "What news?"

"You know how Aunt Cleva and Dad go around in their teasing each other about Aunt Cleva coming to live with us? They were at it the night you came for dinner, remember?"

"She's changed her mind! She's coming?" I ask. "Great! Isn't that what you wanted?"

"Guess again. Dad's decided he will go live with her! They are like a couple of kids running away with the plans they have been making. Dad says it will be better for her, and she can keep her eye on him more regularly." Lance changes lanes.

"Jamie, he's going to move off the ranch and turn it completely over to me. He says my cooking isn't that good! This rather frightens me in a way. Dad and I have always been a team. I know I shouldn't dump on you. When I saw you last night, I didn't know all this." Lance definitely has a very concerned look on his face.

"I'm sure you are capable of taking charge. Mack said you have been running things there anyway. Your aunt can't keep living alone, so it probably is good for both of them." At this point I don't want to say anything wrong.

Barbara Twibell

"You're right, I guess, but I just hate changes! Look at the ones you've faced in one year. Can't things go along the way they are? Enough of this. Are the wedding plans still on? I shouldn't be bawling about my problems, when you have enough on your mind."

"They are, and thanks to you, I feel better about what Mom plans. I can see how lonely she has been, and how thrilled she is now. She certainly will have many things to keep her busy. Ranch life is really what we both feel most comfortable with. As long as she has a calf to hug, and some rolls to bake, she will be happy." I glance out the window from inside the Interstate Bridge, looking down on the wide Columbia. The whitecaps are fighting with the front of a large barge headed up river. Two fishing boats, no, one is a tug boat; almost look like they're racing each other on the way to Portland or Astoria, Oregon.

There's an island called Government Island, off to the left. A big sign says, No access... What is a government owned island? And why no access...why do they have to say anything if they don't want you there, what's there? My mind always rolls over foolish questions!

"This is great. Glad you were able to come with me!" yells Lance over the noisy grate on the bridge decking.

"Me too!" I yell back.

"Too bad I don't have air conditioning, but in a truck who needs it? Just an added expense as I see it! See that big wooden roller coaster? Some time we'll come do that!"

Daughter of the Gorge

"I don't think so...they scare the dickens out of me. I do love Jantzen Beach though, so someday I'll take you up on that offer." Shaking my head I ask, "Did you ever go through that rotating barrel? I always fall and roll all over until I manage to crawl out the other end. The Fun House is a scream, especially the Room of Mirrors. I always take my time going through. Then I feel I get my money's worth."

"YOU'RE CHICKEN ABOUT THE COASTER?" laughs Lance.

"Yes, I am, and unless you'd want me to throw up on you, you'd never try to get me on that thing! Ferris wheels are about my standard. Ever eat over there at Waddles Great food. It's so big inside."

I love being able to chatter on with this man, I think to myself.

"My dad and I have a few times, when we took some beef over to the stock yards," admits Lance.

There isn't much that is attractive along this route. The Vanport Flood a few years ago pretty well swept this clean. I'm thinking it will never develop with people knowing how high that river can get. The stock yards stayed pretty good. But, anything left has that high water mark on it, and it smells funny all around.

"Lance, are we going to St. Johns?" This is an area where my fathers mother had a small restaurant called the "Chili Bowl" back in the late forties. I remember walking all the way across the bridge there. That's all they served- chili with the little round crackers." I am feeling anxious and expectant.

"Actually yes, then I'm going across that bridge, and on to Montgomery Wards. I need to get Dad some things and some stuff for the house. I need to do some minor repairs. If you like, because I do, we'll eat inside. Have you ever eaten at one of these new cafeterias?"

"I've been there, and I'd love to go again! I think I can get my fill of food and shopping! All in one place...what a concept!"

"Wake up Little Goose! Did I tire you out that much? Not that I mind your head on my shoulder. That I like a whole bunch, but I thought you might help me stay awake on the way home," asked a concerned Lance.

"Ummm, where are we?" I ask dreamily.

"Just about Mt. Pleasant cutoff. So if you wake up now, you can keep me awake until we get to your grammas. The wind has come up, and I don't need to be sleeping at the wheel. This road can get a little dangerous. At least it's not winter time. I always hate the threat of black ice and a thousand foot plunge to the river!"

"That's why my folks take the Washougal River road. You need to be alert on it too, but they always said the river was closer!" I laugh at the thought I'm about to share with Lance about the time Gramma had a big rock come through the passenger side front window of their truck when they were on their way into Vancouver. They went to Vancouver all right. To the hospital! Gram had stitches on her face, where later large bruises came after the grapefruit sized rock passed through the front windshield. Glass left her with quite a few cuts on her face. What angered her most were not the injuries to her person, but the fact that it scared her so that she needed a change of clothing!

We both heartily laughed over this tale and had no problem staying awake to the farm.

"I had a great time, Jamie. Let's do this again after the wedding. I know you'll be busy for awhile, so I'll give you a whistle sometime next week. Would that be all right with you?" queried Lance.

"I had fun too. Don't take too long to whistle." I kissed Lance and left for the house.

When I got in the house, it was very quiet. Everyone had gone to bed. It seems like a good time to have some cold milk, and cut a piece off Gram's great bread. If I look in the cupboard, I'll be able to find some homemade jam, too. With any of these foods, I have the most delicious picture of my grandmother busy preparing these goodies. Raspberry jam is topping this big slice of yeast smelling, moist textured slice of bread! Cutting the piece twice the size it should be might have something to do with how wonderful it tastes. Even my cold milk, Gram skimmed and poured into the pitcher. Everywhere I see her handiwork in making a home. My mother also has these talents of making things "from scratch" that I don't fool with. It seems that in school they are teaching us invaluable skills for jobs, but not pressing the skills of homemaking as much as a mother would. I find my life colliding at times. I know I looked for a career instead of a husband.

Barbara Twibell

Why am I working instead of homemaking? For one, I wanted to get away from living at home, and I needed a job to afford that move. So in pioneer days did the daughter live at home until she found a husband? Where did she find a husband? I haven't located a husband patch yet! Unless he sells Watkins products, he is not knocking down my door!

A soft red glow emits from the heater here in the living room. Mack has stoked the fire and shut down the dampers so the fire will put out some heat until morning. Heat rises so bedrooms upstairs do stay warm most of the night, but not all night. Something has to happen to make bedrooms so devastatingly cold by the time you get up that you get that country frozen feeling. It is not difficult for me to think about the Christmas story about the house being so quiet, not even a mouse.

Living in Montana? My mother asked if I had given any thought to that as a job market. Until now with Mom's marriage, why would I have? Just giving it a passing fancy now, I don't think so. I really don't want to be that far away from Gramma. Living here with her this summer has made me think how much she means to me. I love my mother; I don't fool myself. I am a daughter of the Gorge! I know that now. This is where I feel complete, where I was born, and where I want to live.

Therefore, Miss Jamie, you'd best think about finding work. You can't go on forever being a guest at Gramma's. I know my mother will be living her life, and I will go visit her. I feel good now about her marriage. I am anxious for it to come off, and be done. I like Monty. I even like Louise (From a distance.) In our conversations day before yesterday, she even asked me to come up to her college and visit! She said by then she would have some boys noted. I think she and I could become friends. These things I don't push.

The body has wound down now and sleep would come if I let it. I think I'll stay here on the couch and wrap in an Afghan rather than wake everyone going up the stairs. Gramma will fuss at me tomorrow, and I will love it!

25

Land sakes, Child, what are you doing here?" yelped Gramma. "A lot of places I could envision you, since you weren't in your bed. Some were rather exciting, but not huddled in a cold room by a cold stove. Are you all right dear?"

I was expecting to be shocked out of sleep, so she didn't do too much damage as her voice penetrated my sleep world.

"Good morning, Gram! I wanted to enjoy the fire and have some time to myself, so I decided not to wake you by stumbling upstairs. You mean you didn't hear me come in last night? You didn't hear the screen door?" Now I was enjoying a good tease with her.

"I thought perhaps Lance had swept you away last night. Never know." Gram could tease one step ahead of anyone.

"We had a lot of fun, and I got the things Mom wanted. It was so much fun to see parts of Portland that I have not seen for years. There is so much building going on. Anyway, on to the next day. Right Gram?"

"Better get upstairs and change. You might beat a couple of people from the barn. I need some more cackle berries from those ole biddies in the chicken house, too, if you don't mind doing that for me. I had Mack pick up some of that good sausage from the Steel Bridge Store, and we'll have that for breakfast this morning."

Daughter of the Gorge

Gram's mind is already in full gear for plans and meals for this day! THE day of my mom's wedding.

"I'm off like a bunny. I'm going to wake Mom up." I called to Gram as I hit the first step.

"Hey Mom, wake up!" as I hit her bed full force in the middle. She always sleeps as if she is about to fall off the side. "Mrs. Carpenter, wake up! Life's changing." By now I've managed to snuggle down beside her. There is a smile on her face in spite of the fact she is pretending to be asleep.

"Is there no rest for the weary?" she asks.

"Nope, not today, Mom, not today! Aren't you excited?"

"Yes, Dear, I'm just thinking how my life will be different. I hope I've not hurt you by doing this." She stretches.

"Absolutely not! Let's go for it! You'll be out of my hair, with someone else taking care of you in your old age." Moving a wild strand of hair from her face, I know she will be better with this marriage.

"It's time for you, Mom. It's about time you have a life for you. Thank you for the years of devotion and commitment you gave to me. I know you and Daddy had a difficult marriage, and I know you stayed in it for me. Well, I'm grown now. You've done well, Mom. Carry on!"

"When did you become so wise, and how do you know all of this? I tried so hard to protect you." The concern grows on her face.

"Mom, kids have ears. See?" I show her my ears. "I knew from years of catching you crying, or hearing Daddy tear you down. I had to hide from you what was pretty plain for a child to notice too.

The rest I asked Gramma about and begged her to tell me the truth. Don't be angry at her. It was time for me to get some answers about how I felt about things. It's all okay, Mom. It's all in the past...we both have our tomorrows!"

She reaches out from the covers and gives me a big squeeze.

"I love you, my dear Jamie; don't ever forget that! Now off with you. It's my wedding day, and the groom should be coming in from the barn!" With that and gales of laughter, our day begins.

Gram wanted to leave the dishes in the sink and just hurry the party at getting dressed. None of us listened to her, and the dishes were done and put away. I don't believe Louise has ever washed dishes in such a primitive way. We managed to throw water at each other, and get it cleaned up before we were caught.

There is always a disadvantage to being a hairdresser around any gathering where hair does not co-operate with its owner. Mack needed a trim, Mom needed a complete do, Louise had hay in her hair, and something needed to be done with me. The morning zipped by quickly, and somehow we were a handsome group as we poured into the cars.

The day was warm and sunny. The trip to Bonneville flew by our windows. Everything was ready at Mr. Brown's home. A local pastor stood in for the service. Mr. Brown was so good to my mother while Daddy was overseas. Many an evening he would show my mother and me his

Daughter of the Gorge

fabulous collection of Rosary beads, collected from all over the world. It seemed so right to use his yard and have his company. He is truly happy for my mother.

The wedding went off without a hitch. (No pun meant, of course. There was a hitching!) We all were on time including the preacher. Mom looked beautiful, and Monty was joyous. Gram was gussied, and Mack was nearly unrecognizable in his suit. His beautiful gleaming Italian black hair was slicked down with some kind of sauce that would not let a hair move. Mack has the naughtiest smile or grin I've ever seen. It truly makes you wonder what he is up to or what he has done.

Monty had a big surprise that bowled us over. He announced that the new Mr. and Mrs. Carpenter were treating everyone to dinner at the Multnomah Falls Lodge restaurant. We would caravan over to the Oregon side. Such a surprise! The only thing missing was I kept looking for my friend Lance. I knew he was not going to be there for the wedding, though maybe he might have shown up.

We crossed over the wonderful Bridge of The Gods and continued along the spectacular two lane scenic highway that leads to the fall, and on to Portland. Along the side of the highway is a stone barrier covered with moss and the delicate licorice ferns. Trees clamber to the side of the highway, edging each other aside for more sunshine. Long tree limbs weighted from years of snow reach out to touch one another. Glimpses of poison oak greet the trained botanist. I so enjoy the dark beauty of these densely growing evergreens. There is no place to pass, so even the most impatient of drivers must relax a little and enjoy the glorious scenic pleasure.

The gift shop is on the ground floor, and of course we girls want to hit it. But we've just been herded into the fabulous glass- enclosed dining room with the full view of the falls. A bamboo screen is across one corner of the room. I don't remember that ever being there, but...

"Surprise!" Down comes the bamboo and here are people standing with outstretched arms and happy expressions on their faces. Faces I am now beginning to see that I know. Mom is shocked, to say the least! Her new mother-in-law, Monty's family, cousins, etc. are all lined up with huge smiles. I'm certain some are my mother's friends, friends she has not been in contact with since the funeral for my father. Lance and his father and Aunt Cleva.

Lance is here, and my heart makes its familiar jump!! What a fabulous surprise!

"How in the world did Monty manage this?" As I inquire, I hear my mother ask him at the same time. He laughs his easy laugh and says good friends are invaluable, and so are swiped address books! This is so good for Mom. People needed to know about her changed life, and I'm not sure she could have described her new found happiness. "Lance, you devil. You said nothing last night!" I blurt.

"Sworn to secrecy, all of us were! It has been fun. My aunt was so thrilled to be included. Even though we had only a couple days notice. Did you know he rented out this whole place?" There's going to be a dinner and everything! I think Monty's very happy." Lance's excitement is contagious.

"Did you see the huge wedding cake in the corner?" My mother never had a wedding cake. I never ever dreamed he would do so much for my mother. She looks absolutely radiant. She is wandering around, introducing Louise, and Monty and her new in-laws and "outlaws" to her friends. I'm not jealous! She has great people to share, and they are my family now, too!

After endless introductions and renewed friendships and explanations of her new home, my mother was guided skillfully to the place of honor at the head table. Monty asked all to find seats and prepare for dinner. The staff started pouring water, to be followed by waiters bringing on the Champagne. Each waiter looked so crisp and professional. Bowing to each guest, smiling to all they served. I doubt that many here had ever witnessed first hand this kind of service. Each glass was filled to a precise level. Then waitresses came back into the room with salads.

Monty stood, clinked his knife against his glass two times, then lifted it into the air. "To our future, to my wife." He smiled warmly as he touched her glass.

"To the best of times for the happy newlyweds!" Mack rejoiced. The toasts went on and on. The glasses returned to the proper level by watchful waiters. Most of the ladies sipped their way through the toasts. No sipping for the men!!

Eventually all quieted, and everyone was soon busy with their salads. Plates were collected, and we all waited in anticipation for the main course.

"Look at that prime rib! Man that took a whole herd." Mack sighed.

The men were particularly pleased at such a sight. The ladies were concerned how they were not going to be wasting such a fine meal. A twice baked garlic potato and asparagus garnished each plate. Everyone was speechless.

The word got around pretty quickly that Monty had provided the meat for the dinner. This was Montana Black Angus Beef. Right off his ranch and the restaurant really enjoyed the privilege of preparing it for him.

This new Dad of mine does it all right!!

Monty again stood, and again clinked his glass. "Attention please, Maurine and I will be leaving tomorrow for a trip to England! Don't look for us for a month at least. We will leave from Seattle, and fly to New York, spend some time there, and fly on to London. See if there are any bridges to look at! I mean castles!"

Everyone laughed hard and loud. My mother's face was scarlet. I was so proud of her at this moment, as I know most people were. She thought she was going to wait awhile for her honeymoon. It didn't sound that way to me. What a guy!

Lance was enjoying himself thoroughly. He and his dad knew how to have a good time. Lance came up to me and asked if I was having a good time, and was everything going as I hoped? His eyes just glowed with excitement. "How long has it been since you attended your mother's wedding?" he teased. Adding, "Maybe all kids should wait; it's got to be more fun!!

His Aunt Cleva found me and congratulated me on my mother's fine choice of a man. She thinks Monty is a knockout and so kind. She also asked when I was coming again for dinner. How much they had enjoyed me the last time. Her smile is so warm, I find I believe her!

Monty asked for attention again and we all looked his direction.

"Since God was so good to give me another fine wife and since Maurine has nothing to match her new wedding band, (reaching into his pocket) I think she needs this to wear with it!" Out came a gold and diamond necklace, and a gold bracelet, with matching earrings. Mom flew into his arms and kissed him.

"And since he gave me two beautiful daughters, I have these for them." We each were given matching bracelets of gold! "Now then, since I don't have any money left, no one can expect it when I die!"

Again happiness abounded. It was a wonderful wedding, so much more than any of us would have ever dreamed.

Louise was to be taken into Portland to catch the bus for home and I was with Mack and Gram. I was pleased when Gram said it was time to go. I was exhausted. Lance stepped forward and said, "I'd like to take Jamie home, may I?

Mack was quick to say, "Of course. Better partake of that wedding cake first though!"

The cake was a four tier white, with gorgeous white flowers circling around the sides. Mom and Monty cut the cake together, and all people were fed more than they knew they could eat at one setting! My mother's wedding will certainly be a great memory for me! I said my goodbyes, hugged both Mom and Monty lavishly and made my getaway. It seemed so warm in that restaurant. I just wanted some fresh air.

The ride home with Lance was quiet. Both of us were thinking about the past day.

"I didn't need anything but the prime rib and Champagne as far as I feel." Said a stuffed Lance. "I haven't seen as big a piece of meat like that ever! Some party!"

"Yes, I agree with you! Some party, I'm wiped out! I don't ever remember being so tired, or have my feet hurt so badly. Thank you for bringing me home. I really appreciate the quiet ride! The noise level was beating a drum in my head!"

"Perhaps the Champagne helped the drum beat a little. Get lots of rest tomorrow; you'll be a lot better soon!

"Jamie, I'll be taking my horses down to California and showing them around. I'll be gone for a couple of weeks, maybe more if my sales go good. I really enjoyed the wedding, and I'm glad I was included. I need to get as many horses sold before winter sets in as I can. My favorites I keep.

"Speaking of a favorite," Lance pulls me very close, at the same time tipping my head back, and running his lips across my cheek, nuzzling down to my neck. "Did I tell you how great you looked today? How great you look right now?" My mind had trouble keeping the location of his hands. They were moving about my back and shoulders so smoothly. This is a most delightful way of loosing concentration that I've ever enjoyed. I 'm enjoying the warm feelings flood my entire being. Something happens to me when Lance gets this close. With others I felt a fear, never this feeling of warmth and comfort as now.

Lance turns more of me to him, as he slides my jacket off. His lips have found mine again and there is an urgent message in them that I am unable to decode. "You are so incredible, so different, so full and warm." My own hands betray me as my arms are over his shoulders and my hands are caressing his hair as I remember how a kitty will knead with its paws. His face has slight stubble and his eyelashes are so soft.

His lips are on my face, my neck, and my shoulders. My ears even get a nick of affection. His lips are so soft, yet strong enough to hold what they want. I would maybe expect a bruising, but feel none. Feel? Did I say feel? I don't feel anything but an ache all over. I note how strong his back feels, how broad his shoulders, how deep I feel myself falling. No one has ever touched me this way...

"TOUCH, my gosh, what are you doing, Lance?" I bang my shin on his dashboard. Gathering my blouse back to button form, I hiss out at him. "I'm not that kind of girl, why I never!"

"Thought it was time you did," grinned Lance. "You're really quite delightful!"

"Oh. Man, this is wrong." I begin to tremble. Most of the feelings I shared with Lance I still felt.

"It was not wrong, and we were just getting started." Lance was helping me gather something. "How did you have a boyfriend if this is such a surprise?"

"He never, I mean we didn't, I wouldn't anyway."

"Jamie, I told you I would never hurt you."

"It didn't hurt!" It felt good, too good. "I want to wait until I get married before I do that stuff." I am so embarrassed. I feel so guilty.

"Honey. You hardly did anything. I will admit you made me want to forget where I am. You are most innocent and desirable."

"I am not innocent." I know from listening to girlfriends what leads to unwanted pregnancies."

"My God, Girl, one must do more than hold hands for that to be possible. Now quit shaking, you're fine, and you're beautiful." Lance gives me a quick peck on my nose. "Just lean against my shoulder, Jamie, and we'll talk a bit.

"Jamie, what do you dream of for the future? Where after Gram's? Go live with your mom? Stay here? What do you dream?"

Calming down, I feel myself melt into my dreams. "I wanted to become a hairstylist, I'd become a hairdresser, to work my way through college. I need a good career to support a house and maybe an acre or two. Gram always said she could find an acre for me!

"I have always loved log houses. They seem so strong and warm. When I was sixteen, and doing the dinner dishes, I actually prayed to God that I wanted a strong, but gentle husband. Tall and dark! Would he mind if I asked for two boys, two years apart? No girls, I'm too much a Tom Boy! Wasn't that a hoot? But, until then I have to find a way to earn my dreams, and staying at Gram's for a long time will not accomplish that. How about you?"

"Well guy's dreams keep changing. We aren't allowed to dream like girls do. I have to be getting now."

"That makes good sense to me. Have a good safe journey, and thank you again for the ride home." Jamie makes to leave, but Lance brings her to him.

"I'll surely miss you while I'm gone. Take good care of yourself okay?"

His hug and kiss felt so good to my tired ol' body, I nearly fell asleep. Lance's laughter brought me about! "Okay Sleepy, you win!" Go on inside and curl up in those blankets!! See you when I get back."

26

"Can you do a really tight curl?" This over made-up owner, with the blue hair asked. "I don't go with this fancy stuff that doesn't last a day." Her blouse is about two sizes too small and the buttons are gaping.

"You girls don't larn anything in school. If I take you on, you'll do it my way or out you go." Her customer nods in agreement. "I need someone badly, but you young girls today, just work a few days and quit. Your schooling today is not worth a nickel! Also I get the pick of the appointments. I do almost all the perms. Got that?"

I'm thinking, no one would be able to build a clientele or make a living here.

"Wanna start in the morning?" She's chewing gum and somehow makes a loud cracking sound. The noise would drive me crazy if I were working with her.

"Well?" she asks.

"No, thank you. I've worked for three years, and I am well trained. I'm a graduate of Clairol Coloring School, and I am used to working under strict dress codes and liberal sharing of new customers. I don't need your job offer that badly." With that I left.

Owners like that are the reasons so many women choose to work with large chain salons instead of small private home salons. I knew I would not like to work in a small salon, but maybe, just maybe it would be different. Trying to get a job closer to Gramma was not going to be easy.

Daughter of the Gorge

So much for the first ad in the paper. Keep trying, I tell myself. I decide to go into Vancouver.

"We have need for a color technician. You could have that station with the sink right in it if you wish. You also can be in charge of ordering any supplies you wish to use. If you can do that, it will take a burden of my back."

The salon was clean, the girls neat, and there was a lounge to have lunch in. Actually I believe this is a new shop!

"Could I work from nine until six, say four days a week? I work fast so I could be booked a little tighter than some want to be booked. I live about two hours away, until I can save enough wages for a place." I'm speaking to a richly red- haired lady who is the boss. Her hair is impeccably styled.

"Only if I could have you five days a week during holiday weeks, and throw in the Saturdays of those weeks." She's frowning a little. I don't think she is used to negotiations. "I then think we could have a deal, young lady. I like your confidence!" Sixty percent and you help me run this place!" She smiles one of the warmest smiles I've ever seen. I believe this could be my kind of work-place!

"I can't start for another week. Will that be all right with you?" This is so tough; I don't think I'm really ready to go to work. It's been too much fun lazing with Gram.

"Sure. My name is Gladys. How about coming in a day early so we can get things together and you can become acquainted with the salon? There's a beauty supply store about three blocks away. If

Barbara Twibell

you need something within reason, charge it to the shop. Welcome aboard!"

On the way home I think about what I just did. Man, I can't undo this now! I did stop at the beauty supply store and bought some new rollers, a couple of stainless steel combs out finishing combs, a new cape and a separate coloring cape. I want my things to be new and fresh.

Gram will be happy for me, but she will worry about the drive into Vancouver. I figure working fewer days will still give me time to spend with Gram. I paid for my own items. I feel they are my responsibility, plus I don't have to share with people who refuse to care for other people's supplies.

"I did it Gram! I got a good job. Well, the potential is there. I have to keep the customers once I've done them the first time! I asked for only four days a week, and this gives me time to find a nice apartment in Vancouver. No more leaching off of you!"

"I supposed this day was coming, Dear. Too bad society frowns on young girls staying home until they marry and enjoying one another forever! You're so helpful to me; I never would consider it leaching. On the other hand, we can't run around in our undies when you're here!" Gram's got this big smile on her face. "It's time for you to get on with your life, Jamie."

Mack peaks around the corner and asks, "Where is this job, and with who ya got it with?" He tickles me the way he can't hear unless it's something he is not supposed to hear.

"The job is at Stamford's Styling Salon on Third in Vancouver. Pretty new place with lots of parking. It was opened by a lady who managed another salon. She felt it was time to put something really nice in town. They have shampoo sinks right at the stations! You just seat your customer, drape her, turn her around, and shampoo. I love the concept because all towels and products are mine and should stay nice. Plus the customer does not get paraded all over in front of everyone until she is all done."

"You sound really enthused. I'm happy you found something you like. When do you start?" Gram has found some dishes to dry and is putting them away as she talks to me. When she is nervous, she will always fuss at little things.

"Next Tuesday. Gladys wants to help me get set up. It's essential everything is in its place when you get that customer in your chair. Know what I mean?"

"Yes," says Gram. "My hairdresser is so organized she drives herself and those around her nutty! I go in every three months for a perm, no set, just comb through it and show me the door!"

"I bought some things today. Two more uniforms, a new pair of white shoes and I will feel like a stylist again! Yep, new job, new gear!"

"Does Lance know you've gotten a job?" Mack's eyebrows nearly are crossing each other in concern.

"No. Why should this be of concern to him?"

"Well now, who's gonna care for his favorite horses? You know you said you would." Mack is stumbling here for something, I don't think he knows what.

"Gracious," says Gram, "even he must know jobs come first! She owes him nothing other than notice."

"When I got this job, Mack, it was more with the thought of you guys and you're getting your home back to yourselves. Lance was not a thought. Besides, he'll want what is best for me, I think!"

"Did we hear from Mom yet, Gram?"

"Not yet, I imagine she is having too much fun to worry about dropping a letter to anyone." Gram moves on to another task.

27

"I'm so happy I could pop! Imagine my surprise after stopping by the salon one of the girls who works there told me about a friend of hers who owns a funeral home and is looking for someone to live in the funeral home and answer the telephone at night. Gram, I got it!! I went right over there and talked with the owner. He's really so nice, and he said he would certainly like to have me live there. He then took me upstairs to see the apartment. Man, it's so big! Great big kitchen, lots of cupboards, two bedrooms, a bath, and a big living room with bay windows. So they look out on a parking lot! I have my own entry way, and a spot to park out back. I asked what the rent is, and he said NOTHING! Just be willing to answer the phone at night. Dispatch personnel when needed. And stay sober! Also Gram, on the back porch is a washer and dryer and vacuum cleaner for my use!! NO MORE LAUNDROMATS!!

"There will be a little training so I answer the phone right. I do have to pay for the television power and my own phone line. Isn't this great? I can save much more money this way. I don't know how many friends will come visit me. He said not to be disappointed if my new friends don't come knocking down my door to visit, but I can always go visit them. He did say the apartment had to be quiet during the day because of services. If I have plans for an evening, I just need to let him know, and he said he'd cover the phone some other way for that night. All the doors have locks, so I have plenty of privacy. I can move in any time in the next month. It's furnished, too, though I can replace anything I wish. His wife will help me if I'd like her to. I think this will be a very good setting for a single girl." I have a renewed feeling!!

"Goodness, dear, when fortune falls on you, it falls fast and hard! Let's start getting you ready for this adventure!"

"I'm so going to miss the quiet here, Gram, and our times together. Can I keep coming back?" I feel empty as I ask Gram this question.

It is so scary to be in an apartment, as a lone single woman; anyway, that I feel really good about the protection afforded me in this setting. It's not like people will flock to my home to visit, and I will not be bothered by those who come knocking on my door uninvited. NO MORE LAUNDROMATS!! I can't get over the appreciation of that washer and dryer! I've always abhorred going to a Laundromat. I think it is one of the most dangerous places for a single girl to have to hang out. Not all the customers look like they are safe people to be around. Anyway, this fear of being followed or something is always there. I always said if I were to marry, that person had to provide me with washer and dryer soon after the "I Do's."

On this day of great merriment the rain is just pouring. Gram is helping me decide what I must take, and what she can lend to help set up housekeeping.

Heat from the two stoves has made such a cozy setting that it is hard to concentrate on my project and not fall asleep. The windows have gathered their steam, and there is nothing to see out of them.

A trip to the outhouse in the rain is now hazard duty since the path gets so wet that not being careful or on the full run can cause your feet to go out from under you and you slide into first base! The trick is to plan ahead so you don't have to rush. Otherwise, you're not only a mess, but cold and wet. The roof of course always drips water on you as you enter and leave.

The forest right behind Gram's seems dark and heavy in this type of rain. The smell off of the trees is dank, but clean. Their branches hang in shame one upon the other, as they meant to be strong and hold the rain away. I can stand here at Gram's kitchen sink and look toward the river and watch the rain fold in sheets and move over the fields in parallel waves. The evergreen tree tops reflect the wind that is famous in the gorge by bending their tops, sometimes to the point of breakage.

Tonight we have agreed the worst part of a heavy rain is wet cows. They can hold an incredible amount of water on their hides. The smell of wet hair is so much stronger than the wettest dog. The steam virtually rises from a cow. Add about ten milk cows together, along with their very wet tails that are waiting for the person who is going to milk them. Using the little three legged milk stool, one gets into the position to milk. You know, to pull the delicious milk from their udders. The pail goes between your knees and you place your head against the cow's side. I have milked a lot. This is not a new toy for me. I usually help out if I'm here, but the wet cow bit I can live without! I swear they know just when to wrap that wet tail around your head. Now, usually you tuck the tail behind your knee. Left knee. But it's wet. So you kind of think maybe she'll behave and not notice that you have not controlled her tail. Wrong! Slap!!! Here is the tail, wrapped clear around your head ending at you face! If you're lucky, she won't get nervous and step in your bucket of warm, clean milk and spill it all over the barn floor in the process.

Now wet is not so bad, but you also have to get the buckets of milk down to the house. There have been times I either slipped on the path or tripped. The buckets flew into the air, the milk was dispersed God knows where, and I would come through the door of the house with about three inches of milk in the pail instead of the usual full bucket. Therefore, rain, lots of it, can be a pain in the neck.

Funny how a change in weather slips my mind over those happy barnyard memories.

A barnyard in the winter, with a few head of cattle, can be knee- deep in mud. Trying to walk around in it gives that sucking sound with each step. My luck wearing these big heavy black knee high boots often is to lose my balance and fall in that mud. Sometimes face first! Naturally one must find a cold water facet to wash off the muck so others may not recognize your folly. Gram's hot chocolate solves all of those wet problems.

"Jamie, there you are day- dreaming again! I ask you if you need a mixer. I've got two and you

Daughter of the Gorge

are welcome to one if you like." Gram stands there as she does so often with her hands on her hips.

"Yep, I can use a mixer." I probably won't cook after I get off work, but this will make Gram happy to send off the mixer. Then why not. It was most likely given to her by my folks!

Gram is notorious for saving her modern Christmas gifts, and hoarding them in the trunks upstairs. We can only imagine how many "pretties" have been put away. Gram is a wonderful crochet artist. Lately she has used many colors in her doilies. These are found under each lamp and on every table. There are some gorgeous large designs of pineapple on the back of the sofa in the guest living room. Most people make the cream colored or the white thread doilies or table clothes. Anyway she and my mother do this work by the hour, and it would drive me nuts to even try this craft.

In my little housekeeping kit Gram has helped me put together, I now have handmade dish cloths, a mixer, bedding, a potato peeler, two old pillows that smell like moth balls and enough home canned food to last me six months. She has reminded me that I can get fresh eggs on the days I stay here. You would think Gram was the one moving!

"How long till you get your first paycheck?" Gram has this deep frown as she is boxing my kit.

"Probably not for a month, though they said I could be paid more often. I think I'll have them set up a two week schedule. I should be able to set up a good savings plan since I don't pay rent. I thought I'd pick a rent price and put that amount away.

What do you think, Gram?" To me this is especially fun. Gram is so good at jumping in and making anything seem possible.

"Twenty five miles isn't so far away child. If you need us we can be right there, and if we need you, we'll just come to town and get you." Such satisfaction Gram displays on her beautiful wrinkled face.

I think I didn't get my question answered, but she did answer in love, and that is enough for me.

"Gram, I'm so happy and yet a little afraid. Doesn't that sound stupid?"

"No, each step in life is a little unknown, but without that step, none of us would walk! I envy the young women of today. I hadn't the choices of what I would do with my life. For a woman to have a failed marriage and be left with a pretty little girl who knew her daddy walked out on us was difficult. It's hard to move with a youngin' hanging on ya. Nobody going to help ya." Her frown deepens. "Course I would not have give up my kid, no sir."

"I'm thinking you went through some very hard times didn't you, Gram?" I place my hand on her arm.

"Jamie, you'll never know how hard times were. I could tell you what it's like to have no food for your child, and nobody else any better. Sometimes cooking and cleaning just for a meal for my kid, and having to move on. That's why I come to Washington. It was new country. I dreamed a long time before I had enough to make the trip. I figured I was a good cook, and maybe that would get us by. By then your mom was old enough to

Daughter of the Gorge

find work and help out. That she did! God help us, we did survive. You will never understand war and the Depression.

"It's not your generation's fault, not to know. We all tried to forget. I never want to be that cold or hungry again. I never want us to fight a war. They just don't learn. Your father once told me he thought all the leaders that wanted war should go to a barren field, be stripped of their clothing and let them fight it out. Just them alone. The winner then would be the winner. No uniforms. No innocent people killed. Guess that would be a novel concept! No Jamie, I believe a young woman needs to find a way to support herself, in case something should happen to her family. I am in agreement of you working. I want you to find a fine man to make a family with too, though."

"I'll work on the job first, Gram! Thanks for being such a good pioneer for our family!" I'm so proud of Gramma, I could pop.

28

Major and Candy have such beautiful coats. They have had a summer full of love and care. Grooming and cuddling was nearly a daily process. I so love a horse's soft muzzle. It will be hard to see them less often, and ride less often. Today I just want to wander in the fields with them. After the downpour we got yesterday, it's hard to believe its so hot today. Horses are friendly and will drift along around you, munching here and there, lifting their beautiful heads in acknowledgment of noises they may not identify readily.

I made a sandwich, packed more apples than I will eat, and popped a jug of water and a candy bar in an old pillow case of Gram's. Tied it around my waist, so now I plan to play the afternoon away.

The cattle keep a field pretty well mowed. It is quite easy to lope along until coming to a barbed wire fence. Everyone knows you look for a weak spot in the barbed wire and you spread it apart, holding the wires separate as you pass through one leg at a time. Long hair can be caught in the wiring if you're not careful. Your hind end can get raked and rip your jeans or as happened right now, my bag is caught. For me to free, it means I have to let go of the fence. Great! Now my leg is caught! The wire has my back, bag, and one leg. After much working, I have the bag tossed aside. With a few rips and tears, I am finally a free woman standing on the side of the fence I wanted to be on. Of course not without a price. I now have blood running down one leg. The horses? Oh-

Daughter of the Gorge

Now I need to find the gate to bring them with me. Gate? They have just shown me where the fence was down, and we could have walked over! Sitting on the ground I gather a handful of grass, pull my jean leg up to the minor injury, and wipe the blood away. A couple more treatments and the bleeding stops. It's time for an apple for the three of us. I so hate to think of these kinds of afternoons being no more. Why does growing up mean so little time for this? I remember the schedule I was keeping in Seattle before coming here, and I can see it returning. First one customer, the second, then more, and soon no free time. I must work hard to keep days like today available to me.

Well, Laddie must have finally woke up from some place like under the porch and decided to come find me. Laddie is such a pretty dog. He is the typical farm collie, devoted to his owners and a very good watch dog. Nothing sneaks up on Gram with him around. His eyes are so loving, soft brown, and he has a ready laugh on his face all the time. The long sculptured nose just fits into the curve of a troubled friend's neck. Laddie is old enough to make his own decision on what he thinks is an important activity to take part in. Sometimes he'll lope along with me, and sometimes he is noticeably not around. Gram just hates it when he proudly tries to display some new odor he has rolled in. Rather than try to comb burrs from his coat, Gram gets out her shears instead; thus his uneven coat. He loves to chase butterflies and field mice. When he comes across a garden snake, you don't want to be around! He grabs it in his mouth and shakes the be-gee bees out of it. Flaying snake parts to the wind.

Having no brothers or sisters, animals have always been my best friends. Some people have told me I don't talk enough about serious subjects. I don't allow my deepest feelings to be known. I don't share my hurts. I can't help it. I was thoroughly trained by my father about privacy. If I blabbed something about someone and he heard about it, the punishment was severe. He had been so injured in the war; he felt it and anything pertaining to our family was no one's business. I remember my schools would send home inquiries and demand they be responded to. My father would write across the page, "Private information. Not needed by the school." What he earned, what our home was like was not needed to give their daughter an education. Of course, I was the one who took the brunt of feelings at school. Even at the beauty salon I find I can't join in with the gossip about mothers, boyfriends, husbands, or yes, customers. I listen, I think, but I can't verbalize problems. My dad said people don't want to hear them anyway. I think he was right! Trouble is sometimes, someone thinks I don't care or am not concerned, when I'm eaten up inside worrying and trying to solve their problems. That's why I love animals. They listen, they comfort, they love, they welcome, and they forgive. Unconditionally.

These horses, this dog...sharing my day with me. Just being buddies. I suppose if people heard me talking to the animals, they might want to lock me up. Such peace I find in sitting in the grass thinking, and chewing on grass ends. Sometimes a sugar filled clover head is handy, and I gently pull sweet pedals apart to enjoy their taste. My mind can wander over anything past or present. Good or bad. I can talk to the trees, bees, clouds, and blue sky. I love it all. I hunger for the times I can be alone and quiet. In town I can't hear the birds sing or hear a bee flitting from flower to flower or the wind racing through tree branches. A person is lucky if there are flowers near their home or work.

That's why I'm going to love my new apartment. It's like a garden around the funeral home.

Enough soul searching. I'll never understand the twists and turns in my life. I just hope I can keep a good job, save some money, and maybe someday find Mr. Right. I certainly don't want to come home to Mommy if at all possible. Gosh, I hope she's having a great time. Imagine being in England. She and Daddy never took a vacation that I can remember.

"Come on guys! Time to get back to the farm and curry you out, give you your oats." This time I'm going to swing up on Candy's back and ride home. I've walked far enough. Laddie is already in the lead and well back home. He knows the short cuts. Laddie knows all the areas that have deep holes under the fence; it keeps him from getting his coat hung up in the barbed wire.

29

"Thanks for helping me pack the car, you guys. It will be fun getting things put around the apartment. I think you have given entirely too much to me. But I am grateful. I'll be back tonight and pack the second load. Clothes. I hate packing clothes upstairs! Once they are there though, they can stay!" Kissing my grandparents goodbye, I roll down the road. It's a great day, and I feel hyper about my new home and job.

"Hi Gladys! I'm here to get settled in if you still want me!" I dump my box of tools, capes, and clippers on the counter.

"You bet, Jamie. Put your things away, and Doris there will show you around, and show you how we do the receipts and booking. Soon as I can get away, I'll join in, okay?" Her hands are tangled in mass back-combing, and she has hair pins in her mouth. "Did you remember to bring your license for us to hang up?"

"Sure did." I answer, as I place my magnetic rollers in their holder. They are stacked pyramid style on a pre- formed plastic stand. Large rollers on the outside and smaller ones on the inside. Then I place the new pivot-point rollers on their stand. This then is fitted to the top of a roll around base. My capes are folded neatly and placed in the top drawer of the stand beside the counter top. My combs are on a kitchen organizer. When I work, I'll have a jar of blue water sanitizer to drop the combs in after use. I'll fill it later.

The woman called Doris watches me from her station, and when it looks like I'm finished she glides over to me. I don't think I've ever seen anyone walk so effortlessly from one point to another. She has dark brown hair and dark brown eyes. Her eyes are warm and shaped like a does. She seems timid, not the average outgoing hairdresser.

"Hello. I'm Doris. I've worked here about a year, and I love it. You're allowed to be pretty much your own boss here as long as you're keeping clientele happy. Come with me and I'll show you our supply room. As you can see, it's pretty full. We all help put supplies away. This washer and dryer are for our towels. We do our own, but we help each other fold. Just put your name on them. Patty will monogram your name if you pay her fifteen dollars per fifty. We've all chosen to do that because it looks nice." She's studying me I can feel it; "We have a small lounge in here, a table that we better keep wiped up, and a refer in the corner. It's the best I've ever worked with. Gladys insists that we work as a team and not as prima donnas." She moves to the table and sits down.

"Any questions?" Her smile is sincere and not threatening. Some hairdressers are leery of someone new until their ability is assessed. Professional pride. No one really wants to be shown up. I have not wanted to be the best; I like to watch others and be challenged. I do want to be second best!

She moved as if she had forgotten something. "I forgot to tell you the cash register will have a code number for you. You will have to use it to open or close the register. Receipts are numbered and have to be counted and matched to the customer each night. If each of us does this, it saves Gladys work. She is determined to make businesswomen of us. She thinks we need to know what it costs to keep this place open. I think she's smart. I've learned to know what I'm earning, and why."

"Thanks for your help, Doris. I needed a good cook's tour. I'll probably goof up sometime!"

"We all do. It's nice to have you here. When will you start?" Doris queried.

"Day after tomorrow."

"Thought so. Gladys already is booking you!"

I looked, and sure enough there was one color, two sets and a haircut already on my first day. This woman was going to see that I worked all right!

I felt that Doris would be a friend. Some people are that way. I don't think she has a mean bone in her body. I respect her already.

The girls all yelled, "Goodbye, see ya soon, and good luck." They seem like a good work force.

Waiting until after lunch, I ran my things to the apartment. I knew they might have a service, so I decided to check in at the office. One of the funeral directors spotted me and said he was assigned to carry my belongings up the stairs. They didn't want me to fall or be carrying these things by myself. Man! Who would have expected this service?

"My name is Al Hammond. Glad to meet you. I'm harmless, married, and have children, plus, my wife is jealous!" He seemed tickled with himself.

Daughter of the Gorge

He was just as round as he was tall. Dressed in a blue suit, white shirt, and a loud tie, he was harmless

"I hate to have you work so hard. You're all dressed up." He has a box balanced on his knee.

"Miss, these are my work clothes! My jeans are dress. I have to live in a suit!"

Placing my belongings here and there, Gram's doilies on tables that they covered stains on, and making my bed up made it feels like home. Amazing how much the refrigerator has in it after Gram packed! There were things I hadn't put there. I flop back on the bed with my hands under my head, and try to relax.

Knock, Knock.

Opening the door, I find my boss from the funeral home standing there in the hallway.

"Everything all right? Glad to have you! Got a minute? If you do, can you come down to the office? I have a little instruction for you and some paper work to study.

"First off, though, this is your home. You need not answer the door if it is inconvenient. There is a buzzer on your phone if we need to talk to you. So don't let anyone upset your days off. Sometimes children get loose from their parents and they head up these stairs, hence the combination locks. Had a drunk come upstairs once? He wanted to see the patio. So always check. Normally we check the doors. When you work here at night, don't answer the door. There's a posted phone number for people to call. We want you to feel safe. Come on down to the office as soon as you can." He was off in a flash down the steep stairs without a second thought.

The training session was easy. Just act professionally when speaking on the telephone. Speak clearly because, so many customers have hearing problems. Be patient and kind. Write information legibly and take complete telephone numbers and names. Ask for clients to spell their names. I am not to assume I know how to spell names as it would probably be wrong! Don't let the time of day or night concern me if I need to dispatch someone. Death has no time limits and observes no holidays. This is a twenty four hour job!

I was told I would always find a daily schedule posted on my door. Just remove it and keep it inside. Knowing when funeral services are and when families are coming in to make arrangements lets me know when to be quiet in the apartment. Well, with my job all that would be over anyway by the time I got home. On my days off, that would give me an excuse to read! I can understand why they ask a person not to be clomping around over people's heads. For free, I can sit down and relax for an hour now and then.

Now I feel like a divided person. Part of me lives in Vancouver and part of me lives in Cape Horn.

Not bad timing. I'll get home in time for dinner. Boy will I miss Gram's cooking!

Setting up my apartment has been fun. This is the first time I've really been on my own. With Mom being in another state, I feel more answerable for myself. There is so much space in this apartment that I feel maybe I'll put my television and bed in the living room. Make it a giant master bedroom. I think I will probably live in one room anyway, as opposed to stringing everything out over the whole upstairs. Yes, this is much cozier. I like the feeling of being closed in about me. By myself now, I notice I have less fear about being alone.

My records are in a box that seems neat to me. Cement blocks bought on my way back into town hold the shelves I put on them. This gives me four shelves four foot long to put my books and collectibles on. My television is high on the dresser so that I can watch it from bed. Why sit in a hard chair when I can lay down in comfort? The closet in the hallway is large. Everything I want to store away from view fits in it! I have put my uniforms and other clothes in the bedroom closet. It will probably seem odd to friends that I use my living room for a bedroom. Who cares? Not me! My record player is on a table in front of the bay window. I have made my bed and put on the pretty quilt Gram gave me. The wedding ring pattern in soft pinks and greens looks fantastic with the throw pillows I bought to match.

The kitchen is blue with white walls. My refrigerator is plum full of everything Gram could push off on me. Including plums! Milk, butter, jams, bread, meat, and all the things to go with it! I purchased pop on my way to Vancouver, and some condiments I needed.

Tonight I will fix my own meal, and clean it up! It's such a small thing to be proud of. Anything I want, all I have to do is decide what to fix! Finally I

Barbara Twibell

open a can of hash and throw in a hot dog. I told Gramma I probably would not fix many meals!

Oh man! I have watched television much too long. I have to get up in five hours to go to work!! Maybe this living on my own is going to be rougher than I figured.

30

"Hello, Jamie. Welcome to your first day at work." My boss is all smiles; she looks well rested and ready to roll. "Your first client is in a half hour, plenty of time to get your booth ready!"

"Hi Gladys! Isn't it a beautiful day to start a new job, in a new town, with new friends?" Hanging up my jacket and checking my hair, I turn and go to my booth.

Shampoo bottles are filled and a conditioner bottle sits nearby. In the cupboard under my counter top in the first drawer I place my new combs and brushes. The giant comb for long hair tangles and the teasing combs are next to each other. Bobbie pins and hair pins are placed in their compartments. The holder for perm papers is in its compartment. I have always prided myself in being very organized with my equipment. I can work much faster knowing where each item is, and not having to take time searching for something. I have purchased a tray made especially for holding my plastic pivot point hair rollers. They are tapered from one end to the other. The tray can be moved around my work area as I move around my client. Three sizes of my curling irons and my blow dryer are mounted under my counter. This is a new way of doing hair, and not all stylists are using them. My teacher was insistent about me learning this new concept. Below this drawer are my towels for placing about patron's shoulders. On top of my counter is the neck-strip dispenser, a paper strip made of stretchable paper that is placed around a patron's neck to help keep leakage from reaching her clothes. To top off my equipment is a late model pair of scissors, a safety razor, and the best of the line clippers. If customers only knew how much this "little" bit of equipment cost their hairdressers! Ready to get started, I wait for customer number one to arrive. And I wait.

"Jamie. Your customer is here."

Taking my client's coat, I put it on the coat rack and lead her to my booth.

"You'll never guess why I am late," this client chirps. "My husband asked me to stop by the bank for him. He had to have some money by lunch time, and there were already long lines at the bank, and would you believe I ran into my neighbor? Why I haven't seen her all summer! Such a start this morning." "Who are you dear? Where is my regular girl? I always have the same girl. Are you shampooing me for her?"

I tell the lady her girl is ill, and I have been assigned to do her today. She is springing about in my chair as if she has fleas. The lady is plainly upset.

"May I speak to the owner please? I really don't like being given to a new girl like this. I mean, you are a new girl aren't you?" Now she is acting like I carry the plague.

Now, when a stylist is ill or playing hooky, her customers are left out in the cold. Maybe a salon should just call them and tell them they can't be done, and their appointment is canceled. Usually early morning ladies can't be reached before they have already left for the salon. So, kind, caring operators try to fit them in their schedules along with their own clients so they will get their hair done anyway. This is the most thankless of all appointments. It always is!

Now guess how I feel? I don't want to do her either! You never can do as well this one time, as her girl who has been doing the exact same hairdo for years or months. I need the money though, and my boss knows it. With all sweetness, this spoiled lady is given the next hour to badger and harass her new operator. I have learned to listen carefully to how each curl is to lay, and to give her the best shampoo and scalp and shoulder massage I know how to give. I will venture the guess her regular hairdresser does not do so with her.

She pays her three and a half dollars, and leaves me a quarter for a tip. She says she will see me in a couple of weeks. Thank you, I have just left instructions at the desk, I will always be booked. She is not worth the punishment I just took.

My next customer was for a permanent. We talk about which perm would be best for her type hair and we begin the process. She is a new client to the salon, and we ask the usual questions of one another. Light subject matter. I like her, and her perm turns out bouncy and quite reactive to her new hair cut and hairstyle. She allowed me to style something new for her, and she loved it! This is the hairdressing I love!

Lunch was spent with a new friend at the salon named Doris. We had a great lunch, something hairdressers seldom get when they have a large clientele. I think Gladys had something to do with us not being busy for awhile. Doris is also single. She has an apartment not too far from mine. She is a quiet girl, but a very nice person. She's someone I will enjoy working with.

When I get back to the salon I have a little girl booked for her first haircut. This will be either heaven or hell! She is a one year old sweetie. Her name is Amy. Her anxious mother and father look on. They want bangs cut...straight! Amy has a mouth the size of any gater in Florida, once she is in the chair. You could hear her scream clear to Portland! I ask if the father might hold her in his arms and whisper sweet nothings in her ear. I also add the disclaimer that one jump and her bangs will not be straight. Amy does pretty well, and looks cute when done. At least I didn't put the scissors through her eyes! All are happy when they leave.

The first day is done, I have no one else. My boss tells me I may leave. She feels I had a good first day, and she likes my work. I refill my shampoo bottles, and all the rest of the hair stuff bottles from the large plunger bottles in the back room. My towels are thrown in the wash, and my sink cleaned. I sweep up and sterilize my equipment and leave for home.

Home, my new apartment! I can walk to work in this weather, and I will until the hard rains. Vancouver is a pretty city. Many older homes are now made into apartments. They have wide full porches and three story Midwest looking styles. Greenery is abundant, with all colors of flowers in the flowerbeds. Most homes are made of timber, since we have so much of it. That leads to fabulous paint jobs. Many homes are of colors like yellow, green, blues, white, and many trims. Just think, inside of each home is a family. Each one different from the other. All these lives living their dreams, or disappointments.

On my way home I pass the Lucky Lager brewery and the signal station. Also on my way are drug store I will need to go into, a cleaner, and a movie theater. "Psycho" is playing right now. If payday comes before the movie moves on, I want to see it.

There's the funeral home. No extra cars are around, so I think I will go in the front door and say hello to everyone.

"Hi," I say as I enter the office. Everyone is sitting around the coffee machine. A box of glazed doughnuts stands open on the desk.

"Hello yourself," says one of the directors. Pull up a doughnut, and have some coffee! All done with work?"

"No," says another director, "she came back to hold our hands!" Laughing he went to get a comfortable chair for me. Something I have learned already is these hard working people, who hold so many peoples grief know how to enjoy each other with light banter. Now is coffee time, down time.

"How was your first day?" The owner asked as if he really cared.

"Great!" I felt wonderful. "I think I've earned a couple of steady customers. I came out okay, really. I felt a little nervous because the whole place was new to me, but all in all, I had a good time."

"Will you be able to catch the phones tonight?" he asked?

"Sure thing, no problem."

After enjoying nearly an hour with the guys downstairs, I excused myself, and headed up the stairs to my home!! Once there, off came the uniform and on came the shorts, tank top, and bare feet. I was dying for a coke. I want to just enjoy doing what I want! When I want!

Shadows skip along the building sides and move in and out of doorways, ever picking up the sounds of cats chasing each other and leave singing their last hurrah of summer. All new sounds to me. I felt I needed to get out and take a walk in my new neighborhood and acquaint myself with my surroundings. Something about living alone makes me more nervous, like I need to be doing something all the time. Just sitting there watching television is not satisfying. I had called my boss, and asked him for an hour off for this walk since I was supposed to take over the phones. He told me, "Go ahead. He needed to come back to work and finish some paper work needed to send into the Government, and that he had put this chore off during the day. He said, "I'll ring the doorbell special so you know it's me!"

The Interstate highway, I-5 is only three city blocks over, so there is a constant rumble of traffic, kind of like the roar of the ocean. It is not offensive, just noticeable. A large city park named for Esther Short is about two blocks from the funeral home. I won't walk there in the dark, though. I'll stay on the street. I'm close to a large red brick hospital St. Joseph's... The fellas at the funeral home told me that a couple of years ago a young nurse had been kidnapped in the vicinity of the hospital. Very nice apartments are next to that. Oh! There is a grocery store close to me how convenient! Television dinners around the corner! All in all my corner of earth looks pretty fitting for this girl. I feel more at ease now that I know my neighbors. I take a good long look at the moon and head home for a solid night's sleep.

31

"Gladys thanks for that color customer. It has been awhile since I colored someone's hair. I think she was really happy with that soft brown color, instead of that mousey grey. She was too young to look so drab." I knew this was a walk in lady Gladys handed over to me. There is more money in a color than just a set. This is what it takes to pay bills!

A short time later I was called to the telephone. Some man wanted to talk to me.

"Is your name Jamie?" says this male voice.

"Yes," I reply.

"You just colored my wife's hair. Right?" He sounds a little excited. "Well, I'm going to stop chasing her just long enough, to say "Thank You." She looks great! Thank you very much! We both love the color and her new style. She looks really sexy!"

With that, he hung up.

The girls all hung around the phone to hear what this was about. After relating the story, we all had a good laugh. Doris and I left to have some lunch at a Holland motif restaurant. We both agreed we were starving.

Sometimes when things are slow at work, we girls do each others hair. It's a good chance to try out new hair styles and hair cuts. It's a time for learning. We tease each other, we laugh a lot and we can get pretty dramatic about the hair styles we are designing. When we finish, each of us looks pretty good. Other times, when we are busy, like

Daughter of the Gorge

for holidays, we can look pretty poor because we don't have any time left to do our own hair! Standing for hours and holding our arms up as much as we do, leaves us open for many arthritis problems later in life.

"Jamie, there's a man up front who insists on talking to you," announced Claire coming into the hairdresser's lounge area.

"I don't know any man. Is he a salesman?" I questioned. "I mean I haven't been here long enough to have someone ask to see me."

"He assured me you would know him. He does not look very patient. Any way he is by the desk out front." With that Claire turned on her heel and quickened back to the front of the salon.

I only had to step around the corner when I saw him. His hands were in his pockets, and he was shifting from one foot to another. Lance was clearly having a hard time being in a beauty salon. As I walked toward him, I noted his eyes change to gentle surprise at seeing me dressed professionally.

"Hello, what brings you here?" I did not mean to sound quite as I sounded. I meant it to be lighter hearted.

"Your grandparents told me where I could find you." He coldly answered me, assessing my appearance as he talked. "I want to take you to dinner tonight. We need to talk. His eyes bore into mine. "I'm not one bit happy about how you moved out of town."

"I don't think my job is the place for this discussion, and I resent your high handed way of coming in here. There is no reason I have to defend my actions to you is there? Tell me why I need to go to dinner with you when apparently I'm going to get my head bit off. Besides there is now at least twenty pair of eyes looking at us." The heat is racing up my neck to my face.

"You're right. I'm sorry," says Lance. "I am not about to bite your head off. You can't know how I felt, to find you were gone. Can I pick you up for dinner, Jamie?"

"Well, I don't get off work for another hour, and then I need time to change. How about six o'clock? Wait in the parking lot, and I will come out the side door." Then I wrote down the address for him, and bid him goodbye.

After Lance strode out the door, the twenty eyes made their appearances.

"That is one great looking man," Said Mabel.

"Where did he come from, Jamie?" asked another.

"Your holding out on us kid," said even another. The bantering continued on until Gladys came up to me.

"Are you all right she asked?" "You look a little upset." comforted my boss.

"He's upset I didn't tell him I was moving and had gotten a job. He's a friend, and he had been out of town. There is no problem. He apparently thinks he looks out for me." I had a warm feeling for a moment, covered over by fear of the following dinner I had accepted. Thinking to myself, why had I not told Lance?

"You're done for the day anyway. Why don't you go on home and take a cool bath and relax for awhile?" Gladys's concern was more than comforting to me, there was a maternal care displayed that I needed at this moment. Not that I was going to disclose that to her.

Walking home I'm trying to concentrate on the beautiful maple trees guarding my route, trying to set my nerves at ease. I feel almost like I'm being watched. My mind kicks off to the many times as a child that this feeling would encompass me and I would find myself running to my destination. I will fight down this urge. After all, I am an adult.

It's amazing how wonderful a leisurely bath is to a woman who is a knotted mass of nerves! My bubbles are secure under my chin, my toes reach the faucet knobs, and my head rests against a rolled towel at the back of my head. Gram's rubber tub was not this comforting.

I find myself wondering why Lance seemed so upset. It would be so much nicer if he had surprised me, and asked me to dinner for fun. He did look handsome. He always does. He seems to command attention everywhere he goes, without even knowing it. Now, what shall I wear?

Lance is waiting by his truck door as I come out. The look on his face is unreadable.

"Hi! You found me, I see." I give him a quick kiss on his cheek and take his offered hand up into his truck.

Lance mutters an unintelligible sentence as he closes the truck door and swings around to his side and jumps into the truck as if he were springing into a saddle.

"Hi yourself. It's good to see you. We're going out to the Stage Coach Inn for dinner." The truck moves smoothly under Lance's direction. I wonder what happens if a car does not react as it is supposed to.

"Table for two, right this way," motions the waitress as she sashays down between the rows. Does she mean direction or follow the way she's walking? Oh well, guess I'm in a silly mood. I don't think my hips could roll that far.

I order fried chicken, and Lance orders prime rib, rare! Here comes the blood! He said little to nothing on the way to the restaurant. Fun evening ahead.

"Why did you just leave? Couldn't you wait until I was back home?" Lance leans forward in his chair and speaks so that diners near us cannot hear him.

"I did not just leave. You knew I needed to find a job to support myself. We talked about it! When I did look for one, this one opened up, and it's exactly what I wanted." I leaned forward to match his lean. We probably looked very romantic to onlookers.

"You live in a MORTUARY!" Growled Lance. "For PETE's sake woman, WHAT ARE YOU TRYING TO PROVE?" Lance has not blinked that I've noticed.

"There is no Pete, and you're starting to yell at me." I'm getting a little annoyed now. "Just what is this about? I have secured proper employment, and I have a fantastic apartment."

Daughter of the Gorge

"You want to be picked up at a MORTUARY?" sneered Lance. "I'm supposed to pick you up at the Mortuary, visit you there, brag about where you live?"

"Number one, Mr. Lance, where I live should not be the focus of casual conversation. It is only my business. Whether you visit or not, are only my business, and I am not, have not been, and never will be a pick-up. My apartment is free, for answering the telephone after work hours, and I get paid for that. The man who owns the funeral home is kind and honorable. How can you be so stupid?"

"How can you be around those dead people? How can you work for those weirdoes?" There goes Lance's hand through his hair.

"I can't believe we are having this discussion." The waitress returns to ask if everything is all right and fusses with the coffee. Should I tell her the truth?

"Lance, if your father would die tonight, who would you call? You are entrusting him to someone's care, while you make up your mind to what you want carried out for him. Is he now something creepy because he died? You have watched too many horror shows!"

"You can't tell me you weren't afraid when you went there to look at your fantastic apartment?" challenged Lance.

"Yes, of course, you're right, but after hearing ordinary men and women who chose to go into this work, I feel a lot different. They really do feel they are helping people when others shy away. They feel the human body is kind of like a house the furniture has been moved from. Like that person has gone on. The person is not suffering anymore, he or she doesn't hurt or cry anymore. Nursing home staff sees more pain than we do. That's a job I couldn't do! Someone really loved that person, and that person loved back. The dead person is to be respected, and cared for as the family instructs. I have seen nothing scary. On the contrary I see well educated, kind people.

"Lance, I feel protected where I live. I have privacy and an opportunity to save money. This is tiring me out. I see no reason I have to defend my choices."

"Jamie, I just don't know if I can accept, I mean, I don't know what I mean any more. When your gramma told me where you were, that you now lived in Vancouver, it seemed as if you were so far away, as if you ran away from me. I thought we were going together. I thought..."

"You thought?" I bit back. "You have never done one thing, including tonight, to make me feel special to you. Not once have you said anything a girl would take as a clue that she was your girl."

"But I thought we would someday. I thought you cared for me." Now came the anger back in Lance's voice.

"You thought! You thought! You were thinking, not saying! Neither one of us knows what to think! Except I think you will take me home now. Nothing of this evening has been enjoyable, and I refuse to argue one more minute." Nearing the tears I don't want Lance to see, I push my chair out from the table and run for the front door.

A couple emerges from a cab, and I give my address to the driver as the cab speeds away from the curb, with me inside.

Crying my eyes out for the last hour has not solved anything except make my eyes swell half shut and streak my makeup. I don't know where Lance and I ended up tonight, except there was no goodbye, and he hasn't come here. Of course not. He can't tolerate where I live. Well, I like my apartment, and that's who is living here. I reach for my robe and get out of my clothes as fast as I can. Barefoot and a coke in my hand, I'm ready to watch television and forget this evening as soon as I can.

32

"Believe you me," said Doris the next day, "I'd let that guy go back to the farm. Who does he think he is? Some nerve to treat you like he owns you. He's not thinking of you at all and what might be good for you." Doris is so quiet that this really shocks me that she has said so much in such a short time of knowing me.

It has been difficult to sort out the things Lance said to me last night, and be able to work as hard as all of us had to today.

One young married woman wanted her hair cut but not cut. Everyone has cut too much off in the past. She has barked about nothing else as I shampoo her hair. As I part her hair for the cut she reminds me that this time she will sue. Doris leans back from her booth to check out my customer and I wink. I tell the lady I will be right back, and Doris and I head for the back of the salon. I tell Doris to keep a close eye as she might have to witness my actions. Back with the customer, I again ask what she desires. No length, no thinning, just make it a good haircut. I proceed to talk to her about her job, where she is from, and the usual dialogue. There is much measuring, and movement of hands, combs, and scissors. I put some conditioner on her hair and blow style her coiffure. Now, I turn her in the chair with a mirror in her hand and joy breaks out on her face. She is thrilled and I get a five dollar tip. My secret is, no hair was cut!!! Doris had made a big show of sweeping my station along with her station, with hair from her previous client.

Daughter of the Gorge

I don't think I will ever forget my very happy customer. I ask Doris if she has time to go to the early show tonight. We have some extra change thanks to my tip.

The Broadway Theater is only a short walk from my apartment. I love the hundred or so lights under the Marquee where you purchase tickets. Inside the theater the fresh hot buttered popcorn splashes up the sides of the popper, begging to leap into big white paper bags that are anything but noiseless while watching the movie in bright dark red plush seats. Never have I been in such a rich setting.

33

Finally I have earned my keep! Awakened at two-ten in the morning, the hospital has just called. A young woman has been killed in an auto accident and is ready at the hospital morgue for us to remove. I ask the name of the spouse or parents, their phone number, and the name of the charge nurse. Then I call Terry, my boss. He thanks me, and says he'll be right down to the funeral home. He told me to be sure and put this information by his desk. It took me quite awhile to go back to sleep thinking of this poor girl and her family. Around four in the morning the phone rings again and this time a nursing home called. The family has requested we be called.

"Hello. I'm sorry, Terry, to wake you again..."

All I did was answer the phone, but the energy level in me is nil this morning. I need to be at work at eight today. I have a repeat customer! This means I am starting to build a clientele, and that is good for a steady paycheck.

I actually move around with much more certainty at the work place since the first week or two, and I am very happy with my new friends. A couple of customers have sons or friends have sons they insist I must meet. There are many fix-you-uppers out there. Ladies invariably want to know why I'm not married yet, am I going with someone, or am I divorced. I say I am new to the area and have had no time to look around. I'm too busy working. I'm left with the distinct impression they

Daughter of the Gorge

are not through with me yet. Another day gone, and I happily head for my apartment.

After I get off work and get home and change my clothes, I find I like going back downstairs. The people at the funeral home are so much fun. In spite of the seriousness of their work, they sincerely enjoy one another. They raze each other over whose turn it is to dust, or out-wait one another on taking the cars down to gas them up. After working with women all day, it's nice to hear what men yak about? In fact I've learned a whole lot more about politics since moving here. Taxes, regulations, and building repairs, something is always subject matter I have no experience with. I am heartily included though, as if I did know something. When everyone heads home, I lock up and return to my apartment. Television dinners are popular now to my age group. They are fondly called T.V. dinners. My boss says they are a flash in the pan, and will not last in popularity.

34

Today is a joyous day off. I'm going to head to Gram's, and unless Mack has taken her Camas today, she will be at home. Things would certainly be easier if she had a telephone! I need to do one wash tub of clothes, make my bed, and do a little dusting and away I go. I've not driven my car lately, it might be full of bugs by now! As long as the weather is this nice, around seventy degrees, I will walk back and forth to work. That means the car just sits. Tank and I both need a day off in the gorge.

I've decided to take a weird way to Gram's. I feel like driving up over McLaughlin Heights, a hill east of the main part of Vancouver. When my father first came home from overseas, we moved from North Bonneville into some military housing in the McLaughlin area. I hadn't been back since then. My, it's amazing how this area has changed in a few years! Lots of new homes and grocery stores are going up. Tank and I wander around and then go back to the main highway.

My ride continues by going up the Washougal River Road. This river is so clear the rocks burst forth with white top hats as the water rushes by. Deep corners pocket the sides of the river looking dark green and peaceful, with a whirlpool here and there lying about its safe look. The drive is so beautiful; one could drive off the road for looking at the river. Some summer homes along the river surprise a driver with their un- announced driveways. Stacks of firewood leaning against nearly every cabin make the passerby aware of a winter threat. It must be wonderful to have a getaway such as this to come to after a week of hard work. Mack says it's nice, but these people have to clean yards, gutters, and repair before they can have fun. He thinks that's dumb. He would rather go fishing on the river when he wants, and not have to do the cleaning!

I stop at the Steel Bridge Store and by some ice cream to take to Grams. I know Mack loves ice cream.

"Hi there!" Says Fred the owner. "Heard you moved to Vancouver and got yourself a job. Good for you." He's already putting the ice cream in a paper bag and folding it over for me. "That all today?" he asks remotely.

"That's all, Fred. Yes, I found a job. This job is a lot closer than Seattle was. I can be closer to the folks now, and I like that," I answer as I step away from the counter.

"Not as close as living with them; they miss you!" said a familiar deep voice behind me. His presence overwhelmed me. I felt I would pass out if I stood there any longer. Why didn't I see his truck when I drove in?

"I parked in the back," as if reading my mind, he replied.

I don't know if Lance paid for his goods, or left them, but he was right on my heels as I got to my car. The hair literally stands on end on my arms as he comes closer to me.

"What are you up to today?" queried Lance. "Coming to spend the weekend with your grandparents?"

His arms surround me but don't touch me. They might as well, as one arm is on the door jam and the other is on the roof of the car. He leans in enough that I can't change positions or stand up. The cologne Lance wears teases my senses with a familiar rarity that invokes all kinds of warm feelings.

I wonder if men understand that there are times they are capable of throwing our minds into mind-jams where it is impossible to think clearly.

"Yes. That's my plan! I miss them terribly myself." I was just getting some ice cream as a surprise. What are you doing here?"

"Do you know how many times you ask what I'm doing someplace? This is a community store, and I stop here often to see friends and buy things. Nothing to say about needing gas for my truck. I was glad to see you again. I didn't know how to solve the problem from the other night. I'd like to apologize for being so thoughtless."

"What?" I crane my neck up to look at him.

Lance shifts to a squat beside the car door. His eyebrows take on that hurt puppy dog look. "I've thought a lot about the way I came on to you at dinner. It was stupid. I'm really sorry. You're right, I had no right." He waited. He remained where he was, waiting for me to answer him. I'm not even thinking of what he asked me, how do I tell him that? I can't think of anything but how cute he

Daughter of the Gorge

is. How sharp he looks, and how good it is to see him again.

"Jamie," his voice growing softer, "I want to get to know you better. I want to date you, and I want you to be my special girl. I'm sorry I took you for granted. Do you think we can start over?"

"We needn't start over, just don't yell at me! I like you, too. I'm just not very good at this boy girl thing. I think I would miss you a lot if you weren't in my life somewhere. YES, I'd like to be special to you." I feel a whole lot better now that I have run into Lance, and we've settled where we are to a more satisfactory point.

"What are you doing this weekend? Would you like to do something?" asked Lance.

"I really have planned to spend the whole weekend visiting with my grandparents. How about next weekend?" I can barely contain the joy that is whelming inside of me. I determine at this point though I'd not like Lance to know how much this conversation means to me.

"I'll come over some time this weekend. I promise not to stay. Think about what you would like to do together, and you can let me know then. It's time I come load up my horses and take them home for the fall and winter. I don't want Candy and Major to forget who owns them! Mack has enough to care for in the winter time. I'm glad to see you, Jamie. You're sure a sight for these sore eyes."

With that he leaned inside the car and gave me a most difficult to forget kiss, and strode away. With not even a backward glance.

I love being around Lance. I feel happier when I am. But, I don't like it when moods change and then I think he's mad at me. Sometimes he makes me feel as if he doesn't even like me. Then I run into him, and all is well again. Why this roller coaster feeling to this friendship? Oh well, I have a lot to learn about male friendships!

Slamming the car door as I leap out, I remember the ice cream and return to the car to get it!

Gram's on the porch already, wiping her hands on her apron, and pushing a strand of loose hair out of her way. She looks so good, her farm worn hands outstretched in loving welcome. For the amount of work she does each day, her hands are so soft. I dearly love the all consuming hug I get from her heart and her ample bosom.

"Oh Gram! Spaghetti! I can smell it clear to Vancouver!"

"You are a child of vast exaggerations! But I love you anyway," chuckles Gram as she shuttles me inside the house.

Gram's spaghetti is to die for! She slow cooks it for two days. The sausage smell strings your mind right on into the hamburger smell overwhelmed by the special tomato sauce, garlic, onions, and cloves. Oh this is painful to the smell sensors! I salivate just thinking of being able to roll this onto my fork in a few minutes. This is so worth the drive! Gram makes her own sausage each year. She also grinds her own hamburger. She has prepared all this sauce in a big canner pot. She will can a goodly portion of this for later meals. The wood stove is really on a roll tonight. The windows of the house are all steamed up. What a glorious smell!

"Jamie, do you want peaches or prunes for desert?" queried Gram.

"Prunes. I think your canned prunes are just tangy enough to top this meal off perfect." I bet she even made homemade bread to complement the dinner.

"Step into the formal dining room, and get a loaf of fresh bread for the table. Honey, you'll find a cutting knife in the second drawer. Be careful because Mack just put new edges on my knives."

"I can't believe I chose a hard job and T.V. dinners over what you have here, Gram. What is happening to our homes? It's so warm and cozy here," I lament.

"Is your apartment cold, Honey? Do you need an extra quilt?" Gram is totally concerned.

"Naw, I'm just not there all day, how can it be cozy? It seems all right to me until I come here. I really am fine, Gram. I don't know why I whine about what I have been accomplishing. A great job, a fine apartment, a car that runs, and I am making new friends."

"Meet any men in that job?" says Mack as he comes around the corner. "Seems to me you're working on everything but what really matters. Someone to come home to. What's so great about being alone? You never say anything about love. You need some man to warm you up, not a paycheck!"

"Land sakes, Mack, until Mr. Right comes along, she can get as much from a pup. Don't you go having her rush off with some darn city slicker?"

"I ain't rushing her off, but the rate she's moving, she won't know Mr. Right because she's too busy making left turns. She's twenty now, in her prime. She needs to strut her feathers some. She's damn good looking, and no dummy. Ain't fittin' these women out working on their own." Mack checks the sauce pot, and ambles on over to the kitchen table.

"Well," says Gram, "you sure find the table when dinner is on. I think you owe Jamie an apology. She didn't come home to have you preach to her."

"Nope no apology, meant no harm, just want her to think." Mack clenched his jaw.

"Hey guys, Lance will be over sometime while I'm here. Said he wants to pick up the horses, and take them home for the season. We will be going out together next weekend. I wanted to spend my spinster weekend with you this week! I felt my love life could be on hold while I visit you! Is that all right Mack?"

"Oh..."

"Ha, ha, Boy, that was good, Jamie," laughed Gram. "That was well deserved for sticking our nose into your business."

"You're dating Lance?" Mack mumbled. "Thought you left him in the cold."

"We have our differences. Apparently we enjoy something about one another!" I am really tickled by this interest each is showing.

Daughter of the Gorge

"He thinks my living in a funeral home is terrible for my reputation. Evidently he has rethought that out! Anyway, we are friends again!"

"Mack, will you pour the milk? We're ready to eat up!" Gram is in charge at mealtime.

"Your job going good? Are you getting a decent paycheck yet, Child?" Gram rolls her spaghetti expertly. Left hand holding a spoon with the tip of her right hand fork touching the bowl of the spoon, catching a couple of long strands and turning her fork around and around until all the noodle is wrapped around the fork, then she pops it into her mouth and quietly chews leaving no muss at all. I do it the same way as I was taught by her. It makes eating this meal so neat and clean.

"The paychecks are improving each week, and with the check from the funeral home I'm going to be able to save at least a hundred dollars a month. I bought a life insurance policy that will make me save, too. It's not term. It will build for a future, if I decide to go on to college, or whatever I want." I noticed Mack and Gram nodding their heads in agreement. Maybe they can see I'm trying hard to do what is right for me at this time in my life.

35

Saturday came and went, so did Sunday. No Lance. Gram and Mack were pretty quiet. We had a great time together, played lots of games, and wondered about my mom and how she is doing. We've not heard from her in awhile.

Gram caught my arm as I was ready to leave. "Look Honey, don't you let Mr. Fancy Pants get to you, and don't you go pining for him. Awful thing he done you this weekend. Go out with some other fellas. Some men just have no feelings about girl's hearts. Let him just play with his horses and ranch. Don't mean nothing to my girl anyway, right?"

Swallowing back a little sob, I punctuated her statement with a slight nod. A kiss and hug, and I turned the car around and headed back to Vancouver. My car was full of jars of sauce and newly baked bread. My heart was empty.

When I got home, I turned up the heat in the apartment. I thought it might make my home cozy. My bed looked inviting, but it wasn't anything special either. Nothing on television is appealing; in fact, I can't even get interested. How can he kiss my brains away, and then just not care to show up? I have never ever been touched or kissed like that before. My heart sang from the memory, and cried from the reality. Maybe this is experience. The more you date, the better you kiss and fondle. I'm just another girl to him. He has plenty, probably. Why come back to a little know nothing? So desperate as to let any touch mean too much. Such a duck I am! Well, tomorrow it's back to reality. Maybe I can meet someone to go out with.

36

Lance had never had such a hangover. He hardly drank anymore. This was serious drunk. How long had he been this way? His buddy Larry had come from Idaho and they had motored up to The Dalles, Oregon. Good rodeo country. Good cowboy atmosphere. Great beer! Larry loved a good time. Lance raised his head and looked around. His shirt was off, his belt lay on a table and his jeans were unbuttoned. Where were his boots? Sitting up, he flopped on his back again. The jack hammer in his head was broken and pieces of it were hitting the sides of his brain. Sleep mercifully overtook him. Then came the nightmares, staggering to the bathroom, while trying to keep his jeans up, and trying to hold the seat cover up at the same time. Damn thing slipped out of his hand and slammed down onto the stool with an earth shattering clatter. His head should have been left on the bed!

The hotel room was okay by sorts, but nothing special. It had a big draped window looking out on something. Pulling open the drapes was a monumental mistake as a blow torch of fire hit his eyes. Throwing his hands to his face, Lance peered out carefully between his fingers at the view. A shabby junked up yard filled with big black crows met his eyesight. Nothing at all nice to look at!

Barbara Twibell

Lance was beginning to feel better. To remember was to feel horrible again. He flipped on the T.V.

It can't be Monday! Larry came by early Saturday morning. The day was clear and beautiful, a super day to take his friend up the river to The Dalles. They played pool, went to another place, drank with some cowboys, shot some darts, drank some contests, and he and Larry had won! Drank with some nurses, drank them away too. Laughed and laughed. Drank some chasers. Drank with some town girls...

Don't remember anything else, except getting sick.

Lance found his shirt. It smelled like cigarettes, beer, sour wine, and faint perfume. He slipped his heavy buckled belt back on, found his boots and socks, and lastly a note scribbled by Larry.

"Hey partner, you can't hold your booze like you used too. I gotta head back to Idaho before my wife gets wind of this party. Plenty of girls, but don't worry- we made it to our room without them!"

Larry is married? First I knew about this! All my buddies are married. Guess I'll go get something to eat and head home.

"I'll have that steak special, baked potato, green beans, and salad. Bleu cheese please. Coffee, black. Yes, I'm alone." The gum smacking waitress with the know it all look nods her acknowledgement of the order.

All alone, Man, have I ever blown this! I'll never get Jamie to talk to me again. I don't need this pressure. I had all the company I could want. Any of those girls would be my girl, with half the sass. I'm just not going to feel guilty, man's got a right to a beer now and then. Don't have to ask any woman if I can have one. Larry and I had fun, didn't ask anyone, didn't need any excuse. Little Jamie can go drink her milk and play with her dolls with the rest of the little girls.

Bet she's mad at me. I can see her beautiful eyes dancing with anger and condemnation. The toss of her sleek hair, the sway of her hips as she slams though a door. My head and backside would both have a chunk bit out. She doesn't kiss like a little girl. Don't mean nothing. I feel sick.

By the pool she didn't look like a little girl. Her lips are so innocent and soft. So trusting. So warm. No... Angry! You stood her up, Dumb Butt. Left her high and dry. You lost it, Buddy. Forget her. She's not your type.

Finally Lance is making sense to himself. Go home. Dad's waiting.

37

It didn't take long for me to get back to the swing of things at home or at work. I suppose those who knew me better said I had my days of pity parties. It is very difficult to try to forget a warm friend, very warm indeed. If I saw a couple kissing in the park, I knew how the woman felt. I liked feeling desired, feeling on top of the world. Now, I feel a little discarded.

"Fantastic, you're coming with us tonight, Jamie!" You'll love my boyfriend's buddy. He has been looking forward to meeting you. I think we're being taken to dinner, and then the movies," Marcy exclaims.

"Ya, right," I think. Just to shut up the girls around here, I have agreed to double date. I need to get out a little. He can be no different than I am to him. He has not seen me either. This is awfully close on the heels of Lance. No harm was done; I mean we were not a ticket item together. Just friends.

Tonight I am wearing a nice soft green cotton dress and a pair of light flats. I'm not sure where we are going, but this outfit should fit anything we end up doing. I am going to stand out by the corner. I don't want any funeral jokes. I have sworn Marcy to secrecy as to where I live. There is always the chance I won't want to see this person again. I have my taxi money in my purse. Exact change. This is one thing my father taught me-Phone money and taxi money! He would be proud.

Daughter of the Gorge

They're not on time I say to myself. (One strike) Shortly a grey sedan slows down and Marcy yells, "Hop in!" The front passenger seat is empty and Marcy is in the back seat. I have to pull open the door and seat myself. (Strike two) Hardly seated, the car rolls off in a hail of muffler smoke and noise. Laughter abounds.

"Hi Kid. My name is Jack. Jack be nimble, Jack be quick! Ha, Ha. Relax Kid, you're in good hands, or you will be. Ha, Ha. (Strike three)

"You look great, Kid. We're gonna chow down first. Then the evening begins!"

"Marcy?"

I hear the tumble of clothes, the embraces, the smacks of kissing, and the groans of pleasure. What have I gotten into? I don't dare look back.

"Whew, hold on there, Mighty Guy. We haven't had dinner yet!" Marcy gathers together and hangs over the front seat.

"What did I tell Ya, Jamie? Such fun we are going to have!!! Woooeeeee!"

"Come on over, Dolly. I can't steer with you clear over by the window. Ole Jack likes his woman close." Jack has this leering grin that sends chills clear up my spine.

Timberman Café is a dive. I've not been in one before, but this has to be a dive. Smoke is so thick I'm choking, and everyone yells over each other. The music is the only redeeming quality I can see or hear. It is western, and, I do enjoy western.

Marcy leads us off to a reserved table not yet cleared from the last diner. Jack is yelling at someone, and then lifts his crotch with some obscene movement of his large ugly hand. Laughter ensues as he dives at me with a huge bear hug that bends me back over the table. "Yes Sir Babe, you're gonna love ole Jack."

I come up off the table with a scream and deck Jack in front of everyone in the café. My wrist feels shattered. My heart is beating out of my chest. I feel like some strange animal, screaming for survival. "Don't you ever come near me again? Ever! I'm leaving now. I never want to see your lurid face again, or I'll call the cops and press charges!" I scowl at Marcy and step over the very surprised Jack, still lying on the floor. I can't swear to it, but I think I left with wolf whistles and applause. The management provided the taxi home.

There is a light on in the funeral home. I hope no one sees me coming in.

"Hi. Hey, why the tears?" Terry and his wife have come back after hours to work on bookkeeping.

Now, I do cry. I can hardly stop. Terry's wife Sherry has her arms around me. Honey, are you all right? Have you been hurt? Please tell us, we want to help.

How can I tell them, they have only caused me to want my mommy! They are so kind and comforting that, that is what my mind is thinking! What a horrible night. I manage to spill the whole evening out to them.

Terry gets an ice pack for my wrist, and Sherry reminds me that double dating can be dangerous. "One couple is always faster than the other, and that alone can cause show-off behavior." Terry is ready to take this man to court.

"I think considering how her wrist is swelling, you better take her to the hospital," Terry says as he reaches for his car keys. Sherry nods a yes and I fall in behind her sniffing all the way to the emergency room.

Yes, I did it! Broke four bones in my wrist. On comes the cast. The doctor seems very proud of my short boxing career. He recommends more training before my next date. DATE?! I don't need that!

38

I can't work for about three weeks. Gladys is really mad at Marcy. Marcy has called in ill.

Meantime I have a letter from my mom! Wow is she happy! She wants me to come over when I can. Well, I have three weeks. I immediately phone her.

"Mom, how about now? I will be off work for awhile, and I really miss you. I can? You'll wire me money to take the train? I guess I shouldn't drive; you're right! It will be a two way fare, won't it, Mom? I love you too! Bye, Bye."

I will have to drive to Gram's and let her know where I'm going.

"You did what, to break your wrist?" Gram is horrified. Mack is laughing. "Do you realize, Young Lady the humility that Jack Pratt has to suffer? Decked! One punch! How much of a wind up did you take on him?"

"I had to land him, Mack. I was so scared, and mad. I really don't want to talk about it anymore."

"That kind of man would have probably raped you. I'm so sorry. Not all men are like that, Honey. Very few. He belongs in jail. Bet he lands there before long!" Mack has his arm about my shoulder.

"Had some bad news in our neighborhood too, Child." Gram turned from her fussings and headed for the living room. I followed.

The wood stove feels so comforting. The little red glow from the damper has a hypnotic effect.

"There was a fire. Lance's home burned to the ground."

"Good Gawd, what did you say?" I stared at Gram in total disbelief.

"You know that weekend Lance didn't show? Mack heard about it at work. Seems Lance and an old school buddy of his had too good a time in the Dallas. On the day he got home, it was just in time to watch the walls fall in. Too far gone to do anything, to fast burning. His pa was just sitting there watching his life go up in smoke. All he and Lance owned was inside that house. The barn and animals were safe since the barn was so far from the house."

Mack now spoke, almost reverently. "Guess his dad tried to jump start the kitchen stove with some gasoline. He burned his arms and hands. He of course then tried to put out the fire. Lance suffered some inhalation burns and burns to his hands, too. He managed to save a picture of his ma, and some little things. It was bad. His dad is at his sister's now, but, no one has seen Lance. The animals get fed. But no sign of that boy. It's said he feels at fault. Blames himself."

I couldn't describe the feelings in my heart right now. How could such an awful thing happen to such fine people? Yes, fine people.

The rest of the evening we jabbererd about my impending trip to Montana and the care of my wrist. I knew I shouldn't have driven here, but how would they know I'd be gone if I didn't drive out to let them know? I look forward to my flannel sheet bed, with the exposed nails over my head to count myself to sleep.

Bacon, eggs and toast! What a smell! My very own piece of heaven. Today I have decided I will drive to Lance's ranch. I don't care if he is there or not. Somehow I need to pay respect to that beautiful, lost memory. Gram and Mack both say they have been there and need not return. "Such a loss," mumbles Gram

I promise them I will be back in time for lunch. The morning has a grey heavy fog hanging just above the river. It reflects a promise of a coming winter. Heavy cold air like this makes me feel winter is just around the corner, even if it is quite awhile before snow will be seen. I have rolled down the window on the driver's side because, I want to feel cold. I want to absorb loss. I want to share what two men must feel is gone.

There it is. At first there's no change. Cattle and horses graze in the pasture. The barn is dark grey and large. The trees are damp with fog and sorrow. Sorrow, hangs like a curtain over everything. The fireplace stands alone with dark brooding shadows of a burnt stove here, a bent hot water heater there. A charred chair overturned by heat. Black bed springs crumpled there. An overwhelming smell of soggy smoke with black soot clinging everywhere the house once stood. What a terrible loss! No one to say you're so sorry to.

The loss of Lance and the loss Lance must feel saturate my being. I have lost him, and with the loss he suffers, I now know I had loved him. Why does this proclamation not surprise me? Now, I believe I know what love is. It's the loss of someone you wish not to live without. Only too late, this discovery for my heart.

39

The train trip to Montana is fabulous. I never knew mountains could be so high, water so blue, or people so gracious. Now, Mt. Rainier is no dud. It stands at over fourteen thousand feet. It stands alone. I've now seen mountains, one after another, rows of them. Wheat fields, thousands of acres of grass land with an Antelope and, buffalo with orange colored babies running beside them. Here I go again, thinking of the Indians racing across the prairie, playing war games together. Freedom to roam, hunt, and live in family cooperatives. Each sharing in the duties. I feel for the pioneers too. They wanted the same thing. Who can say what could have been?

"Mom, Monty! How neat to see you again! Gosh, Mom you look radiant! Before I forget, thanks for the tickets. This means so much to me.

"The train was the way to travel! I slept a good part of the way. Oh Mom, this is such glorious country with such wide open spaces! I'm a chatter box. I'm sorry!"

The trip out to the ranch in the station wagon took two hours. I think Monty said an hour ago we were on the ranch land. Finally, coming up over a knoll, tucked in among poplars and white birch, sits a large orange log home with a huge front porch. Off to the rear of the house is a tall wind-mill, turning in slow easy turns. In front of and slightly to the left of the house are the barns and corrals.

"I've set my corrals so they open east or west," says Monty. In bad weather I need to get cattle in and not have them die in a storm. You'll notice back there a ways, a box canyon. It's Nifty for round ups."

"Now you can see first hand why I can't write all the time, dear," nudges my mother. "We keep so busy year round."

Monty pulls into the main yard, on a big full circle turns around and let my mother and me out at the front of the house. "I'll be bringing in your luggage, Jamie."

Mom and I enter the house. It is drop dead fantastic. It has high open ceilings, wide hallways, and a gorgeous shiny stairway winding around in a slow curve to the landing upstairs. The living room greets you with the western motif. Even a complete saddle and gear are in one corner! Two wooden rocking chairs, a table and benches, and wooden couch with large overstuffed pillows to make the arm rest and backs make for a cozy living room. A free standing fireplaces at least ten feet wide dominate the living room. A day or two's wood supplies is waiting to be burned. I think my mother has the most outstanding home anyone could have to live in!

"Come Honey; let me show you to your room. There is a bath and shower next door." We climb the stairs, and I can see at least three bedrooms. Mine, I am shown could be called a suite.

"Is it all right if I never come out of this room?" Monty has entered behind me unnoticed. Pride shines from his face, as does it from my mothers!

"I told you at the wedding, this is your home too! In this country there is always room for one

Barbara Twibell

more. Louise is going to be pea-green with sorrow that she cannot be here to show you around. We called her, but they are just going into finals, and you girls will just miss each other. I'm sure this won't be your only visit!!"

"You wash up, rest, and come down for dinner when you are ready. What I have fixed will hold well. I am so happy you are here, Darling. I love you so much."

"Mom, you deserve this happiness. I am so thrilled for you! Now, when I write and you write, I can picture where you are, and what you may be doing. You're right; I can use a little quiet time. My wrist is starting to throb. Do you have any aspirin? I won't rest too long! Love Ya, Mom!"

40

"Mom, I'm having such a good time with you. Why couldn't we have known each other like this earlier? I never even knew you could ride a horse!"

"Your dad quit living, and he wouldn't let me live. He did not mean to; he just hurt too much to find joy in anything. My marriage to Monty has been so wonderful. He always has something new to do, or people to see, etc. I feel younger, stronger, and so secure in what we are doing together. I only hope the same for you, dear. How is your young man?"

"Not well I don't think. I don't know. I haven't seen Lance in more than a month. It's over anyway, Mom. I think I am too young and inexperienced for a man of his stature. I will never regret the time we did have together; I think it was good for me to meet someone like I would like to marry some day. His home burned, you know."

"Yes," Mom slowed her mount some more so that we were just slow walking.

"Mom wrote to me about the fire. What a shame!"

A turkey vulture circled overhead, with long lazy sweeps of the canyon. Shadows from the hills on the other side were working their way across to our side where we were riding. A little wood bridge came into view. It rose only slightly from the ground, it suspended over a slow moving creek with its rocks raised up out of the water. Tame and slow.

Barbara Twibell

"In the winter and spring, you would not know this creek." Mom pointed down. "It becomes a gully rusher. Monty has built a dam up a ways that holds back a good amount of water through the summer. We go swimming there." She continues, "You know how I love trees, don't you? I have had a crusade here in the county and on the ranch to plant as many as we can afford to. We are also building as many springs and small dams as we all feel we can to keep more runoff and help wildlife with water supply.

"I think we best head back to the ranch and start dinner." The woman riding beside me, is a wonder...I love her!

Daughter of the Gorge

41

"Mom even though I've had a super time, I must go home and see what I can do with my life. I have a great job, as soon as I can work again, and I want to keep an eye on Gram and Mack. Maybe they don't need me, but I need them."

"I hope you will be careful of who you date from here on," laughs Monty. "Of course getting someone to go out with you with that right hook may turn out to be a challenge! We guys hear about girls like you and stay far away!"

"That's okay by me, Monty. I just want to get back to work and earn some money so I can come back here to play once in awhile! Maybe Gram can come for a visit with me. I'll probably drive next time."

The drive back to the train station seemed to take no time at all compared with the trip out the first time. Waving goodbye to Mom still stuck in my craw, she seems so far away. She is happy though, and that's what is important.

Seeing Mt. Hood with the morning sun on it is glorious! What a way to wake up! Portland is the next stop. This love affair with Mt. Hood has just run full circle. My Mother also woke up to this view years ago when she started her life over.

Across the river is home! I can see Washougal, the mill, Camas, Ft. Vancouver complex, and the famous Interstate Bridge. Clackity, clack go the rails, slower and slower, working in and around Hollywood district in Portland, Oregon and other small suburbs of Portland. Then I can see the Willamette River.

Gram and Mack are waving. They don't usually come from so far. For me they do, though! On the way home to Vancouver I get treated to a steak at the Stockyard Restaurant. Oh, so yummy! Big Idaho baked potatoes! We talk and eat for over two hours. Gram's hanging on to every description I can remember of the ranch and her daughter.

How it is wonderful to be back with my junk, and records. My appointment with the doctor is tomorrow. At that time I will know how long until I can go back to work.

42

Marcy has been fired. I don't know why. Doris seems glad to have me back and the girls take turns shampooing my customers. I am back to full time now. The wrist still hurts when I back comb, which is often. The doctor says that will dissipate with time. My clientele is strong, and my reputation grows every week. I drive to Portland for private lessons. I believe a person should strive to be all that she can be.

I love the easy banter at the funeral home. They have even asked if I can work some services on my days off. There is not much I can do to help, but I can stand at the door and be pleasant and hand out memorial folders and ask people to sign the family record of guests.

The money I have earned has helped me furnish my apartment nicely. I actually have a nice couch. I also bought a good set of dishes and cutlery. Winter has been wet this year, with not as much snow as usual. I've noticed the spring buds growing fatter with promise.

Doris and I have seen far too many movies. "South Pacific" was my favorite. Tomorrow we will be closed to customers because we will be having a hair styling demonstration class. They want us to do better work? Pay us more!

"Jamie, gall dang, I've never seen so many flowers! Hurry up front! You gotta sign for these!"

There must be three dozen yellow tight budded roses. Each and every one perfect. All is quiet, dead quiet. I sign for them and am handed an envelope.

My hands are shaking as I rip open the envelope and read:

Announcing the Birth of a new Foal
Father...Major
Mother...Candy

A remarkable white maned black stockinged, buckskin. Needs T.L.C.

As will owner. This man promises to love, honor, and annoy the lady of his choice, one Jamie Allison.

To wit he is providing one four bedroom log home on "Our" hill near the river, surrounded by "our" Gorge. Furnishings to be chosen by said wife. Only need be present to win. Future should include at least two "BOY" ranch apes, and any others wife might wish to endow.

I cannot conceive living my life without you. Please respond A.S.A.P. I love you very much! Lance.

I read and re- read the letter. Tears are slipping from my cheeks. I can hardly breathe. Nothing has or ever will blow my senses away as this letter has in these few moments.

I can't move or think clearly, I'm numb. I can feel a big chocking sob climbing up my insides. Absolute joy is bursting in my heart. The chills in my spine needing to shout an answer is shaded only by the realization I'm not standing here alone.

"Jamie, what's wrong?" questions a voice.

"I'm sorry, so sorry. You Guys. I love you all, but I gotta go. I mean quit right now!! I've got a ranch to build and two sons to raise!

Yes! Yes.

End

Barbara Twibell

About the Author

Barbara lives in Aberdeen, Washington with her wonderful husband of forty years, Douglas and their Sheltie Chester. The Twibells two fine son's Keith and Paul and their wives Heather and Lavonne also live in Aberdeen, along with three lively grandchildren of Keith and Heather's. Barbara was born in Vancouver Washington and raised by her parents and grandparents in the Columbia River Gorge area.

Printed in the United States
936900002B